TELL ME PRETTY LIES

CHARLEIGH ROSE

Tell Me Pretty Lies
Cover Designer: Letitia Hasser, RBA Designs
Cover Model: Agustin Bruno
Photographer: Clément PJ Schneider
Interior Formatting: Stacey Blake, Champagne Book Design

TELL ME
PRETTY
LIES

PROLOGUE

Shayne

I CLING TO MY BROTHER'S ARM AS HE LEADS ME UP THE RAIN-slicked steps and through the door to Whittemore, thankful for the support. My shaky legs have threatened to go limp beneath me more times than I can count today, between the wet, soft ground at the cemetery that tried to swallow my heels and the fact that I've never been good in anything other than sneakers to begin with. As soon as we enter the foyer, the smell of one thousand casseroles hits my nostrils. Why do people think food makes everything better? *Sorry your loved one died. Here, have some fucking potato casserole. Hope that helps!*

"I'm going upstairs," Grey says flatly, unlatching my grip on his arm. His eyes are bloodshot, and I'm pretty sure he's still in a state of shock. And probably a little high.

"You okay?" I ask. Stupid question, considering. But it's more than Danny's funeral. He seems distracted and distressed.

"I'm fine." He gives me a perfunctory kiss on the top of my head, and I spot Thayer over his shoulder, casually swiping a bottle of brown liquor from the bar. Grey heads for the stairs and I glance around, wondering if I'm the only one seeing this. Holden and their cousin Christian sit on the white sofa, glassy-eyed and ties loosened, elbows resting on their knees. I look to my left as Greyson's intercepted by Mom and her fiancé August—Thayer and Holden's dad—before he can make his escape. Mom pulls him in for a hug, and August claps him on the shoulder, and Grey tenses. Dozens of people I've never even met before are gathered in the house we've called home for the past two years, mingling and remarking on what a tragedy it is to lose someone so young.

I want to throw something.

A crashing sound brings my attention back toward the bar where a glass has now shattered on the hardwood. Thayer steadies himself on the edge of the bar cabinet, staring blankly at the broken glass. His grandfather appears, pulling him upright, and Thayer tries to shake him off.

"Man up," he orders in that quiet-but-deadly tone that brooks no argument. "Your family needs you." His hands tighten around Thayer's upper arms, shaking him a little.

"Move," Thayer says through clenched teeth. Instinctively, I hurry over to him, trying to attract as little attention as possible, ready to intervene. I know two things for certain by the look on Thayer's face. One, he's two seconds from punching his own grandfather at his brother's funeral, and two, nothing is going to stop him from leaving right now.

"I'm so sorry for your loss," I rattle off the cliché line, stepping between them, even though it's the last thing I want to do. William Ames is as powerful as he is old, and not nearly as nice. He eyes me like I'm a nuisance, but he brings me in for a polite hug and a kiss on the cheek, knowing people are most likely watching. I fight the urge to wipe my cheek.

"Thank you, Shayne," he says as if it pains him to play nice, his hands still holding my forearms. When he tries to release me and walk away, I tighten my grip on his arms, sidestepping with him in an effort to buy Thayer more time.

"Is there anything I can do to help?" I ask innocently. His piercing blue eyes bore into me, and his wiry, white eyebrows are set in two permanent, angry slashes, giving him a villainous appearance.

Thayer takes advantage of his distraction and prowls for the door without looking back, and I let out a relieved sigh once he's out of sight. Crisis averted. For now.

"I think we have it covered," William says shortly, bringing my attention back to him. I let go quickly, taking a step back. His nostrils flare and he makes like he's going to go after Thayer.

"Let him go," I say, my voice firm even though this man scares the shit out of me. I've never been this assertive with him. I don't know where this is coming from, and judging by the unimpressed look on his face, he doesn't either. "He'll only cause a scene if he stays here," I say, trying another tactic. No one wants that, least of all William. His family acquired this estate in the early 1800s, making the Ames family one of the first, and he won't let you forget it. Owning the oldest and most trusted cargo airline turned passenger airline makes for a very rich man, and being a rich man means people are always watching, waiting for you to fall from grace. To a man like William, appearances are everything.

He scoffs, walking away, and I don't waste any time hurrying for the door in search of Thayer.

"Thayer?" I call out, closing the front door behind me, but I don't see him anywhere. Thunder rumbles in the distance, the weather mimicking the somber day, and I scan the front yard, knowing in my gut he isn't here. My eyes lift, gazing out at the trees surrounding the property. These woods are massive, but I know exactly where he went. Without thinking of the consequences, I hurry down the steps and take off in a sprint, but I don't get far before my shoes trip me up. I pull them off, bracing one hand against a tree for balance, before tossing them into a pile of leaves.

The wet ground seeps through my knee-high tights, but I don't care. I push through, running as fast as I can. My hair whips in the wind, and I don't realize I'm crying until the cold air hits my tear-streaked cheeks. Raindrops fall slowly at first, but by the time I get to the old barn, my clothes and hair are more than a little damp. When I see that the barn door is slightly ajar, I slow my steps and breathe a sigh of relief, knowing he's here.

"Thayer?" I say softly, pushing on the old weathered wood. The door opens with a creak, like something out of a horror movie, but this barn could never scare me. This barn is my sanctuary, in all its leaky-roof, spider-having glory.

It's dark, but the sliver of daylight remaining allows me to see his shadowed form on the couch, bottle of liquor in his left hand. I bend down, reaching for the lantern we left here last night, and turn it on, closing the distance between us. I don't ask if he's okay. I'm not even *okay*. I set the lantern down at his feet, then climb onto the couch next to him, tucking my legs underneath me as I lace my fingers with his. Our arms rest between us, but his hand is limp, not squeezing back.

"Go." His voice is flat—lifeless—and he stares straight ahead, avoiding eye contact.

"No." I'm not leaving him. Not like this.

He takes a swig straight from the bottle, wiping his mouth with the back of his hand. "I mean it, Shayne. Give me some fucking space. I need to be alone."

His brusque tone makes me flinch, but I take the bottle from him anyway, tears welling in my eyes. "Then let's be alone together." I bring it to my lips, letting the liquid burn my throat, unable to keep from sputtering and coughing on the bitter taste.

His jaw locks, and I can tell he's holding back unshed tears. He didn't cry at the funeral either. Setting the bottle down, I pull his head into my chest, his wet hair chilling my already icy skin. I kiss the top of his head, my fingers curving around the nape of his neck, holding him close. He takes a shuddering breath, sagging into me, and I swallow hard, trying to keep it together. I've never seen Thayer Ames show emotion. Before now, I wasn't sure he was capable of it. Seeing him like this is enough to break me.

After long seconds, his hands find my hips and his lips find my chest when he turns into me, pressing a kiss to my bare skin. A shiver rolls through me, and he does it again, this time a little lower. Dark eyes look up at me as he peels the low-cut fabric of my dress away from my body and kisses the swell of my breast. My eyes fall shut, heart pounding, and then he's gripping my waist and pulling me onto his lap.

I cradle his cheeks in the palms of my hands and lean in, pressing my lips to his jaw. Hands squeeze my hips enough to leave a mark as I do it again, this time on each of his closed eyelids, then finally, his lips. As soon as my mouth brushes his, he snaps into motion. His tongue slips into my mouth as one of his hands snakes up my spine and grips the nape of my neck. He shifts his hips upward, causing a moan to slip free, and then he's unbuckling his belt, lifting his hips to shove his dress pants down just far enough. Rough hands bunch my dress up my thighs, and then he's flipping me over, settling between my legs.

My body's buzzing with barely contained lust in record time, and when he grinds into me, I lose all rational thought. I lock my legs around his waist, and he dips his head down, kissing me again. I flick my tongue across the two lip rings curved around his full bottom lip, and he groans, yanking the top of my dress open. I arch up into him as he swipes his tongue across my nipple. My clumsy fingers fumble to the buttons of his dress shirt, pushing them through, one by one. Thayer pulls back just long enough to tear his shirt off, and then he's back between my legs.

"Touch me," I beg, wanting more.

He snakes his hand between our bodies, using his fingers to rub the damp spot on my underwear. "I need you."

My legs fall open, drunk on the feeling. We haven't ever gone this far—never been this desperate for each other—and somewhere beyond the haze of lust, I know this is wrong. Not the fact that we're together, but it shouldn't happen like this. Not when we're sad and he's drunk and we're on the verge of catching fucking pneumonia in this cold, wet barn. Most people would frown upon losing your virginity this way. Most people would also frown upon losing it to your stepbrother.

Thayer jerks my underwear down my hips, and I capture his jaw in my palms, bringing my lips to his. My eyes fall shut as his tongue slips inside my mouth to dance with mine. He pours everything into the kiss. I feel his pain, his heartache, his need, his love. I recognize it because it matches everything I'm feeling inside.

"I love you," I whisper against his lips, and I feel him tense at the words. When he doesn't speak, I lift my eyes to his. His eyes are squeezed shut, brows pinched together in pain, jaw clenched tight. Dread unfurls inside me as he pulls away, sitting back on his heels.

"Get out."

"What?" I bring my arms up to cover my chest. Thayer's eyes look almost black with only the light of the lantern, his cold expression sending a chill through me. Thunder cracks outside, making me jump, but Thayer remains unmoved, a blank expression on his face. It's as if a switch flipped.

I right my dress, then pull my underwear back into place. Thayer stands, his open belt hanging loosely from his unzipped pants. He pushes a hand through his hair before pulling a pack of cigarettes out of his back pocket. Lighting one, he brings it to his mouth and inhales before he makes his way to the door. He pushes it open, the sound of the storm getting louder, and props one hand against the frame. Rain falls in sheets in front of him as he continues to smoke as if I'm not even here.

I bite down on my lip to keep it from trembling as I stand, straightening out my dress. My tights are askew and still soaked, my dress is stretched out at the chest, but I don't care. I don't care about the fact that I don't have shoes, or that it's storming. All I care about is getting out of this barn. When I pass him, Thayer catches my wrist, stopping me. I turn to face him, but he says nothing, his eyes zeroing in on the state of my dress at my chest. I jerk my wrist from his grasp and run out into the rain.

It's coming down much harder than before, and I'm instantly soaked from head to toe. The sky is dark grey and angry, barely visible above the trees. Thunder booms again, followed by a flash of light that illuminates the forest for a fraction of a second.

"Shayne!" Thayer's voice breaks through the heavy rain. I cross my arms and continue toward my house.

Thunder rolls and lightning follows again, much sooner this time, telling me the storm is moving closer. I push wet hair out of my face, squinting to see through the rain.

"What the fuck, Shayne," Thayer booms, running up behind me. I turn to face him, his dark, wet hair falling in front of his eyes. "Are you crazy?"

"You told me to leave!"

"Well, now I'm telling you to get your ass back inside the barn!"

I shake my head as the thunder booms once more. I know I'm being unreasonable. Now is not the time to hold anything against him. But I can't help it. I turn back around, heading for the house. We're only slightly closer to the barn anyway, and I'd rather get somewhere warm. But then Thayer's hand is gripping mine, pulling me back toward him.

A loud crack splits my ears as another flash of light appears, interrupting us. Both Thayer and I look over to see a bolt of lightning hit a tree only feet away. It blazes down the tree in a straight line, chunks of bark flying off. I stand there, wide-eyed, staring at the smoke that follows.

"We need to leave." Thayer grabs my hand again, jerking me out of my stunned state. When we touch, I feel a jolt shoot through my thumb and down my wrist, and I drop his hand like it's on fire.

"What was that?" It doesn't exactly hurt, but I definitely felt something.

Thayer frowns, bringing a hand up to grip his bare shoulder, but he doesn't respond. *He felt it, too.*

"What the fuck are you guys doing?" Holden calls out, running up to us from the direction of the house. "The old man's about to lose his shit." He looks between the two of us, Thayer shirtless, his belt buckle still undone, and me, shoeless, looking more like a wild animal than a girl.

I freeze, not knowing how I'm going to explain, but Thayer's quick on his feet, even three sheets to the wind.

"Pretty sure she just got hit by some ground lightning," he says, gesturing to the tree that's still smoking. "She should probably get to the ER."

"What? No, I'm fine," I insist, shaking my head.

Ground lightning? Is that what that was? I barely felt it.

Holden rushes over to me and Thayer takes off, giving me one last look over his shoulder as Holden inspects me for damage. I can't pry my eyes away from Thayer, standing there in the pouring rain with his bare, tan chest heaving, perpetual frown in place. Somehow, I know that for the second time this week, everything is about to change. I feel it in my bones.

And I can't shake the feeling that Thayer just said goodbye.

For good.

After Holden and I walked back to Whittemore, my mom took one look at my appearance and quickly shooed me into the upstairs bathroom, demanding answers. I sat there like an infant on the toilet seat while she helped me out of my drenched clothes before turning on the shower, letting steam fill the room. I didn't need the help, but I knew she was hurting and concerned, so I let her tend to me the way mothers do before I assured her that I was okay and asked her to leave.

I don't know how much time has passed since she left, but I sit here on the tile floor with my arms wrapped around my bent knees, letting the hot water fall over me. Tears stream down my face as I think about Danny.

Daniel Ames is, to put it simply, the town's golden boy. Star basketball player. Loved by all and had his whole life ahead of him. Until everything changed in the blink of an eye. He fell from a cliff that he'd jumped off so many times before, but this time, it killed him. Six broken ribs. Two punctured lungs. The official cause of death hasn't been released, but from what the police told August, he most likely drowned.

My lungs constrict and my chest grows tight at the thought of how panicked he must have felt. I shake the thoughts from my head, not allowing myself to imagine his final moments. When the water runs cold, I peel myself off the floor, reaching for the towel hanging on the wall and wrapping it around me.

Eyes puffy and emotionally exhausted, I quietly tiptoe out of the bathroom, planning to duck into my room without anyone noticing, but I pause in the hallway when movement inside Thayer's room catches my attention. The door is cracked, and Thayer sits on the edge of his bed, inspecting his arm, and I gasp before quickly slapping a hand over my mouth. It's red and blistered from shoulder to wrist in a pattern that almost resembles branches.

Or lightning.

Instinctively, I look down at my wrist. It bears the same exact pattern, except mine is smaller, running from my thumb to the inside of my wrist—and much less severe. I frown, running my thumb across the tender flesh. If it wasn't for the slight tingly numbness, I might've forgotten about it altogether. Thayer's, though…the skin is raised, oozing, and angry, and definitely in need of medical attention.

I decide to tell him as much, taking a small step forward, but I hesitate when someone else steps into view. Her back is to me as she saunters toward Thayer, but I recognize the dress from earlier. Taylor Sanders. My already wrecked heart takes another beating as I watch her drop to her knees in between his spread legs. Something inside me cracks open as her dainty, manicured fingers reach for the button of his pants. How can he let her touch him like that when he was with me only hours ago?

As if he can hear my heart breaking, Thayer's eyes lift, meeting mine through the crack in the door. They're angry but somehow vacant, the crease between his eyebrows deepening. I shake my head, my nose flaring as I attempt to keep my tears at bay.

"Let me help you feel better," Taylor purrs, tugging at his jeans while Thayer holds my stare.

My stomach rolls, and I turn around, unable to see any more. I quickly cross the hall into my room and slam the door shut behind me before flipping the lock. I don't bother to get dressed, instead climbing into my bed with my towel still wrapped around me. I curl up on my side, pulling the blanket over my head.

He had to know I'd see them. Why else would he leave his door open like that? He wanted to hurt me. He did it on purpose. And for what? For telling him I loved him? God, I'm stupid. I don't know what I was thinking. It's not like I thought this thing with us could actually go anywhere with our parents being engaged. I wasn't under the illusion that we'd somehow live happily ever after. I just got caught up in the moment, overwhelmed with the intensity of it all.

The truth is, I do love Thayer, and not in the same way I love Holden and Danny. But admitting it out loud was a mistake, because right now, I don't think it's possible for things to get any worse.

ONE

Shayne

I WAS WRONG. THINGS GOT WORSE.

The night of the funeral was just the tip of the iceberg. Like a row of dominos, everything fell apart after that. Thayer ignored me at school, and on the rare occasion he was home, he'd reek of cigarettes and whiskey. Holden pretended nothing happened, burying himself inside anything with a pulse, Grey shut down, freezing me out completely when he went back to college, and the icing on the shit cake? After three weeks, our parents called off their engagement, and five days after that, I was back in Shadow Ridge. By that point, I can't say I wasn't a little relieved. Staying at Whittemore felt more uncomfortable and less like home with each passing day, and going to school was my own personal hell. It was as if everyone could sense the shift, and suddenly, I wasn't one of them anymore.

But leaving Whittemore also meant leaving Thayer, and leaving Thayer was the hardest thing I've ever had to do.

I reconnected with my friends from middle school and finished out my junior year in Shadow Ridge while my mom worked constantly, taking as many flights as possible to make ends meet. She slowed down when she was with August, but she never completely quit, despite his insistence. Now I know why. She didn't want to be dependent on him. It makes me wonder if deep down, she knew she'd need a safety net one day. I was proud of her for it, but I'd never felt more alone. I didn't have her, I didn't have Grey, and I didn't have Thayer. I still had Valen. Our friendship was solid, and the hour drive did nothing to weaken that. And, of course, I had other friends, but it wasn't the same.

I spent the summer working at the country club to help make ends meet, even though my mom insisted that we were fine. I thought maybe if I could bring in some extra cash, she wouldn't have to leave so often. And just when I was finally getting used to my new normal, resigned to the fact that I'd probably never see Thayer again, fate had other plans. My grandmother passed away, and despite their vast differences, she shocked us all by leaving her house on Heartbreak Hill to my mom. It wasn't until we moved in over the summer and saw the state of things that my mom realized it was my grandmother's last fuck you. Turns out, Amelia Courtland was a bit of a hoarder in her old age. The downstairs was in decent condition, but upstairs? Upstairs was in shambles. We're still nowhere near finished, but it's livable and better than our place in Shadow Ridge. Not to mention paid off.

"It's going to be fine," Valen reassures me for the thirty-seventh time in as many minutes as I stand here hesitating before the imposing red-bricked building. Sawyer Point has a reputation for scary, haunted, and historic buildings. But not one of them is as intimidating as the one I stand before, and not for reasons of the paranormal variety. Ghosts have nothing on the rich and beautiful teenagers of Sawyer Point High School. I haven't faced any of these people in nine months. I know the second I walk through those doors, the whispers will start.

As if that's anything new.

"I know," I say, shrugging, aiming for casual when I'm feeling anything but.

"No one's even talking about you guys anymore since Bryce Anderson knocked up Melissa Matthews over the summer," Valen says when I still don't make a move. She produces a lip gloss from the tiny pocket of her equally tiny skirt before she drags the wand across her full lips. Valentina Solorio looks more like an Instagram model than a high school student with her olive skin, the perfect number of freckles across the bridge of her nose, and the dimples in her cheeks. Her thick dark hair is rolled into twin buns on the top of her head, leaving two strands hanging in the front. If I tried to pull off that hairstyle, I'd end up looking like an actual alien. But Valen manages to make everything look hot. Her style is what can only be described as rich-girl grunge. Feminine with a little edge. Meanwhile, I'm looking decidedly less hot in my cut-off black denim shorts, cropped grey sweatshirt, and Chucks. We're complete opposites, but she's my best friend, and the only one who stuck around when everyone else turned their backs on me.

I raise my eyebrows, pinning her with a look. Everyone wants to know what happened to make Thayer and Holden drop me. Myself included.

"Okay, fine. These losers are still talking about it," Valen says. "But that doesn't mean anything. It's senior year, and you're Shayne fucking Courtland."

I shake my head, but a small smile tugs at my lips. My name means absolutely nothing. In fact, it's more of a scarlet letter than a badge of honor these days, much to my late grandmother's dismay. My mom grew up here, and apparently, she wasn't exactly the perfect little debutante they expected her to be. I'm not sure of the details, but after a falling-out with her parents, she moved away at a young age. Both Grey and I were born out of wedlock, which apparently was still frowned upon here like it's 1952. Our father left when I was too young to remember, and all I have left is a single, faded picture.

When my mom returned to Sawyer Point to visit her parents for the first time in over fifteen years, she managed to snag August Ames, CEO of AmesAir, without so much as batting an eye. That made her the talk of the town, and when she dragged my brother and me to live at Whittemore, it made *me* the shiny new toy at Sawyer Point High. Rumors weren't exactly a novel concept for me. I didn't expect it to last more than six months with her track record, but she stuck around for two whole miraculous years. Sometimes, I wonder if she would have stayed with August for good, if not for Danny's accident.

"Solid pep talk."

Valen shrugs. "It's true."

The first bell rings and I hitch my backpack onto my shoulder, straightening my spine. Valen hooks her arm through mine and I blow out a breath. "Let's do this."

We make our way across the student parking lot, through the clusters of cliques, heads held high. It starts immediately— the hushed whispers, the furtive glances. With each step, they get louder, bolder, more obvious.

"I heard she got caught fucking one of the Ames brothers, so they sent her away."

"Well, *I* heard she was having an affair with their dad."

Gross.

"I heard she pushed Danny because he wouldn't date her."

Okay, that last one hurt. But I ignore it all, teeth clenched tight to keep from saying anything.

"You have English first period?" Valen asks as we push through the double doors, heading into the main hall, the familiar scent of cafeteria food and a hint of bleach hitting me immediately. We've compared schedules, and unfortunately, we don't have any classes together this semester.

"Uh, yeah," I say, pulling out my phone to double-check my schedule. "I think my locker's down here," I say, gesturing to the row of shiny red ones that lines the walls.

"Lame. Mine's up there." She points a finger toward the second floor. "It's like the universe is intentionally trying to separate us."

"Do you have first or second lunch today?" I ask, running my finger along the cool metal lockers until I find my number.

"Second." She scrunches her nose.

"At least we have that together. Text me."

Valen salutes me before spinning on her heels, walking toward the stairs at the end of the hall. I hesitate at my locker, watching her space buns bounce through the crowd until she's no longer in sight. This isn't my first year at Sawyer Point. Same school. Same people. But somehow, everything feels different. Because everything has changed.

The minute bell propels me into motion, and I decide to worry about my locker later, keeping my backpack on me. When I make it to English, most people are already seated, and every head whips in my direction. I don't make eye contact with a single one of them. Mrs. Roberts—who's surprisingly intimidating for someone who can't be over four-foot-ten—gives me a pointed look, motioning for me to sit down with her chin.

I drop my bag onto a desk in the back of the class before taking my seat. I pull out my notebook and a pencil, and when I look back up again, everyone is still staring.

"What?" I snap, already fed up, and it's not even eight A.M.

Some smirk and giggle, but most of them look away. Mrs. Roberts clears her throat, redirecting everyone's attention as she starts to pass out the class syllabus, and for now, I'm all but forgotten.

Until next period.

"Okay, so maybe I overreacted," I confess.

"Ya think?" Valen deadpans around the straw of her iced coffee from Dunkin' Donuts. She sucks the rest of it down and tosses it into the trash. Having only forty-five minutes for lunch, our food and beverage options are limited. Living in Sawyer Point narrows the list even further, but you can't throw a rock without hitting a Dunkin'. Most people stay on campus for lunch. Plus, the food here is exponentially superior to the stuff that passes for food at Shadow Ridge. Valen indulged me when I said I wanted to go off-campus today, but I doubt I'll get a pass for long.

"Shut up." I laugh, nudging her shoulder with mine. I've made it through all but one of my other classes relatively unscathed. Honestly, it wasn't nearly as bad as I thought it would be. The curious looks and muffled remarks didn't cease, but it didn't go beyond that. I expected that much—worse, if I'm being honest. I figure if I lie low, someone will screw a teacher or something and eventually, I'll be old news.

We part ways, planning to meet at her car, and when I walk into world history, I'm feeling cautiously optimistic. But the fleeting feeling dies, the faint smile slipping from my face when I see him. Dark brown hair a little shorter than Thayer's and thick lips above his square chin and sharp jaw.

Holden Ames.

He sits at his desk, slouched back in his seat with his legs spread wide, like a fucking king sitting on his throne, surrounded by his loyal subjects. I should feel sad looking at the group of people I used to hang out with, but they were never my friends. Not really, anyway. Holden, on the other hand, he was my best friend. And I miss him more than my pride will allow me to ever admit out loud.

I freeze, heart in my throat when his eyes meet mine. I

knew I'd have to face him eventually, but I didn't prepare for how I'd feel if we had a class together.

He stares daggers at me, his lips curling up in disgust. My fingernails dig into the strap of my backpack as I glare right back, even though my heart isn't in it. We all experienced a loss. But Thayer and Holden lost a brother. And even though I loved Danny like a brother, it wasn't the same. Grieving him feels like a slap in the face to them. Like I'm not allowed to be sad when they've lost so much more than I have.

After long seconds, Holden shoves out of his chair, gripping his binder at his side and prowls toward me. I hold his stare, my body locking up as he gets closer, anticipating whatever verbal smackdown I'm about to receive.

"Thayer know you're back?" he asks in that low, threatening tone that's usually reserved for his enemies. I'm not used to having it directed toward me.

I shrug in response as if to say, *how should I know?*

A slow smile spreads across his face. "This should be fun." He barrels past me, shoulder-checking me on his way out the door.

I stumble back, frowning, my gaze following his retreating back as a sinking feeling hits my gut. So much for time apart lessening the blow. So much for a fresh start.

"Mr. Ames!" Mr. Garcia calls out. But Holden doesn't stop, throwing up his middle finger behind him in response. If he were anyone else, he'd be suspended. Or at the very least, he'd get hit with detention. But he's Holden Ames, son of August Ames.

And me? *I'm screwed.*

TWO

Shayne

MY LAST CLASS COULDN'T END QUICKLY ENOUGH. I FELT THE weight of everyone's attention on me like a thousand bricks on my back. As soon as the bell rang, I made a beeline for the parking lot, shooting a text to Valen to let her know I decided to walk home instead. I didn't want to tell her about my run-in with Holden. I knew she'd try to fix the problem, for one thing, and I wasn't in the mood to be fixed.

I wasn't ready to go home and play twenty questions about my first day back with my mom either, so I walked around the wooded area behind my grandma's house—*my house now*, I remind myself—wasting time, lost in thought. On the other side of these woods is Whittemore, and the barn sits in between the two estates, but it's technically on their land. I don't know what possesses me to go to the old barn, but that's exactly where I end up. Old habits die hard, I guess. That, and the fact that I'm a glutton for punishment.

Slowly, I approach the injured tree from that night, pressing my palm against the bare strip of bark that's much lighter than the rest of the tree, amazed by its resilience. I decide right here and now that I want to be like this tree. A little scarred, but still standing strong. When I left Sawyer Point, I was Grey's little sister, Amelia's estranged granddaughter, and the girl who lived with the Ames brothers. I just want to be Shayne. And I want to stand on my own two feet.

Walking in the direction of the barn, I pause when it comes into view, an unexpected wave of emotion rolling through me at the sight of it. From the outside, it looks exactly the same, as if no time has passed at all. I haven't been here since that night, even when I wanted nothing more. It felt like *his*.

I jiggle the padlock, defeated, but then a thought occurs to me. I make my way over to the rock that used to act as our hiding spot. It's a long shot. I doubt Thayer left it here. He knows I know where it is, and he wouldn't pass up an opportunity to hurt me. I pick it up, and the fact that I have to wedge it free from the dirt tells me that it hasn't moved in a long time.

"Holy shit, it's still here," I whisper to myself, plucking the key from the ground and shaking the excess dirt off. Thayer kept this here so I'd always be able to get inside. *Does this mean there's still some part of him that cares?* No. I shake the thought from my head as fast as it came. Why do I do that? Romanticize what I thought we had? He's made it more than clear that whatever it was meant nothing to him. *I* meant nothing to him.

Even still, this place means a lot to me. He doesn't get to take that, too.

Turning back for the door, I stick the key in and twist. The lock pops free and I don't waste any time letting myself in. The moment I step inside, I know it's been vacant for a long time. Maybe even since the last night we were here together. The night everything changed. It's cold, dark, and…lifeless. Empty and stale.

Memories flash into my mind, unbidden. Thayer smoking his cigarettes while we took turns listening to our favorite songs. The first time we kissed. The first time he touched me. In here, we didn't have to worry about our parents, or about what people thought. In here, we were just...us. In here, we were free.

But now it's just an old barn.

I walk over to the worktable and swipe my finger across the layer of dust coating the top. *He really hasn't been back here.* Unexpected sadness creeps in at the thought. I stayed away for obvious reasons, but before it was ours, this place was his. I swallow hard, turning to leave.

Pulling out my phone, I scroll through my missed calls and texts. Two texts from Mom asking me if I'm okay, one from Grey telling me to call Mom, and three from Valen demanding more than the vague excuse I gave her earlier.

After tapping out a quick text to all three, letting them know I'm fine—and Valen that I'll call her later—I take one last look at the barn, then close the door behind me.

"Where have you been?" Mom asks before I'm even fully through the door. I shoot her a look, confused. She's never cared much about my whereabouts before, and one could argue that Shadow Ridge is a hell of a lot more dangerous than Sawyer Point.

"I went for a walk. Why?" I shrug my backpack off my shoulder, tossing it onto the couch before making my way to the kitchen counter that doubles as our dining table. I take the stool next to her as she sips on a glass of wine.

"I was just worried. Being your first day back and all."

Right. "It was fine. No one seemed to notice, or if they did, they didn't care," I lie.

She narrows her eyes, not believing me.

"I'm fine, Mom."

"I can't believe you're turning eighteen soon," she says, pinching my chin between her thumb and finger. "You get more beautiful every day."

I give an uncomfortable laugh and try to pull out of her grasp, but she holds me in place.

"Promise me you'll be careful." Her eyes are red and weary, and for the first time in my life, my mother looks... tired. She's still beautiful with her blonde hair and heart-shaped face that will probably always make her look younger than she is—both traits I inherited from her—but the spark has faded from her eyes. There's no denying that I am my moth-er's child. The only thing I didn't get are her chestnut eyes. My father, whoever he is, must be responsible for my blue ones.

"What could possibly happen—"

"Not just with your safety," she clarifies. "With your heart."

That heart she's referring to starts to work overtime in my chest. Does she know about Thayer and me? I swallow hard, then shake off the thought. There's no way. We were careful. Mostly. Toward the end, I couldn't hide my heartbreak if I tried, but everyone assumed that I was grieving. And I was. In more ways than one.

"You don't have to worry about that," I assure her.

"Shayne?"

My head pops up when I hear the teacher's voice to find her standing at the front of the class, holding a slip of paper in her hand.

"You're needed in the guidance center."

Flipping my binder shut, I don't waste any time pushing out of my seat. I might be more nervous about what I'm walk-ing into if it wasn't for the fact that I'm just grateful for the excuse to get out of this class and away from Holden's scrutiny. I make my way down the aisle, between the desks, and stop short when a beige closed-toe wedge with a dainty ankle strap shoots out in front of my path in an attempt to trip me. *Really?* I arch a brow and Taylor Sanders simply pouts, shrugging a shoulder. Images of her dropping to her knees in Thayer's room pop into my mind, and I have the sudden urge to rip her hair out.

"Oops."

I roll my eyes, forcing myself to not react. *It's not worth it, it's not worth it, it's not worth it.* Without a word, I step over her foot, ignoring the snickers coming from Alexis and the rest of Taylor's cronies. When I get to the end of the aisle, I catch Holden's gaze. I expected him to be laughing along with them, but instead, he seems...bored out of his mind. I break his stare and head out the door, into the hall.

The halls are quiet, my shoes squeaking against the vinyl floor the only sound. I'm torn between dragging my feet or getting it over with, because I know what this is about. I'm surprised it took this long, to be honest. Deciding to rip the Band-Aid off, I go with the latter.

"Come in," Ms. Thomas says, standing from her desk in a fitted Guns N' Roses tee, and I'm thrown off when she pulls me in for a hug. She smells like vanilla lotion and coffee, and her soft, black curls tickle my cheek. "Sorry." She clears her throat, pulling away from my stiff form, keeping her hands on my upper arms.

"It's okay," I say, letting her off the hook. Ms. Thomas isn't your typical guidance counselor. She can't be older than twenty-five. She's dry and sarcastic and kind of a hard ass. Suffice it to say, hugs are out of character for her.

"Have a seat," she instructs, moving back behind her desk.

I do as she says, sitting in the chair in front of her. She folds her hands together, elbows braced on the desktop.

I clear my throat, uncomfortable under her attention.

"So," she starts. "How was your summer?"

I roll my eyes. "Come on, Ms. Thomas. Cut the crap. We both know you didn't call me in here to make small talk."

She mashes her lips together to hide her smirk. "No, I didn't," she agrees. "I do want to know about your summer, but if you'd rather we cut the pleasantries—"

"Please do."

"Okay, then." She sits back in her chair, crossing one leg over the other. "I called you in here to see how you were settling back in."

"Fine?" I say with a shrug, but it comes out sounding more like a question. She lifts a brow. "Nothing I wasn't expecting," I amend, giving her a slightly more honest answer.

Ms. Thomas nods knowingly. "I can imagine. Your situation is certainly…unique."

I snort. That's putting it lightly.

"Have you talked to anyone?"

I cut my eyes at her. "You mean, like a therapist?"

She nods again.

"No."

"Is that something you're open to?"

"Not especially. Why am I here?"

She frowns, not understanding what it is that I'm asking.

"I'm not the one who should be here," I clarify. I highly doubt Holden or Christian has to meet with a counselor.

"You know I'm not allowed to discuss other students with you," she starts, choosing her words carefully. "You've been gone a while. I just want to make sure you're adjusting well."

"Well, like I said, I'm fine." I can't keep the defensiveness out of my tone.

"Hmm." She cocks her head to the side, considering something. I avert my eyes, focusing on the collage of cheesy, inspirational quotes pinned to her wall instead and bouncing my knee.

"Those came with the office." She motions to the signage behind her.

"Right." Makes sense. She's not exactly Oprah.

"What about a diary?"

My foot stops its incessant bouncing. "A diary," I repeat, skepticism lacing my tone.

"Diary, journal, whatever you want to call it." She waves a hand through the air.

I shake my head, dismissing the idea. "I don't see how that would accomplish anything."

It's her turn to shrug. "It's therapeutic, sometimes, to get it all out. Even if no one will ever see it. It will also push you to be…introspective."

I can practically hear the unspoken second half of that statement. *Instead of pretending like nothing happened.*

"I'll think about it," I say to pacify her, then stand to leave.

"I'll be frank with you," she says, stopping me in my tracks. I pause, waiting for her to continue. "I'm supposed to meet with you on a weekly basis—"

My mouth drops open. *Did my mom put her up to this?* "That's a little excessive," I say, cutting her off.

"I agree." She surprises me by saying. "So how about a compromise?"

I cross my arms, unhappy with where this is going. "Such as?"

She leans over to open a desk drawer, pulling out a black composition notebook, then holds it out in offering. "Instead of dragging you in here every week, you write in this instead. You'll check back in with me every *other* week. I won't read a word you write," she promises. "As long as I can see that you *are* writing, that's good enough for me."

"That's it?" I ask, waiting for the catch.

"You don't have to talk before you're ready, and I don't have to waste my lunch break trying to make you. Fair trade, I'd say."

You are the worst guidance counselor, ever. And I'm thankful for it.

I hesitate, weighing my options. Be forced into baring my soul to an unqualified high school guidance counselor, or scribble in a notebook every once in a while? It's a no-brainer.

She lifts a brow, extending the notebook further, prompting me to take it. My shoulders deflate, and she smiles, knowing she's won.

"Fine."

"Come back and see me in two days. Then, every other week from there on out."

I mumble a thanks, then turn for the door when her voice stops me again.

"And Shayne?"

I pause, looking at her over my shoulder. She leans in, lowering her voice. "I was a student here once, too. I know better than anyone how brutal these entitled assholes can be."

My eyebrows shoot up to my hairline and I almost crack a smile. I did not see that coming.

"So if you ever need to talk…" She leaves the invitation hanging and I give her a grateful nod before closing the door. Stepping out into the now-busy hall, I fish my phone out of my back pocket to text Valen, but she beats me to it.

Valen: Eating on campus. Meet me in the cafeteria.

I groan, internally debating on ditching school for the first time. To my right are the double doors that lead to the cafeteria. To the left is the exit. My phone vibrates in my hand, interrupting my thoughts.

Valen: Don't even think about bailing.

I groan, stuffing my phone back into my pocket, and reluctantly make my way toward the cafeteria. Apprehension settles in, growing with each step, but I shove it down and square my shoulders. It's not that I can't handle it—I'm more than used to being a spectacle. Being the new girl in a small town is bad enough, but living with the Ames brothers was another thing entirely. Everyone either hated me because they were jealous or they wanted to befriend me in an attempt to weasel their way into the brothers' inner circle. And their pants. Everyone, that is, except Valen.

So, no. It's not the whispers and jokes and stares I'm worried about. It's the unknown that unsettles me, and this is just another giant question mark in my life. Without Thayer, Holden, and Danny, where do I belong? Best-case scenario— the masses will no longer perceive me as a threat nor an in, and I'll become invisible. Worst-case? The gloves will come off, now that I'm not in their good graces.

Taking a deep breath, I school my features, slipping my mask into place, and pull the door open. Showing weakness isn't an option. The minute I seem intimidated, they'll pounce. Head held high, I scan the crowded tables and lunch lines for Valen. I spot her near one of the counters and head her way. Instantly, I feel eyes on me, but I keep my eyes straight ahead, not stopping until I reach Valen.

"I hate you," I say, leaning in close so only she can hear.

"You love me," she argues. "Besides, you had to get it over with sooner or later." The girl in front of us turns to leave after paying for her food, and we move up to the register. "Chicken salad and a Diet Coke, please."

"And a turkey sandwich," I say with a pointed look at Valen. If she's going to force me to spend extra time with these assholes, I'm at least getting something out of the deal. Valen rolls her eyes, nodding her permission to the lunch lady.

Cling-wrapped sandwich and container of salad in hand, we make our way over to one of the few empty tables. The minute we sit, my eyes find my old table and, sure enough, Holden and his crew are there. He straddles the bench sideways with Taylor Sanders between his spread knees, her back to his front. It shouldn't surprise me to see her with Holden after she hooked up with Thayer, but for some reason, it does. I guess it doesn't matter which one it is, as long as they're an Ames.

Holden slides a finger down the top of her shirt to get

a good look at her chest and she giggles, slapping his hand away, even though she's loving the attention. *Clearly, some things never change*. The kid across from them laughs, and my eyes snap up to his face.

"Who's he?" I ask, nodding my chin in his direction.

Valen glances over her shoulder. *"That,"* she laughs, pointing her fork at him, "is Chris Baker."

My jaw drops and I squint my eyes, trying to find the resemblance. "No way. Since when did Chris Baker start hanging out with Holden?"

"Weird, right? And it's just *Baker* now," she says in a mocking tone.

"Beyond weird. Wonder how that happened."

Chris Baker was the last person I'd expect to join the ranks of the pretty and the popular. They're not exactly a welcoming bunch. I had a couple of classes with him, and he was always kind of a loner. Shy—or maybe just quiet—but nice on the few occasions we did speak. He was usually cloaked in all black, had chin-length, dark hair, and I don't think I ever saw him without his headphones and a camera. Now, he's sporting a close-cropped haircut, fitted jeans as opposed to his usual baggy ones, and a plain white V-neck stretched across his chest.

"Damn," I say appreciatively. "He looks good."

"It was out of nowhere. He sat at our table during lunch one day last year and just…never left."

I unwrap my sandwich and pinch a piece of the corner off before popping it into my mouth. The rest of lunch goes by uneventfully, and Valen catches me up on the rest of the Sawyer Point drama that I missed. I still catch a few people staring, but I think for the most part, the masses got bored once they realized there wasn't going to be any action.

When the bell rings, I stand, and Valen's eyes lock onto something behind me. I know it's Holden before I even turn around. He towers over me, leaving only centimeters between us. I fight the urge to back away. I know Holden, and I know this is nothing but an intimidation tactic.

"Hey, little sister," he says, peering down at me with a Cheshire smile—a stark contrast to the way he reacted the last time he saw me.

"What do you want?"

"For you to fuck off back to Shadow Ridge, but apparently, you didn't get the memo."

"Working on it," I quip. As soon as I graduate, I'm leaving Sawyer Point. And with any luck, I'll stay gone this time.

"Good."

THREE

Shayne

"I REALLY DON'T THINK THIS IS A GOOD IDEA," I SAY, watching Valen primp in the mirror of her vanity.

"I disagree. Hiding isn't going to make things any easier."

"I'm not hiding," I argue. I didn't come back to Sawyer Point to go to parties and football games. If it were up to me, I would have opted for getting my GED or finishing my senior year online.

"The sooner you show them that you're not an easy target, they'll move on to someone who is."

I sigh, leaning against the edge of her bed that's fit for a princess. "Don't you ever get sick of this?" I ask. After Danny died, my whole life changed, and now everything that used to matter seems so...trivial. Between my daddy issues and the fact that I was thrown into a school where everyone is richer and more beautiful, I became a professional at overcompensating. I used to strive for perfection. Maybe if I had the right clothes, the best hair, the best grades, I'd be good enough.

Admitting that even to myself makes me cringe. That girl was weak. Seeking validation in all the wrong places and from all the wrong people.

Valen secures her dark, silky hair into a tight, high pony-tail before turning around to face me. "It's senior year—"

"How could I forget when you remind me every thirty seconds?" I tease, interrupting her. She twists her glossy lips and stands, walking toward me, gripping my shoulders.

"You might not realize it now, but you're going to miss this one day. Don't let Holden and a couple of jealous assholes ruin it for you. Or *me*. I finally got my best friend back and I want to have some fun."

She's right. I know she is. And how bad could it be? It's not like Thayer's around anymore, and he's the one I should be worried about.

"Fine," I concede.

A devilish smile spreads across her face.

"What?" I ask, suspicious.

"Aiden will be there tonight," she hedges, watching me for a reaction.

"*Okay.*" It comes out sounding more like a question than a statement. Aiden's one of Thayer and Holden's closest friends. He's gorgeous and one of the more bearable guys to be around in this town, but we've never hung out one-on-one.

"He's single now."

"Cool." I scrunch my nose.

Valen shoots me a look. "You're a lost cause. You're lucky you're so pretty." She pinches my cheeks, speaking in a voice reserved only for talking to babies and animals, then gives me a once-over.

I look down at my cut-off jean shorts, white Converse, and a tight, white, long-sleeved shirt. "What?" I ask defensively.

She tilts her head to the side, assessing. "One minor im-provement," she says, pulling my hair out of the messy bun on top of my head. My long blonde hair falls to the middle of my back, a slight wave to it since I didn't bother to blow-dry it af-ter my shower. Valen ushers me to sit in the chair at her vanity and I watch in the mirror as she uses her still-hot flat iron to straighten only the ends. She pumps something into the palm of her hands before rubbing it into my hair, making it shine, then finishes it off by spraying my roots with something that gives it much more volume than I have naturally.

"Voila," she announces, using both hands to ruffle my hair. "Instant Victoria's Secret Angel hair."

I nod, impressed. "You have a gift."

She curtsies, dipping her head. "Thank you. Now let's go."

Twenty minutes later, we're walking along the rocky beach toward the blazing bonfires a few feet away. Music blares from somewhere, and there are clusters of people scattered everywhere, spread out from the beach to the cliff above us. There's no way all of these people go to Sawyer Point. I don't recognize half of them.

Valen's boyfriend, Liam, is surrounded by a gaggle of college girls by the looks of it, and a couple guy friends when he spots us and breaks away.

"Hey, baby," he says before promptly shoving his tongue down her throat with a hand on her ass. Liam's at Northeastern, but you'd think he's been on the other side of the world by the way he greets her.

Valen pulls back, breathless. "Hi."

"Well, look who's back from the dead," Liam says as he wraps his arms around Valen from behind, just now noticing my presence. Valen elbows him in the ribs, sending him a disapproving glare for his poor word choice. "Shit, my bad. Welcome home, Shayne."

"Much better," Valen praises.

I roll my eyes, hating that she thinks people should walk on eggshells around me now. I'm not some fragile little flower. "Hey, Liam."

"You ladies need a beverage?"

Valen nods and Liam gestures for us to follow him.

"So that's going well, I assume," I say, walking a few paces behind him.

"Yeah." She shrugs.

He leads us over to a group of people surrounding a bonfire, the tall pieces of wood used to kindle the fire forming a teepee. Liam bends over, grabbing two plastic cups from a bag.

"I hope keg beer's okay. We're out of the hard stuff." He plucks the hose while his friend pumps the keg, filling up the first cup for Valen. His friend takes the second one, filling it up for me.

"Matt, this is Shayne," Liam says, nodding his chin at me. "My girl's best friend." Then he looks at me. "Matt goes to Northeastern."

"Nice," I say, unsure if I'm supposed to be impressed by that information, or if he's just making small talk. "Congrats," I tack on. I almost ask what they're doing back in Sawyer Point instead of at some college party, but I keep it to myself, not wanting to offend. Matt's the typical Bostonian, preppy frat boy with his long sleeves bunched up on his forearms, khaki shorts, Ken-doll hair, and boat shoes to top it all off. In other words, one million percent *not* my type.

He sends me a wink, handing me the cup. Liam tugs on Valen's arm, taking an empty chair around the fire, before pulling her onto his lap.

"You still in high school?" Matt asks.

I nod.

"Very nice."

I look away, uncomfortable with the way he leers at me. I stare out at the fire, hearing it crackle before it spits out a few embers that seem to disintegrate into the night sky. I'm hypnotized by the flames, the scent, the sound, as Matt drones on about something beside me. Something beyond the flames catches my attention, snapping me out of my eye lock.

Holden, Christian, and Thayer.

The sight of them together sends a jolt of sadness through me. Danny's absence is almost tangible.

The three of them couldn't be more opposite, each of them having their role. First, there's Holden. The playboy. The comedian. Has a heart of gold somewhere underneath all that debauchery. Then there's Christian. The athlete. On a fast track to success. Entirely too serious for someone our age. Has his entire future planned out. Lastly, there's Thayer. The black sheep. The bad boy. He rejects his popularity, as if it's a stain on his reputation, but despite that, he's arguably the most coveted of the Ames boys. Or maybe because of it.

As if he can sense me looking at him, his eyes find mine through the fire. My breath hitches, heart stalling. I bring my thumb to my opposite hand, rubbing the faint raised scar on my wrist out of reflex. He seems shocked at first, as if he's seeing a ghost. But then those eyes go cold and pass over me as if he didn't see me at all. My throat gets tight as memories of forbidden love and loss and ultimately heartache hit me all at once. But I shove them down, closing my eyes to gain my composure.

He's just a boy you used to know. You will not fall apart at the sight of him.

A hand on my shoulder breaks through my panic. "Are you okay?"

"Hmm?" I look over to see...what's his name again? Matt. "Sorry." I shake my head. "I spaced out." Like a magnet, my gaze is being pulled back to Thayer, and Valen is suddenly at my side.

"I thought you said he was gone." My voice is barely above a whisper.

"He was," she says, sounding as confused as I feel. "I swear. I haven't seen him for months."

Thayer's sitting in a folding chair with a girl draped across his lap sideways, her arm curled around his shoulders.

Holden's in the spot next to him, oblivious, getting his neck sucked on by a petite brunette in his lap.

"Maybe I should talk to them." I nod to myself. "Rip off the Band-Aid. Right?" I ask, looking over to Valen for confirmation. It's been almost a year. We've had time to move on. *So why does it feel like only yesterday Thayer was rejecting me in the barn?*

"Yeah," she says, but she doesn't sound convinced.

Before I can talk myself out of making what is sure to be a colossal mistake, I'm moving toward them.

When I come to a stop before them, neither one reacts. Thayer's eyes lazily lift to meet mine, and there's nothing but apathy shining back at me. His fingers glide up the girl's thigh, and my eyes lock in on the movement, unable to look away. The hurt that slices through me catches me completely off guard, and my stomach twists with jealousy. I feel tears stinging the backs of my eyes, but there's no way I'll let them fall. I'm not the girl I was last year. At least that's what I keep telling myself.

"Umm…" A feminine voice snaps me out of it. "Who is she?" she asks Thayer.

"No one." He says the words casually, but I know they're meant to hurt me. And they do.

"Can I talk to you for a second?"

Holden's eyes shoot open at the sound of my voice before narrowing mischievously. Christian ignores my presence altogether as he pretends to listen to something Chris Baker says.

"Talk," Thayer says, his fingers continuing their path on her bare thigh.

I swallow hard, trying to look away.

"Alone?" I try again.

"As you can see, I'm busy."

I almost walk away. It's clear this won't end well. But I stay, determined to say my piece and get it over with. I shift nervously on my feet, uncertainty pricking my spine.

"Just because our parents aren't together, doesn't mean we can't be—"

"What, *friends*?" Thayer cuts me off with a bitter laugh. "Is that what you were about to say?"

That isn't what I was going to say—not in those words, anyway—but everything sounds so...generic. He stands abruptly, the girl on his lap tumbling to the ground with a shocked yelp, but he doesn't so much as spare her a glance. He gets in my space, close enough that prying eyes and ears won't hear his next words.

"We're not friends. We're not anything."

"My mistake," I say, shaking my head. He's right. I don't recognize this cold version of him at all.

I don't know why I look to Holden for his reaction; it's not like I'd get any backup from him. But he was my friend once, too. He's staring at me with silent amusement painted across his features as the girl in his lap continues her assault on his neck. *Disgusting*.

"Run along now, Shayne. This isn't your home anymore."

"Yeah," I agree. "I can see that."

Turning around, I make my way to the opposite side of the beach that leads into an open wooded area. I catch Valen's concerned eyes across the fire, and she stands up like she's going to come over, but I give a slight shake of my head, letting her know I'm fine.

"You're back," a deep voice coming from my left says. I turn around to find Aiden standing there in a black shirt and fitted jeans. I have to admit, he isn't awful to look at with his dark, curly hair, full lips, and light brown eyes.

"Yep." I stuff my hands into my back pockets.

"What was that about?"

"High school politics," I say. "Apparently, I've been demoted."

"I wouldn't worry about it. How've you been?"

I frown, trying to figure out his motive. I don't know why

he's talking to me when I've been all but declared a pariah. It's not like he hasn't noticed. Looking around to see if anyone's taken notice to us, I spot Taylor and Alexis scowling in our direction. "We have an audience," I whisper conspiratorially. "You probably shouldn't be caught talking to me."

He scrapes his teeth across his bottom lip to bite back a smile. "I don't give a fuck. I've been meaning to talk to you."

"And why's that?"

"Because you no longer have a small army of guys cock-blocking any and every potential suitor."

He says it as a joke, but it only serves as a reminder of how much things have changed. Not that I think there was any actual cockblocking happening.

"Shit, wrong thing to say."

"No, it's fine." I wave him off.

I glance over at Thayer once more, unable to resist getting another look at him. He's staring right at me, the warmth that I usually see in his eyes nowhere to be found.

Suddenly, I feel the urge to bail. I don't want to be here anymore. I consider asking Valen for a ride home, but she's currently lip-locked with Liam, and I can't bring myself to ruin her night. She doesn't get to see him as much with him living at the dorms.

"Hey, are you sober?" I ask Aiden.

"As a judge."

"Feel like giving a girl a ride home?"

"Only if we can get some food first."

"Sold."

After I tell Valen that Aiden is going to take me home, she reluctantly agrees to stay. We hop into Aiden's lifted black truck and he turns to look at me.

"Any requests?"

"Pizza," I say without hesitation.

"Say no more. There's a bomb-ass pizza place in Haverhill."

He throws the truck into drive, heading down the winding,

narrow path that leads to the main road. It's easy to talk to Aiden. He's cocky and witty, but respectful, and not too pushy. After we split a large pepperoni pizza and a pitcher of Pepsi, I feel stuffed. And in slightly better spirits than earlier.

"I'm so full," I groan, leaning my head back against the booth.

"That mean you're not going to eat that?" he asks, flicking his chin at the last piece on the silver pizza tray.

"It's all you." I laugh.

Aiden folds the slice in half, devouring it in two bites, dusts his hands, then stands. "Ready to go?"

I dig into my purse, pulling out some cash, but he stops me.

"I got it," he says, throwing three twenties down onto the table.

"Let me pay for half at least."

"Nope." He stuffs his wallet back into his back pocket, then motions for me to lead the way.

"Thanks," I say, turning to face him, walking backwards toward the front of the restaurant. "For the ride and the food." He smirks at me, but then his eyes focus on something over my shoulder.

"Isn't that your mom?"

I turn around, fully expecting him to be mistaken, but low and behold, there she is, all dolled up, walking through the parking lot on some guy's arm.

What the hell?

"Do you want to go say hi?" Aiden asks.

I shake my head. "No, that's okay."

The guy helps my mom into the back of a car before climbing in behind her, and then it takes off out of the parking lot. If this is a date, why go out of town? It's not for the fine dining, that's for sure. And why wouldn't she mention it? Maybe it was a meeting, or a client? I roll my eyes at myself. Not likely. Not at this time of night.

Looks like I'm not the only one with secrets.

FOUR

Shayne

I MOUTH THE WORDS, SILENTLY SINGING ALONG TO "QUEEN OF THE Night" by Hey Violet as I make my way toward the lunchroom when a hand darts out, jerking me into an empty classroom. I squeal, surprised, and yank my earbuds from my ears.

"Happy birthday," Thayer says, pushing me up against the wall next to the door. I slap at his shoulder, craning my neck to look out the rectangular window in the door.

"Someone could've seen you."

Thayer shrugs, bending down to grab my thighs and lifts me to his height. My legs automatically wrap around him, my hands gripping his shoulders, and then his lips are on mine, hungry and demanding. I open for him and his tongue pushes inside. I moan, feeling his length twitch between my legs, and shamelessly grind against him, seeking the friction that I need.

He pulls away, breaking the kiss far too soon. "So, birthday girl, what do you want for your present?" he asks, his voice gravelly.

"Anything?" I bite down on my lip.

"Anything."

I lean forward, bringing my mouth to his ear. My heart is pounding, but I'm going to say it anyway. "I want you to touch me again," I whisper.

"Shayne," he groans. "You can't say shit like that."

"Why?" I pout. He touched me once, and I've been dying to feel it ever since.

"Because now I have to walk around with this all day," he says, pushing into me to demonstrate his point.

"I guess I'll just have to take care of it myself…"

"Fine. Meet me in the barn after we have cake and presents with our parents. Then I'll give you your real *present."*

"Ready?" Valen asks, jerking me from my memory. I tear my eyes away from the classroom that triggered it to find her frowning at me, probably wondering why I'm staring at the empty, dark room.

"As I'll ever be."

That was a year ago today, when things with Thayer and me first started to heat up. I did meet him in the barn that night, and he gave me exactly what he promised. Thayer wasn't exactly known for his morality, but for some reason, he fought going any further with me. It was fun and exciting and reckless to sneak around at first. But eventually, as our feelings grew, having to hide got old. But we couldn't stop it, no matter how many times we tried to end it.

We head out to the student lot, making our way through the crowded parking lot to Valen's pearl white Mercedes. Since it's my birthday and my mom had to fly out for a quick two-day trip, I'm celebrating with Valen. I wouldn't have it any other way. It doesn't feel like my birthday, anyway, without Grey and my mom around.

When Valen asked me what I wanted to do, I suggested touring the Lizzie Borden house in Fall River. She thought I was joking. I wasn't. As we brainstormed on things I could do as an eighteen-year-old, it came down to either a strip club, an eighteen and over club, or a piercing or tattoo. The thought of something as permanent seemed too intimidating, but a piercing? A piercing I could do. I'm actually excited.

"Have you talked to Aiden at all?" she asks once we're inside the car, starting the engine.

I shrug. "Here and there." It's been a week since he brought me home. We say hi to each other in passing, and he's texted me a couple of times, but that's it. I think he knows I'm not interested.

"Well, that's disappointing." She pulls out of the parking lot, heading for her house. Our appointments aren't until later tonight.

"Why?"

"Because I don't want you to waste your whole year hung up on your ex-stepdick."

I gape at her. Valen's always suspected, but after the funeral, it was obvious something had happened between Thayer and me. I played it off, chalking his behavior up to grief, even though I wanted nothing more than to confess everything. Judging by her comment, she didn't buy it.

"I'm not!"

"Mhm."

"You saw him last weekend. He despises me. They both do."

"Which is exactly why you should focus on other boys. Specifically, ones that look like Aiden."

"I don't want to date *anyone*."

She lifts a shoulder. "Whatever you say."

Four hours later, we pull up to the red-bricked building with the large picture window. There's a sign that reads *Heartbreak Ink* with a purple neon sign underneath that flashes the words *Tattoos and Piercings*. Behind us are a bunch of cars parked in every direction, some I recognize and some I don't. When I see Thayer's Hellcat, my stomach swirls with nerves. There's a string of bars and restaurants in this area, which means everyone congregates here. It's pretty much the only other thing to do in town besides the beach. It's also a pre-party meet-up point, and my guess is they're all about to head out to some college party.

Valen cuts the engine and we both hop out of her car, making our way toward the brightly lit shop. Just as we're approaching the building, Thayer, Holden, and Christian come out of the convenience store next door. Thayer sees me first, his eyebrows tugging into two angry slashes. Holden notices the shift in his demeanor, and he follows his gaze. Amusement flashes in his eyes, as he says something I can't hear. Christian's the last one to catch on, barely acknowledging us with a glance.

Lovely.

"Ignore them," Valen says from my left.

I tear my gaze away from Thayer and walk up to the sidewalk. The door chimes when we walk in, and a guy with a Celtics jersey and arms full of colorful ink greets us.

"What can I do for you?"

"We have appointments for Valen and Shayne," Valen supplies.

"Right on. I'm the piercer here, so you'll be with me. Name's Nate. I'll need your ID's and you'll both need to fill out everything on these forms," he says, pulling out two clipboards from behind a counter. He hands one to each of us, and I scan over the consent form, feeling a slight rush of excitement. "I'll be ready for you in just a minute," he says, and then he's disappearing into one of the back rooms.

"What did you decide on?" I ask as I fill in my information and pull my license out of my back pocket before clipping it to the board.

"Nose," Valen says, pointing to her nostril. She's not going to be eighteen for another couple of months, but she has fake ID. Because, of course, she does.

"Hoop or stud?"

She twists her lips together, seeming to consider it. "Stud. What about you?"

The door chimes again before I can answer, and even before I turn around, I know it's Thayer. Sure enough, he and Holden walk inside, surveying the place.

"I think you're in the wrong building," Thayer says. "The Chuck E. Cheese is on the next street over."

I turn back to Valen, pretending like they're not here, and touch the shell of my ear. "I'm thinking about getting a little hoop up here. Or maybe an industrial."

Valen crosses her arms over her chest. "We did not come here to get something you could've gotten when you were thirteen, Shaynie Baby."

I roll my eyes. "Fine. My bellybutton then." I like the idea of having a secret piercing. Something I can hide easily.

"Way to live life on the edge," Thayer deadpans.

I whirl around, pinning him with a glare. "I don't remember asking you."

Nate, the piercer, walks back out, nodding his head at Thayer and Holden. "Getting a touch-up?" he asks, directing his attention to Thayer.

He has a tattoo?

Thayer shakes his head in answer.

"We're with them," Holden says, flicking his chin toward us.

I roll my eyes, handing Nate my clipboard.

"Birthday girl?" Nate asks, glancing down at my license.

"Yep." I rock back on my heels, suddenly feeling a little nervous.

"Happy birthday then. Who's up first?"

"Me," Valen announces, holding her clipboard out for him to take.

"All right, brave girl. Pick out your jewelry." He gestures to a glass counter display with all kinds of different jewelry, along with the shop's merch in the form of stickers, beanies, and t-shirts.

The two of them walk over to the counter and I follow suit. While Nate shows Valen the nose ring options, I browse all the different types of jewelry. Some, I don't even recognize.

I snort when I see a curved bar with a Playboy Bunny dangling from the bottom.

"You'd be surprised how many people still get those," Nate says, smirking. "Mostly divorcees in their thirties or early forties with a newfound wild streak." He winks.

"I'm not judging." I laugh. To each their own.

Once Valen settles on a dainty, little nose ring, the two of them disappear into a piercing booth somewhere down the hall. I scan the jewelry some more, my eyes stuck on something in particular. Two somethings, specifically.

"You're too scared," Thayer says from behind me, his voice next to my ear, and I jump, not realizing he was so close.

"No, I'm not." I swallow hard, feeling him move in closer.

"Liar," he accuses.

"Don't act like you know me," I grind out.

"Oh, but I do. I know that secretly, what you really want are those," he says, stubbing his fingers onto the glass countertop, his arm brushing mine in the process, "but in the end, you'll back down and play it safe, because good little girls don't get their nipples pierced."

I don't know what I hate more. The way he's talking to me or the fact that he's right. But that doesn't mean he knows me. He saw me eyeing them. That's it.

"Done!" Valen chirps, skipping back toward us. Thayer backs off, and Holden watches us intently from the couch on the opposite side of the lobby. Oblivious, Valen frames her hands under her chin, batting her eyelashes dramatically. "What do you think?"

"That was fast," I say, walking over to inspect the little diamond that sits on her slightly red nostril as if my heart isn't going crazy inside my chest. "That might be the cutest thing I've ever seen."

"I love it," she declares, turning for a full-length mirror to admire it some more.

"Looking good," Holden says, appreciation in his tone.

"Bite me."

"Yes, please."

The door swings open, cutting off their bickering, and Christian pops his head in. "We're heading out."

"Enjoy your belly ring," Thayer taunts, and then they're both walking out the door.

Asshole.

I turn back around, noticing two leather booklets on top of the glass case, one reading *Tattoos*, the other *Piercings* in silver Sharpie. I flip through, checking out all the different facial piercings, but about three pages in, I pause, unable to look away.

I've always thought they were pretty, but never something I could pull off. I never even considered getting them for myself, but for some reason, now that the idea has taken shape, I can't shake it. It's been gnawing at me ever since I saw the jewelry in the case. *I want to do it. I'm going to do it.* Something slightly rebellious, but not as permanent as a tattoo. And I can't deny that there's something appealing about knowing no one else will ever see, unless I decide to show it to them.

Nate comes around the counter, asking which jewelry I like, and I point to what I want.

"That's not what you're looking for." Nate chuckles. "The naval rings are here," he says, stubbing a tattooed finger down onto the glass.

"I know. I want these."

His eyes snap up to mine.

"Those are for nip—"

"I know." I widen my eyes at him.

Nate clears his throat, but the professional in him recovers quickly, plucking a tray of various barbells out of the display case. "Let's get you back in the booth so we can discuss it further."

I nod, then Nate leads me to a very bright, very sterile-feeling room with a chair that reminds me of the exam table at my OB/GYN.

"Have a seat," he says, closing the door behind him.

My heart doubles its pace, and the nerves start to set in as I hop up onto the chair. Nate eyes my shaking hands and I clasp them together in my lap in an attempt to steady them.

"You sure about this?" he asks, lifting a brow. "Quite a leap for your first time."

Good little girls don't get their nipples pierced.

Thayer's words play back in my head. Is it a cliché rebellious teenager move to get piercings in questionable places? Probably. Am I going to do it anyway?

I swallow hard, then give a firm nod. "Yes. Let's do this."

A smile tugs at his lips, and for some reason, it's that smile that makes me suddenly realize that this guy is going to be up close and personal with my nipples. Nate drops down into a rolling chair and scoots toward me, tray of jewelry in hand.

"But we should hurry. Before I can talk myself out of it."

He chuckles, reaching over to pull a rolling stand over, then sets the tray on the top before refocusing his attention on me. "Can you lift your shirt for me? Your bra will need to come off, too."

I nod, taking a fortifying breath. I pull my shirt over my head, then slide my bra straps down my arms and reach behind me to free the clasp of my bra, letting it fall into my lap. My nipples tighten painfully, as if they know what's coming.

"You have perfect nipples," he remarks.

"Um." I don't know what to say to that.

"For piercing," he amends. "They're proportionate and not flat, so they'll look great."

"Okay."

He leans in close, inspecting me, and I try my hardest not to fidget as his fingertips pull slightly on the tip. "I'm thinking we'll go with a fourteen gauge since they're pretty small. I'll leave the bar a bit longer to accommodate the swelling, but you can change it once you're healed."

"How long will that take?"

Nate lifts a shoulder. "It's hard to say. As far as pain, you'll hurt tonight, and they'll be tender for a couple of weeks. No *playing*—" he says with air quotes, making his meaning clear— "for four to six months."

Wow. That's a lot longer than I would've guessed. But it still doesn't sway me.

"Ready?"

"Yep."

Nate stands and does something at the small counter on the opposite side of the room and returns with gloved hands holding white gauze.

"To sterilize," he explains. "It's going to feel cold."

He swipes the cold liquid across my right one first, causing me to shiver. He repeats the motion to the other side, and then he's turning for the counter once more. When he turns back around, he has some sort of metal device in his hands, and I feel my eyes go wide.

"Relax, it's just a clamp. Are you the need-to-know-every-step kind of girl? Or just get-it-over-with-as-soon-as-possible girl?"

"Definitely the latter. Just tell me when it's coming."

"Deal." He sets the torture device down onto the tray and plucks a thin, purple Sharpie out of his pocket, biting the cap off with his teeth. His brows furrow in concentration as he dips his head down to get a closer look. He's so close that I can feel his breath on my skin as he flicks my nipple with the tip of his finger. He draws a small dot on one side of my nipple, then one more on the opposite side. He repeats the motion to the other one, then leans back, inspecting.

"Look even to you?" he asks, handing me a mirror.

I give a quick look, uncomfortable seeing the reflection of my bare chest even though I've been topless in front of him this whole time. "Mhm."

"Lie back."

I do as he says, bringing the backs of my hands over my

eyes as my back hits the table. I hear him rustling around, and then feel cool metal against my skin.

"This is just the clamp," he clarifies. I feel my nipple being pinched, but it doesn't hurt. It's just uncomfortable. "Okay, now take a deep breath for me, Shayne," he instructs, his voice smooth as velvet, but it doesn't do much to comfort me.

I inhale deeply, filling my lungs, and when I release it, hot, sharp pain sears through me. I flinch, squeezing my eyes shut tighter, and my hands fly down to my sides, digging my fingernails into the leather seat.

"Good girl," he praises. "The needle is through. I'm just feeding the barbell through now."

"Don't say needle," I manage to grind out, only half-joking. I feel like I'm going to throw up. My entire body is trembling.

"One more to go."

It's the same process for the other side, and I don't know if it's because I'm expecting it, but I swear it hurts more. The pain is intense, but it's over mercifully quick. Once the initial pain fades, it morphs into a duller, throbbing sensation.

"Breathe," Nate instructs. I didn't even realize I was holding my breath. I focus on taking slow, deep breaths, doing my best to ignore whatever it is he's doing. Screwing the ball onto the barbell, if I had to guess.

"All done," Nate announces, helping me to sit up, one hand holding mine, and the other between my shoulder blades. I look down to assess the damage, but I'm pleasantly surprised with what I see. A small, horizontal, silver barbell decorates each nipple, and there isn't even a drop of blood.

"They look so good," I say with wonder in my voice. *I can't believe I just did that.*

"Yes, they do," Nate agrees before clearing his throat. He leans in once more, reaching out to adjust the barbells. My stomach tightens at the sensation, feeling raw.

"There isn't any blood," I muse aloud.

"There might be a little later. I'll give you instructions for aftercare and go over everything, but I'm going to warn you right now, if you shower with those loofah things, do yourself a favor and throw it out now."

"Okay…"

"There's nothing worse than forgetting you have a fresh piercing and snagging it on one of those bitches. Trust me."

"Ouch." I hop down from the table, reaching for my clothes that must've fallen from my lap.

"I'd skip the bra for a week or two, too."

Going braless at school for two whole weeks? Sure. That won't be weird at all.

I pull my t-shirt over my head—sans bra—wincing when the fabric hits my chest. Nate rattles off instructions about how often to clean them and how long to abstain from certain… activities. And then we're walking back out toward the lobby, with my bra stuffed into my waistband in the back of my pants.

Valen pops up from the couch and springs toward me. "That took forever. Let's see it!" Before I can stop her, she's lifting my shirt, exposing my stomach.

"You little wuss!" she exclaims, laughing. "I knew you'd chicken out."

I pull my shirt back down, walking up to the counter with the cash register. We still have to pay, so the jig is up.

"Fifty for you." He points to Valen, and she digs into her purse for cash. "And it's usually forty-five each, but I'll cut you a deal since it's your birthday. Give me fifty and we'll call it even."

"Wait." Valen's head snaps around. "You got *two* piercings? *Where*?" Her eyes scan my body.

"Somewhere where *nobody* can see," I tease, widening my eyes at her. I hand Nate a fifty and a twenty for a tip…which isn't exactly chump change for me, but it's the least I can do since he gave me a deal. "Thanks again," I tell Nate, changing the subject as I walk backwards toward the door.

Once outside, I'm relieved to find the cluster of cars has left. Valen jogs to her car and hops in, but I can't exactly run, so I opt for slow and steady steps, and I see Valen's mouth drop from the driver's seat.

"You little rebel." She laughs when I pull the passenger side door open. "Show me right now."

I slide in and close the door before angling my body toward her. I curl my fingers around the hem of my shirt, quickly lifting it to my chin.

"Holy shit, they're perfect," she squeals. I drop my shirt, then face forward. "How bad did it hurt?"

"Bad," I admit. "But it was quick. You?"

She angles the rearview mirror down to admire her nose. "Surprisingly not bad at all. My eyes watered, but that's about it."

Valen starts the car and pulls out of the parking lot and begins the drive back home. We talk some more, but all the while, my thoughts keep drifting back to Thayer and how different he is. He didn't even wish me a happy birthday, and I know that's insignificant, all things considered, but it's just another reminder that my life has done a complete one-eighty. Last year, I had Danny, Thayer, and Holden. I had Grey. Now, I don't have a single one of them.

Valen's car slows, snapping me out of my thoughts. When I look up, I realize we're pulling up to her house instead of mine. I glance over at her with a questioning expression.

"Sleepover," she deadpans, as if the answer is obvious. "It's your birthday. You're not spending the rest of your night at home alone. We're going to order pizza, get drunk, watch shitty reality TV, and then I'll probably make you flash me one more time."

I crack a smile. "I'm in."

She cuts the engine, then dangles her keys in front of my face. "As if you had a choice."

FIVE

Shayne

"S O I'VE BEEN THINKING," MOM SAYS, IN WAY OF GREETING as I walk through the front door after school. She came home on Sunday with a grocery store cake, but other than that, I haven't seen her much, and I haven't brought up seeing her with that random guy.

"Well, hello to you, too."

"Have you thought about getting back on the team?" she asks, not wasting any time getting to the point.

"Nope," I say simply, popping the *p*. "But I can see you have."

"I just think it would be a good idea. You're still playing catch-up, and it will look good on your college applications."

"I don't know." I was the captain of the volleyball team for the past two years. I used to play both high school and club before we moved to Sawyer Point, and I loved it. But for some reason, over the past year, I just...lost interest.

"Shayne," she starts, tucking my hair behind my ear and smoothing out my flyaways. "I want you to have everything you deserve in this life. I don't want you to have to depend on anyone. Ever."

Her sudden serious demeanor catches me off guard. It's just a sport. It's not going to make or break my future. "I think you're being a little dramatic."

"If not volleyball, what about something else? Like student government? Or the debate team? I bet you'd be good at that—"

"Mom," I say sharply, cutting her off. "I'll talk to the coach, okay?" I say just to pacify her, even though I have no intention of actually doing it. Spending extra time with Taylor and Alexis isn't exactly at the top of my to-do list. I'd rather join that aforementioned debate team.

"Thank you," she says, smiling, but it doesn't reach her eyes. Not that my mom's ever been the poster child for happy and carefree, but lately, I get the sense that she's worried about something in a big way. And it makes me feel uneasy. I tell myself that she's simply extra high-strung after two funerals in the past year and ending her relationship with August, but something tells me it's beyond that. I make a mental note to call Grey and see if he has any idea about what's going on with her, though I doubt he'll be much help. I doubt he'll even answer.

"So, what'd you do last weekend?" I ask, trying to sound nonchalant as I make my way over to the fridge. I pluck the pitcher of water out and pour myself a glass. "When I got home, your car was gone."

"Oh, nothing special. Just had some stuff to do," she says, not meeting my eyes, followed by her signature sniff. "What about you?"

I slam the pitcher down onto the counter, none too gently, causing her to flinch. I can't exactly call her on her lie. That would incriminate me. I was supposed to be at Valen's house. "Really?" I prod, ignoring her question. "Nothing at all?"

She meets my eyes, suspicion finally creeping in. "What I do in my free time is adult business."

I scoff. *Adult business?* "I'll bet it was," I quip, my innuendo clear.

"Shayne," she scolds, looking at me as if she doesn't recognize me. *That makes two of us.*

I reach down for my backpack, taking everything out except my notebook and a couple pens, then I swipe the throw blanket off the back of the couch and stuff it inside the backpack before zipping it up. I shrug it on one shoulder and head for the door. It's not that I care what she does, but if she's planning to move us in with some new guy, I'm going to have to figure something else out. I'm not moving again.

"Where are you going?"

I turn and look at her over my shoulder. "What I do in my free time is *adult business.*"

By the time I make it to the barn, it's starting to get dark, and I kick myself for not having the foresight to bring a flashlight. The one on my phone will have to do. Lifting the rock, I scoop up the key and make quick work unlocking the padlock. These woods never used to scare me—probably because Thayer was always with me—but now, alone right before dark, I'm a little on edge.

I close the door behind me, instantly feeling safer, calmer, now that I'm inside. I close my eyes and inhale, taking in the familiar scent. Of everything from my life *before*, I think I miss being in this place most of all. *And the person who was here with me.*

I shake away the thought, walking over to the couch. I drop my bag onto the floor and fish out the blanket before spreading it out over one side of the couch. Turning on the flashlight on my phone, I prop it up on the cushion, then retrieve my notebook and the first pen I touch. I try not to think about the fact that the couch is full of dirt and dust, or that this place has probably become home to God knows how many bugs and critters.

I sit down, tucking my legs underneath me, and I start to write. And write. And write. I write to my brother. I write to

Danny. I write to my mom and Grey. And I write to Thayer. I fill pages and pages of all the things I never said—of all the things I'll never *say*. And it's not until I'm done that I notice a tear rolling down my face. I bring two fingers to my cheek, collecting the moisture before rubbing my thumb and fingers together until they're dry. I don't think I've allowed myself to cry since the night of the funeral…for so many reasons. I didn't have the right, and more than that, I was afraid once I started, I wouldn't stop.

Reaching over, I pick up my phone and check the time—ten forty-six—and notice not only that my mom has called several times, but my phone is clinging to life at one percent battery. "Oh my God," I whisper out loud, shoving my notebook and pen into my backpack. I opt for leaving the blanket. I'll come back for it tomorrow.

I rush for the door, ignoring the pain that tugs at my nipples from the movement, and click the padlock shut. Holding one arm across my chest, I sprint through the woods I know so well, hoping like hell my flashlight will last until I get back to my house. I don't make it more than ten feet before that hope dies and I'm blanketed in darkness.

"Fuck," I curse, trying in vain to turn it back on, but, of course, it doesn't work. I take a deep breath, trying to slow my racing heart. "Calm down, calm down, calm down," I chant to myself in a whisper. *You've walked this path a thousand times. You can do this.* I take a single step, and a twig snaps from somewhere behind me. I freeze, whipping around. I can't see anything, but the darkness has made me more aware of every sound. I wait for long seconds before chalking it up to a squirrel or something, but when I start to walk again, I hear a different noise. This time, it sounds like leaves crunching, and it's coming from somewhere in front of me, off to my left. Rustling from my right has my head snapping in that direction, wishing I wasn't stupid enough to lose track of time without a flashlight.

Before my imagination can run wild, I take off, sprinting toward my house once more. I hear footsteps behind me, picking up speed to keep up with my pace, and that's when the panic starts to set in. It's not an animal. These are people. As in, more than one. I go as fast as my legs will carry me, panting with the exertion. I can hear their footsteps getting closer, and when I finally get the courage to look behind me, I don't see anyone. I stop, surveying my surroundings, half-wondering if I'm going crazy. But when I turn back around, a dark, shadowy figure stands right in front of me.

"Boo."

I scream, my heart plummeting into my stomach, but hands fly out, one covering my mouth, one cradling the back of my head.

"Shut the fuck up."

Thayer? I try to force my eyes to adjust. I can't see his face, but I know it's him. I can tell by his voice. His scent—tobacco and pine.

He peels his palm from my mouth and pulls a flashlight from somewhere, bathing my face in bright light. I squint, bringing a hand up to shield my eyes.

"Someone's chasing me," I say, still out of breath, chancing a glance behind me.

"Is that so?" he asks, and I can hear the amusement in his voice. That's when it clicks. It was him. And probably Holden, if I had to guess.

"You guys can come out now," I yell, turning around as fear gives way to frustration and embarrassment. Three more flashlights click on, bobbing through the darkness as they run toward us, cackling like hyenas. Once they're close enough, Thayer's flashlight illuminates their faces, confirming my suspicions. Holden, Christian, and Baker.

"Assholes."

I try to shove past Thayer, but he blocks my path. "What are you doing?"

"Going home," I snap.

"No, what are you doing out *here*?" he clarifies, moving closer. "Were you in the barn?"

I swallow hard, not wanting him to know that I've been going back there. He'd find a way to ruin it for me somehow.

"No," I lie. "I went for a walk. Couldn't sleep."

He smirks, the shadows from the flashlight making his face look all too sinister, and leans in even closer, lowering his voice so only I can hear. "I can help you out with that." His breath fans my ear, and goosebumps spread down my arms. "Remember the last time you *couldn't sleep*?" he taunts. "Want me to touch your pussy again? Maybe I'll use my tongue this time."

My cheeks burn, the tips of my ears getting hot. "Fuck off." I barrel past him, and this time he lets me by.

"Come on, Shayne," he yells after me. "It'll be just like old times!"

SIX

Shayne

"**G**OOD MORNING, SUNSHINE," VALEN SAYS, LOOKING ME up and down. "You look like shit."

"Couldn't sleep," I mutter, not even bothering to act offended by her comment. Lack of sleep coupled with the fact that I opted for a baggy, oversized shirt to let my piercings breathe have me looking borderline homeless.

Last night, after Thayer's little stunt, I tossed and turned all night. I told myself it was the lasting effects of the adrenaline, but it was more than that. *I can help you out with that.* His words played in my mind on repeat. They were crass and offensive, but they made my stomach flip with…something. Ironically enough, I only fell asleep once I finally stopped fighting the urge to relieve the tension he created. So, I guess in a way, he did *help me out with that.* Asshole.

"Dunkin' for lunch?"

"It's a date."

We part ways and I slip into first period, taking my seat near the back. Once everyone's settled, the morning announcements float from the speaker, making me wince. Lack of sleep gives me the worst headaches.

"Goooood morning, SPH," Taylor's shrill voice singsongs. "First thing's first. As you all know, we've had to change our mascot and logo because it was offensive...or whatever." I snort at the way she sounds put out by the fact. "Last week, we all voted, and the results are in! Instead of the Sawyer Point Indians, we are now..." she trails off and I hear a muffled drumroll in the background. *"The Sawyer Point Tigers!"*

Half the class groans; half applauds. Someone throws a wadded-up ball of paper followed by a *boo*. I'm just glad we've finally stopped offending an entire group of people for the sake of tradition.

"The sign out front as well as the logo on the gymnasium floor will be updated to reflect this change in the coming weeks, so we appreciate your patience while we do our best to work around school functions and athletics. Okay, now that that's out of the way, I also have an announcement from Coach Jensen and me. Volleyball tryouts will take place next week in the gym, every day from three-thirty to five. If you need more information, you can visit Coach Jensen in his office."

I'd rather scoop my eyeballs out with a spoon.

Part of me is dying for a sliver of normalcy. Volleyball is something I'm good at. Something familiar, and something I enjoy. But the bigger part of me doesn't want to deal with everything that comes along with it.

I pull out my notebook and a pen, taking a quick glance around to make sure no one is paying me any attention before I open it to a blank page. Keeping my head low, my hair acts as a curtain, and I drown out the announcements as I write.

A piece of paper taped to my locker has dread unfurling in my stomach. I should've known I wouldn't be able to fly under the radar. I march toward my locker, seeing the words written there.

What do Shayne Courtland and cockroaches have in common?

I rip it off, turning it over, expecting to find the punch line, but nothing is there. I hear snickers and look over to see Taylor and Alexis watching me with amused expressions. "Good one," I deadpan, crumpling up the piece of paper before dropping it to the floor. They're losing their touch. Their insults used to be witty, but this one doesn't even make sense. I spin the dial, putting in my combination, and when I jerk my locker open, a bloodcurdling scream rips through my throat.

I jump back, stumbling into someone as dozens of giant cockroaches crawl over each other, spilling out of my locker and onto the floor. I shudder, watching them all over my stuff. I don't have much in there. An extra jacket, a granola bar, some lip balm. All of which will be trashed.

Another note dangles from inside, catching my attention. *They're both impossible to get rid of.*

My head whips over toward Taylor, but her eyes are wide, horrified, as if she didn't know what I was going to find. She wouldn't go near these things. Then, who? My lock is intact, and the actual locker doesn't appear to be tampered with—on the outside, at least.

Thayer.

He's the only one besides Valen that would know my combination. The same three numbers I use for every password and every locker. But why? Why would he go out of his way to torment me at school? He doesn't even go here anymore. Does he really want me gone that badly?

"Damn, Shayne. You really shouldn't leave food in your locker," Holden says, coming to stand next to me, leaning in close to my ear. "You'll get bugs."

Ah. So, Holden's doing Thayer's dirty work. A nasty retort is on the tip of my tongue, but I keep it inside, settling for a glare instead. They want me to cry and run away. They want a reaction. And I'm not going to give it to them.

"Who did this?" Mr. Beeney, one of the science teachers,

demands, running toward us with what appears to be a small glass aquarium. He drops to his knees, scooping up the cockroaches with his bare hands. "These are Madagascar hissing cockroaches and they are *pets*, not pests." Mr. Beeney keeps these in his classroom, and I always avoided looking at them when I had him my freshman year.

"I don't care what they are. Just get them out of my locker." My stomach rolls, my lips curling up in disgust as I watch him handle them.

"Now you know how we feel," Taylor quips. Alexis has the decency to appear contrite, but the rest of their crew acts like it's the funniest thing they've ever heard.

Something shifts, and I realize that my way of doing things needs to change. Lying low, staying quiet, keeping my head down? It didn't make it go away. If anything, it made things worse. People like Taylor, Thayer, and Holden prey on the weak.

"Thank you," I tell her, loving the way her face screws up into a confused expression. "You just made things a whole lot easier."

"Whatever," she says, her eyes shifting to the side, unsure of how to respond.

I walk away, leaving Mr. Beeney to take care of his *pets*, and head straight for the athletic building. Screw Taylor and Alexis. Screw Holden and Thayer. From now on, I'm not going to let them dictate my choices. Starting with talking to the coach about getting back on the volleyball team.

"You're joking, right?" Taylor snaps, seeing me enter the gym in a tank top and spandex shorts. I put on a sports bra for the first time since getting my piercings, and to my surprise, it doesn't hurt.

"Nope," I say innocently, tightening my ponytail. "Feels good to be back." Actually, it does feel good, if not slightly terrifying. But I'm going to fake it 'til I make it. I talked to the coach last week, and taking into consideration the details of why I quit last year, he was more than happy to let me back on the team. Of course, I have to try out as a formality, but we both know I'll make it.

Taylor steps toward me, getting in my space. "If you think you're going to take my place as team captain just because you decided to come back, you've got another thing coming."

"I wasn't aware the team captain had been chosen for this year yet," I shoot back. The thought didn't even occur to me, but she doesn't have to know that.

"All right, ladies," Coach's voice echoes through the gym before Taylor can respond, clapping his hands to get everyone's attention. "First, it's nice to see both new and familiar faces. We're going to start out with a group warm-up, run some laps, then we'll partner up for some passing. We'll finish by seeing where you're at with your spiking, serving, digging, and setting skills. In the coming days, we'll move on to scrimmages to evaluate footwork and how you work as a team. Sound good?"

I nod my understanding and a couple overzealous girls cheer.

"Taylor, lead the warm-up?"

"My pleasure," Taylor says, sending me a smirk before she skips away.

The next hour and a half flies by surprisingly fast, and before I know it, Coach is blowing the whistle and telling us all he'll see us tomorrow. I grab my backpack from the bleachers and manage to make it out to the parking lot before Taylor can come back for another round. I'm sweaty and tired and *apparently* out of shape, and there's nothing I want more than to go home and shower.

TELL ME PRETTY LIES | 61

By the time I make it home, it's dark, and the empty driveway tells me my mom's gone. Again. Unlocking the door, I walk in and flip on the light switch. I go straight to my room, tossing my bag onto my bed before toeing off my shoes. Pulling my shirt over my head, I turn to throw it into my laundry basket, but I freeze when I see Thayer standing in my room on the other side of my bed, my shirt landing nowhere near its intended target.

"What the hell?" I screech, bringing my arms up to cover my chest. "What are you doing?" I slap a hand behind me, hitting the light switch. Thayer stands there, arms crossed, blank expression on his stupid, perfect face.

"Hand it over." His voice is flat and to the point.

"Hand what over?" I feel my eyebrows tug together in confusion.

He rounds the bed, holding out a palm. "The key to the barn."

My heartbeat kicks up a notch.

"I know you were there." He moves closer, and I kick myself for taking a small step backwards.

"My mom will be here soon."

He snorts, not hesitating for even a second. "You think I give a fuck?"

"What happened to you?" I can't help but ask. His dark eyes narrow, a storm clouding his perfect features.

"Don't play dumb, Shayne. It doesn't suit you."

I frown, looking into those sad eyes, and my heart breaks just a little. "I wish I could change what happened—"

Thayer's in my face in an instant, his arms caging me in against the back of my bedroom door. "Don't," he warns, his voice full of venom. "You shouldn't even fucking be here."

"Where else would I be?" I whisper, my chest heaving, both thrilled and terrified to be this close to him again. He's different now. Unpredictable. But physically, he still feels like Thayer. Still looks like him. And my body isn't communicating with my brain because it still reacts to his nearness. His eyes slide down, hesitating on my sports bra.

"What do we have here?" He brushes the tip of his thumb across the thin material, directly over my nipple. I shudder, flinching away. "You actually did it."

"They can't be touched yet."

He lifts his eyebrow at the word *yet*, and I'm quick to correct myself.

"*You* can't touch them at all."

"Relax," he says before I can correct myself again. He pushes off the wall, putting space between us. "You're the last person I want to touch."

I force my face not to crumble at his words. The old Thayer wasn't exactly a boy scout, but this version? This version is cold and cruel and not the boy I fell for in that barn.

"Get out," I say, steeling my tone. "Now."

"Give me the key and I'm gone."

I consider giving it to him, if only to make him leave, but the thought of not having access to the one place that feels like home...

"I dropped it."

"Bullshit."

"It's your fault," I snap back. "Maybe if I wasn't being chased, I wouldn't have dropped it."

He works his jaw before responding. "Stay away, Shayne. From the barn, from Holden, and from me."

I want to ask him again why he's doing this. Why he's acting like I did anything other than try to be there for him, but my pride won't let me. I won't beg for an explanation. I won't beg him to care about me.

"You're the one in my house," I remind him.

"Still got that mouth," he mutters, eyes zeroing in my lips. "But your brother isn't here to protect you anymore, is he?"

Grey practically raised me, with my mom working all the time. He was like a brother, a best friend, and the only father figure I've ever known, all rolled into one. For the most part, I consider myself to be a responsible person. I got good grades and tried to follow the rules. Except when it comes to Thayer. Something about him brings out the worst in me, and I can't ever seem to think clearly when he's around. Not then, and apparently not now. He made me reckless, and I loved it.

No one would ever expect the two of us would fall for each other. He was the bad boy. The loner. The black sheep. I was just...Shayne. Grey's little sister. But he knew the real me and I thought I knew the real him.

"Or maybe you're the one protecting him now," Thayer muses.

What? "What does Greyson need protecting from?" I ask, not understanding what he has to do with any of this. Grey, Danny, and Thayer were closest, being the oldest, but when Danny died, it somehow turned us into the Montagues and the Capulets.

Before he can answer, I hear the front door open half a second before I hear my mom's heels click-clacking through the house. I turn, wide-eyed, to look at Thayer. If he's nervous, he doesn't show it. If anything, he looks annoyed by the interruption. I, on the other hand, am wearing only spandex and a sports bra, and all I can think about is how bad this is going to look.

"Shayne?" my mom calls. "How did volley—" She pushes my bedroom door open, stopping short when she sees Thayer. Her eyes flash to me in question before landing back on the broody boy in my room.

"Thayer," she says, surprised, bringing a hand to her chest, her slender fingers fidgeting with her necklace.

"Elena." He doesn't bother to hide the contempt in his voice or in his expression. My mom eyes him warily, neither one speaking. My mom wasn't ever the Ames brothers' favorite person, considering their father's status and affinity for bringing home gold diggers, so there's no love lost between them. But this feels different, and I can't put my finger on why.

"Thayer gave me a ride home from tryouts." The lie rolls easily off my tongue, and I see Thayer tense out of the corner of my eye. I didn't even see his car outside, but if she realizes it, she doesn't call me out on my lie.

"How nice." Her tone is polite, but her lips tug down into a frown.

"You know me. Always willing to lend your daughter a helping hand." He winks.

My face burns with a mixture of anger and embarrassment, his meaning not lost on me, and he smirks, knowing exactly what memory is playing in my mind.

"I thought you were at Amherst." It sounds like an accusation.

"He was just leaving." I slip between them before he can answer her. The room suddenly feels way too crowded. They follow me down the hall and through the house, not bothering to make small talk. Mom waits behind in the kitchen while I walk him out. I jerk the door open, waving him through with my other hand. His eyes flash toward the kitchen, knowing she's still within earshot.

"See you soon."

I'm under no illusion that it's a simple, friendly goodbye.

It's a threat.

The next week flies by blissfully uneventful...when it comes to the Ames brothers, anyway. Taylor still got her digs in—pun intended—at tryouts, but where Thayer and Holden are more like hungry wolves, Taylor and Alexis are gnats. Annoying, but harmless. The last day of tryouts was Friday, and the results are to be posted this afternoon in the gym.

"Why do you seem nervous?" Valen asks around a mouthful of yogurt. "You know you're going to make it."

"I'm not nervous."

She pins me with a look, and I roll my eyes, giving up the charade.

"It's been a while and I'm rusty. What if they throw my ass on JV?"

"The horror!" she mock gasps, her eyes widening comically.

"Shut up." The truth is, I'm not nervous about making the team. I'm nervous about playing again, period.

"Come on." She throws her yogurt into the nearest trash can, then pulls me up by my elbow.

"What are you doing?"

"We're going to confirm that you made the team."

"We don't even know if the roster's up yet."

Valen flicks her chin toward the hall where I spot Taylor, Alexis, and their friend Addison strutting through the double doors that lead to the lobby connecting the cafeteria and the gym. "I'm betting they do."

"Fine."

When we push through the double doors to the gym, a class who doesn't have first lunch is playing basketball on the court and a group of volleyball girls is huddled around the list in the far corner. As I'm walking, the basketball somehow ends up rolling out of bounds, stopping right before it hits my feet. Aiden spots us, jogging over. We've seen each other in passing, but we haven't said more than a few words together since he brought me home that night. I figured it was a one-time thing.

"Hey," he says, coming to a stop in front of us. I bend over to pick up the ball, handing it to him. "Let's hang out again."

I arch a brow. "Does Holden know you're talking to me?"

He bends down a little so that he's closer to my height, as if he's letting me in on a secret. "Contrary to what you seem to believe, I do think for myself from time to time."

I chew on my lip, unsure. He's one of *them*. And if I'm being honest, there's still a part of me that feels some misguided sense of loyalty toward Thayer, even though he's made it crystal clear that he wants nothing to do with me. But it wouldn't suck to have another friend.

"Fine. I could use a friend," I say, not wanting him to get the wrong idea. Apparently, I wasn't as smooth as I thought I was, because his eyebrows shoot up, and he rubs a hand over his smile.

"Damn, Shayne, you're just gonna friendzone me off the jump like that?"

I laugh, not knowing what to say.

"Relax, I'm fucking with you. Scout's honor," he swears, holding a palm to his chest. "Friends it is." He holds his phone out with his other hand, and I take it, adding myself as a contact.

Before I can respond, Taylor, Alexis, and Addison march up to us.

"Good news, Shayne. You made the team," Taylor says in her brattiest voice. "Now you can work off that fat ass you acquired over the past year." I bite my tongue, eyes rolling skyward and patience wearing thin as she slaps my butt and skips off.

"I happen to think your ass is fucking phenomenal." Aiden smirks, his eyes scanning my body. I try to smile back, but it feels fake on my lips. She's such an asshole.

"It's true," Valen agrees, nodding. "People pay money for asses like yours."

"Aiden!" someone shouts, throwing their arms up impatiently. I hand his phone back, and as he takes it, his fingers brush mine.

"I'll text you later." Then he's jogging back to his game.

I guess Holden doesn't have as much influence as I thought.

"You do realize Taylor's just jealous because you're getting attention, right?"

"I don't really care what her deal is." I don't let Taylor's words get to me. At this point, she'll say anything to make me doubt myself.

We come to a stop at the two pieces of white printer paper taped to the wall. Worming my way through the cluster of girls gathered around, I go straight for the varsity list and run my index finger down the names, stopping when I find mine.

I close my eyes, the tension leaving my shoulders. *Yes.*

"Weird," Valen says, looking entirely unsurprised. "Never would've guessed that the former captain would've made the cut."

"Excited to have you back, Shayne," a voice says from behind me, and I turn around to find Coach Jensen approaching. He gives my shoulder a squeeze.

"Thanks, Coach." I smile, and this time it's not forced. This is the first time I've felt excited about anything at school since last year. Not to mention, it will get my mom off my back.

"Practice starts next week. I'll see you then."

I nod, and then he's walking away.

"We have a few minutes left before lunch is over," Valen informs me. "Want to grab coffee?"

"I'll pass. I actually have something to do."

Her eyes narrow into slits. "Sounds mysterious."

"Hardly. I have to meet with that counselor chick who's up my ass. See you later?"

I head toward Ms. Thomas' office, stopping at my new locker grab my notebook first. I demanded a new one. There was no way in hell I was going to touch the cockroach locker again. Her door is cracked, and when she sees me, she waves me in, phone cradled between her ear and her shoulder. I slip inside, closing the door behind me. When she motions for me to take a seat, I do, pulling out my phone to shoot a quick text to my mom, letting her know I made the team while I wait.

"Sorry about that," she says, setting the phone back onto the cradle on the wall behind her. "How's the journaling coming along?"

I chew on my bottom lip, my hands squeezing the edges of my notebook. "It's not so much journaling in the traditional sense. More like letters and random thoughts scribbled out without any rhyme or reason."

"Oh?" she asks, eyebrows raised.

"It just kind of happened," I admit. "But I'm writing, so it still counts," I say, defensiveness lacing my tone.

"Of course it counts," she agrees. "And letters are a very common, very effective medium. Writing down your uncensored thoughts and feelings that you know you'll never send can be healing." She holds her hand out. "May I see?"

I hesitate, not wanting her, or anyone for that matter, to see me at my most vulnerable. Bringing the notebook to school is risky enough. If these words ever got into the wrong hands…

"I'm not going to read anything, remember?" she reminds me. "I just want to see that you're filling pages."

I huff out a laugh, handing it over. *Oh, you'll find pages, all right.*

She takes the notebook from me and flips through the pages quickly with her thumb, eyebrows pulling together at the sheer volume of words. Some are written like notes you'd pass in class, some read more like poems, and others are just incoherent ramblings written sideways, upside down, and everything in between. My heart thumps harder, hoping she doesn't catch any particularly incriminating information, but then she's handing it back to me.

"Well?" I prompt, impatient to hear her thoughts and annoyed that I even care.

"I think you're going to need a new notebook," she says, her face breaking into a smile. "How do you feel?"

I shrug. "I don't know yet. I don't think I like the way it makes me feel, but when I started, I couldn't stop. So maybe I'm just a masochist."

That earns me a chuckle. "Well, keep it up. See you in two weeks."

SEVEN

Shayne

"**O**KAY, LADIES, WE'RE GOING TO WRAP IT UP WITH A drill some of you will remember well. It's called Hyperventilate."

A chorus of groans echoes throughout the gym because yes, it's exactly as fun as it sounds. Which is to say not at all.

"So you do remember." Coach laughs. "But it's crucial for you girls to be aggressive. You can't be afraid to hit the floor. Shayne," he says, turning to look at me. "Up here."

Relieved that I'm spared this round, I make my way toward the net, my Asics squeaking against the gym floor. I turn around, the net to my back, facing the rest of the team.

"Sarah and Taylor are going to help toss the balls. Since there's six of you, I want you to pair off and take turns. Three at a time."

The team splits up into three rows of two while Taylor and Sarah duck under the net, heading for the cart of volleyballs behind me.

"The objective is for you guys to work together to get ten good passes to Shayne. We'll throw the balls, you pass them to Shayne, turn around and tag your partner's hand, and then turn back around quick enough to pass again. It goes faster than you think, so be ready. Everyone clear?"

Everyone nods.

"All right, Shayne is going to count until she has ten good passes, then you'll switch. If your pass sucks, it doesn't count. It's at her discretion."

Coach blows the whistle, then he, Taylor, and our teammate Sarah are hurling balls over the net and the girls scramble to get there in time.

"One!" I shout, catching one before letting it fall to the floor.

It quickly turns to chaos, balls flying in every direction, the girls running and lunging to dig the ball.

"Two!"

"Come on, ladies. Get there, get there!" Coach shouts.

It seems to take forever to get to nine. I can tell the girls are out of breath from running back and forth. They're losing steam, but finally, they manage to get the last one to me.

"Ten!" I shout, both hands gripping the ball in the air.

Coach blows the whistle, and I turn to face him just in time for a ball to hit the side of my face. Hard.

"What the hell?!" I know before looking that Taylor is responsible, and when I see her fake pout, I know I'm right.

"Oops. Sorry," she says, dropping her head to the side in mock sympathy.

"I'm *so* sure you are," I say, taking a step toward her. But Coach stops me, tugging the back of my tank top to keep me in place.

"Taylor, Shayne, hang back. Everyone else, go home."

I roll my eyes, inspecting my nails while I wait for everyone else to file out. When just the three of us are left, Coach finally speaks up.

"You two were friends last year," he says, waiting for one of us to fill him in.

"Things change," I deadpan.

He looks back and forth between us. Taylor stands there, arms crossed over her chest, bitch face firmly in place.

"Is this going to be a problem?" he asks, a slight edge to his voice.

"No," we answer in unison.

"Good. First game's in two weeks," he warns. "Get it together before then."

"Fine," Taylor relents.

"Fine."

She turns on her heels and takes off for the locker room, but I grab my backpack and gym bag, heading straight for the student lot. I'll shower and change once I get home. I'm sweaty, tired, and I have the overwhelming urge to introduce my fist to Taylor's smug face, so it's best for everyone if I leave now.

With my nose in my phone, reading a text from my mom about getting called in for a last-minute job, I'm not paying much attention to my surroundings. I use my free hand, distractedly fishing my keys out of my backpack, and when I look up, I stop short, seeing Thayer and Holden leaned up against my car, arms crossed over their chests.

My eyes roll, my head dropping to one shoulder. "Whatever *this* is," I say, motioning between them, "I'm not in the mood for it today."

Two sets of hard eyes bore into me, neither one responding.

"Okay…" I say, walking toward my car. Holden is against the hood and Thayer's to his right, in front of the driver's side door. I hit the unlock button on my keys, but when I reach for the handle, I'm scooped up and thrown over Thayer's shoulder, my keys, bags, and phone falling to the pavement.

"What the hell are you doing?" I yelp, trying to get out of his hold, but he has one arm banded around my waist and the other around my thighs, making it impossible.

"Get her shit," he orders before prowling away from

my car. I lift my head, twisting around to see Holden's black Range Rover parked on the other side of the parking lot.

"Put me down!" I kick my feet, trying to wiggle my way out of his hold, to no avail. Holden jogs in front of us and opens the back door before tossing my bags inside.

"Drive," Thayer tells Holden, then dips his shoulder, shrugging me off into the back seat. I scramble onto my feet, trying to jump out, but then he's climbing in the back with me, shutting the door behind him.

I scurry backwards to try the other door, but I hear the locks click into place. I unlock it manually, and when I pull on the handle, nothing happens. Thayer doesn't react. He doesn't try to stop me, doesn't send me one of those smug smirks. Boredom shines in his eyes, as if he's waiting for me to get it out of his system so he can proceed with…whatever his plan is.

"Really? Child locks?" I jiggle the handle hard enough that I think it might break off in my hand.

"If the shoe fits," Holden says from the driver's seat. He starts the car, throws it in drive, then peels out of the parking lot. I fall backwards at the sudden movement, hitting my head on the window.

"Ow!" I rub the back of my head, then situate myself, my back against the door, facing Thayer, with my right hand on the front passenger seat to steady myself. "What, the cockroaches and late-night stalking weren't enough? You're adding kidnapping to the list?"

"Calm down, drama queen. We just want to ask you some questions."

"And you couldn't do that without locking me in your car?" I try to steel my voice, hoping they can't detect the uneasiness I feel. They won't hurt me. This is *Thayer*. Although, I wouldn't have guessed he'd end up hating me either, but here we are.

"What do you know about my brother?"

I cut my eyes toward Holden.

"Not him. My other brother."

Danny.

"What kind of question is that?"

Thayer hits the headrest behind him with the side of his fist and I flinch, not expecting it. "Don't play games with me, Shayne."

"I don't know anything!"

"Her phone's locked," Holden says, reaching back to hand said phone to Thayer over his shoulder.

Thayer takes it, punching in the password, giving me a look I can't decode when it works. I roll my eyes and look away. I really need to change my password...for everything. I don't know what he's hoping to find, but I don't put up a fight because I know he won't find anything. I have nothing to hide, especially when it comes to Danny.

"Your brother ignoring you?" he teases, angling the screen toward me, displaying our one-sided text thread.

"He's busy with school." I lunge for my phone, but he raises his arm, holding it out of reach. A dark look passes over his features, but he schools it quickly.

"I'm going to ask you one more time. What do you know about Danny?"

I shake my head, confused, and open my mouth to tell him again that I don't understand, but he cuts me off before I can.

"About...that night," he clarifies. His jaw is tense, eyes sad, and for a brief second, I forget that he's holding me here against my will. I forget all the mean things he's said and done, and I just want to wrap my arms around him. But then his mask slips in place, reminding me that the old Thayer is nowhere to be found.

"You know what I know," I say quietly, hoping Holden doesn't pick up on it. I was with him when we found out, after all. "He fell at the falls." I try not to choke on the words.

"He fell," he repeats flatly. "Come on, Shayne. You're going to tell me that you—the girl who listens to murder podcasts and has a conspiracy theory for every goddamn thing—thinks it's likely that my brother happened to go for a swim in fucking thirty-degree weather? Alone?"

I frown. "Are you saying it wasn't an accident?" I shake my head, dismissing the thought. I've wondered what happened that night, but people hurt themselves jumping off that cliff all the time. After Danny died, they finally put up signs warning against it. But not once did foul play enter my mind. "Who would want to hurt him?"

"That's what I'm going to find out," he promises. "And if I find out you're lying to me—"

"I'm not," I snap.

"We'll see."

EIGHT

Thayer

"THINK SHE'S TELLING THE TRUTH?" HOLDEN ASKS, EYES locked on Shayne's retreating form as she stomps back to her car. I can't help but feel amused by her newfound attitude. When Holden first told me she was back, I was pissed—no—I was fucking enraged. How dare she show her face as if nothing happened? But now? Now our little encounters are something I look forward to in a way I can't make sense of. Not that I've ever been able to make sense of anything where Shayne is concerned.

"About not knowing anything?" I shrug, watching her ass bounce in those fucking spandex shorts that used to drive me insane, then she's tossing her bags into her back seat before getting into the driver's seat. "Maybe. But that doesn't make her innocent." As if on cue, Shayne rolls down her window, sticks her arm out, and throws her middle finger up.

"No," Holden agrees. "Not so innocent anymore, is she?"

I catch his hungry expression in the rearview mirror and something like jealousy swirls in my gut. He doesn't know Shayne was mine once. No one does. She was my dirty little secret. And I'm going to keep it that way.

Reaching around the front seat, I slap the side of his head a little harder than necessary.

"The fuck," he barks, peeling his eyes away from Shayne.

"Move over. I'm driving."

Holden climbs over the middle console and I get out, jumping into the front seat.

"So what now?"

"Befriend her. Keep your friends close and your enemies closer and all that shit."

Holden looks at me as if I've grown two heads. "How the fuck am I supposed to do that? She's not exactly trusting of us anymore."

"Then *make* her trust you. If she knows something, she'll eventually let it slip."

Secrets never stay buried for long.

Especially not in Sawyer Point.

NINE

Shayne

"SHAYNE?" MY MOM'S HESITANT VOICE CALLS FROM THE OTHER side of the bathroom door. I sink lower into the water until the bubbles come up to my chin, making sure I don't have any special jewelry peeking out.

"Come in."

The door opens, revealing my mom, contrite expression on her face. "Did you get my message?"

Shit. I never responded after Thayer and Holden intercepted me after volleyball. "Sorry, practice ran late, and I totally spaced it."

She buys the lie easily, making her way over to the toilet to sit on top of the closed lid. "That's okay. I just want to make sure it's okay with you. I can tell them to ask someone else," she offers. "Five days is a long time to be alone."

"Mom," I say flatly. "I'm eighteen. I think I can handle it."

She purses her lips. "I know you *can*. Doesn't mean you should have to. It's different now with Grey being gone."

"I'm going to be swamped with school and late practices, anyway. I won't even notice you're gone."

"I'll call your brother and have him come home for the weekend, at least."

"That won't be necessary," I assure her. My brother is in his own fucked-up, unreachable bubble right now, and I'm not even sure she realizes it. The fact that he's two hours away is the perfect cover. "Who is it this time? Anyone I'd know?" I ask, changing the subject.

"Some hotshot athlete," she says with a wave of her hand. "He *actually* stated that platform heels are mandatory for air hostesses."

"Gross," I say, wrinkling my nose. My mom's job seems glamorous on the surface. She gets to spend all her time on private jets, visiting the world and receives tips in the form of expensive handbags and flashy jewelry. But she also has to deal with handsy men who think she's offering other *services*, and the very real possibility of being replaced by someone younger or prettier or thinner at the drop of a hat. I don't know how she does it.

She shrugs. "For what he's paying, I'd dress up like a clown and let him call me Bozo."

I laugh, splashing bubbles at her. I want to press for details about who she's been with and why she's been so secretive, but these moments—when smiles and light conversation and teasing come easy—are few and far between these days. "When do you leave?"

"Monday. At least I have more than a day's notice this time."

I nod and she pats her thighs before standing. "I'll let you finish up." She walks away, stopping in the doorway, one hand on the frame. "Remind me to ask you about college applications later."

"Oh yeah, Coach is setting up college tours for the seniors." Another thing I forgot to mention. Soon, college coaches will start scouting at games, but before that, Coach wants us to visit surrounding campuses to get on their radar and get a feel for the area. I don't know if I'm interested in a volleyball scholarship anymore, but I figure it's good to keep my options open.

"Well, okay." Mom's eyebrows lift, pleasantly surprised, I'm sure. We haven't spoken about plans for college since before the accident. She's been walking on eggshells with me, probably due to the fact that I was a basket case in the months following the accident, and not just because of Danny. Losing Thayer was almost just as hard, and that's the fucked-up truth. "That's great."

I give her what I hope is a reassuring smile, and then she's gone, leaving me in peace. The second the door closes, the smile falls from my face, my thoughts shifting back to Thayer in record time. He's always been intimidating, but I've never been afraid of him before. And although I don't think he'd ever hurt me, he scared me today. This wasn't some stupid high school prank.

What was he looking for, anyway? Does he honestly think something nefarious happened to Danny? His death was ruled an accident, and I easily accepted that answer—we all did—but was it because it was simply too much to bear to consider the possibility that someone hurt him on purpose? Are we being willfully ignorant? The parents in this town are professionals at pulling the wool over their eyes. Their generation is all about keeping up appearances. Speaking honestly and openly about ugly things is considered airing your dirty laundry. Living in denial is par for the course.

I just never included myself in that category. I've always been a little too curious. Ever since I can remember, I've been interested in crime, conspiracies, and most of all, the psychology behind what makes people the way they are. Nature or nurture? Thayer once asked why I was so interested in these things, considering the vast majority of victims are women. He compared it to a fish enjoying *Deadliest Catch*. I told him it's because knowledge is power. It makes me feel safer. More prepared.

But when something tragic happens to someone you know and love, it hits too close to home. Literally. You don't ever think things like that, whatever *that* may be, will happen in *your* town or to *your* family. But tragedy doesn't discriminate. Bad things happen everywhere. To everyone.

Or maybe, Danny's death was just a freak accident. Maybe Thayer's in denial and simply wants someone to blame. Far more likely.

I sigh, slipping beneath the bubbles, submerging myself completely, and squeeze my eyes shut, overwhelmed with the direction of my thoughts. One thing is clear. The Thayer I knew is long gone, and in his place is the ghost of the boy I used to know.

"Hey, little sister."

"Jesus." I jump, not expecting Holden to be there waiting when I got out of my car. "What do you want?" I don't wait for his reply before I weave in between parked cars on my way to class.

Holden falls into step with me, hooking his arm around my neck. "Can't a guy walk his sister slash friend to class?"

I stop abruptly, spinning to face him. "One, I'm not your sister, so stop calling me that," I say in a whisper-yell. "Two, we haven't been friends for a long time. You hate me now, remember?"

"Fuck, Shayne, you want a plunger to bring up some more old shit?"

Old shit?

"You literally threw me into a car and kidnapped me yesterday."

"Again with the drama. And, technically, that was Thayer."

I storm off, shaking my head. *Unbelievable.* Holden jogs up to me and catches me by my elbow, spinning me around.

"Listen," he says, dropping the act. "I've been a dick."

I arch an eyebrow. "That's an understatement."

"We had to know," he continues as if I haven't spoken, running a hand through his thick dark brown hair. "When you came back, it caught us off guard. It's hard to know who to trust. It's been a fucked-up year, okay?"

I sigh, looking up at the sky to avoid his puppy-dog eyes. Leave it to Holden to use the death of his brother to manipulate me into being his friend again. And even still, knowing exactly what he's doing, I'm falling for it, hook, line, and sinker.

"I'm sorry if we scared you."

"You didn't," I snap a little too defensively. I clear my throat, looking around and noticing for the first time that we have an audience. "Let's drop it, okay?"

"Truce?" he presses, not letting me off the hook that easy. I spot Valen pushing through a group of people, heading my way, expression perplexed.

"Fine, yeah," I agree distractedly, not giving him a chance to reply before I break away, meeting Valen. Thankfully, he doesn't follow this time.

"What was that about?" she asks, linking her arm with mine. "You okay?"

"I'm fine." I shake my head dismissively, still confused about the whole thing and not entirely convinced that his motives are pure. "He apologized."

"As he should."

I glance over my shoulder to find him standing in the same spot, staring right at me, except now, Taylor, Alexis, and the rest of their group are gathered around him with various expressions of contempt and confusion plastered to their faces.

"I guess."

The leaves crunch beneath my feet, telling me that summer is soon coming to an end as I make my way toward the barn, and this time, I'm prepared. After school, I made a quick pit stop at home to pack a bag, stuffing it full of things I might need.

A battery-operated lantern, an extra flashlight just in case, a bottle of water, a peanut butter sandwich, and, of course, my notebook. I feel like an ill-equipped toddler who's run away from home.

I pull one earbud from my ear, letting it hang freely so I can better pay attention to my surroundings. The last thing I need is Thayer to pull another one of his stunts. I stayed away for a few days just to play it safe, but after today, I felt an overwhelming need to purge my thoughts, and with any luck, clear my head. As if Holden apologizing wasn't weird enough, lunchtime was even more baffling. Valen had something to do for cheer, so I grabbed a water from the cafeteria before heading out, opting to hang out in my car instead. Holden called out my name from the other end of the cafeteria, and naturally, everyone's eyes were on me. He waved me over, gesturing for me to sit with them despite the dirty looks from Taylor, but I shook my head in answer, brows pinched together in confusion, wondering why he was so adamant.

Once I get to the barn, I pause the podcast I'm listening to about a teenage girl who killed her own parents, ball my earbuds up, and stuff them into the front pocket of my backpack. Taking one last glance around to make sure I'm alone, I reach beneath my shirt, plucking out the necklace I tied the key to the other day. Except when I go to unlock it, I realize that the door's not locked at all. The barn door is closed, but the lock hangs from the rusted hook, the latch open.

I must not have realized it in my haste to get home last time.

I pull the door open, letting a sliver of sunlight in that illuminates a path to the couch. I'll leave it open to take advantage of the sun until it gets dark. I shrug the strap of my bag down my arm, taking a seat on top of the blanket I left on the couch last time, then pull my backpack onto my lap. Unzipping it, I pull out the lantern, my notebook, and a pen. Once I'm situated, my phone buzzes, and my mom's picture flashes across the screen.

"Hey," I answer, bringing the phone to my ear.

"Where are you? I just got home and your car's here, but you're not."

"Yeah, I dropped it off after school. I'm at Valen's house, working on a project."

"Okay. So, I'm assuming you won't be home for dinner then?"

"They invited me to eat here if that's okay."

"Sure," she says after a pause. "Just have Valen bring you home by ten."

The sudden smell of smoke hits my nostrils and I freeze, inhaling deeper.

"Shayne?"

"Hmm?" I stand, trying to figure out where it's coming from.

"Ten o'clock?"

I spin around, dropping the phone with a scream when I see a figure shrouded in darkness against the back wall. My heart stalls then starts again when I realize it's Thayer. I can barely make out his form, sitting on an old stool, one ankle resting on his bent knee, but I know it's him.

"Shayne?" I hear my mom's concerned voice float from the speaker, and I quickly bend down to pick my phone back up.

"Sorry, dropped my phone. I gotta go, okay? Dinner's ready."

I end the call before she can respond, holding my palm to my racing heart. "Jesus Christ, Thayer. Are you trying to kill me?" The insensitive words fall out of my mouth before I can take them back, but if it offends him, he doesn't show it.

He stands, taking another drag of his cigarette. The cherry burns brighter when he inhales, and tendrils of smoke curl through the air in front of him. He flicks it to the ground, stomping it out with his foot before he stalks toward me. "So it's not just me then?" he asks, stopping when there are mere inches between us.

"What?" I ask, eyebrows pinching together.

"You lied to your mom just now. Fuck knows how many times you've lied to me."

"I haven't lied to you."

He closes the distance between us, towering over me, then pinches a strand of my hair between two fingers. He muses, rubbing the strands between his fingers.

"Why do you still come here, Shayne?"

My eyes dart to my notebook on the couch and he follows my gaze, zeroing in on it. We both lunge at the same time, but he's faster. I jump on his back, his front flush with the couch, but he holds the notebook out of my reach and rolls over beneath me. Suddenly, I'm straddling him, breathing heavy, and I can feel him between my legs. My eyes snap up to his. Thayer's nostrils flare, eyes narrowing into slits.

I swallow hard, leaning forward to reach for the notebook again, but he releases it, letting it fall to the ground with a loud smack. Hovering over him, I glance back down, seeing those dark eyes bore into mine. I don't know what possesses me to do it, but I shift my hips, grinding against him to assuage the ache between my thighs. He bites down on his lip, pulling those two silver balls between his teeth, then hooks an arm around my waist, and before I know what's happening, he's flipping me onto my back and sliding in between my legs.

"Is this what you want?" he asks, bracing one hand on the arm of the couch above my head as he flexes his hips. I gasp, feeling his need pressing into me. He does it again and a moan slips free, my thighs falling open. "Fuck, Shayne." His voice is raspy and tortured and I know he's feeling it, too. That need that's always there, right below the surface. I thought it would be gone now—*feared it would be*—with everything considered.

Our bodies do the talking as we start to move against each other. His mouth is so close to mine and we're both breathing ragged, our lips brushing with each movement. His right hand kneads my chest through my shirt, and I gasp, feeling pain mixed with pleasure shooting straight to my groin.

"Do it again," I all but beg. "Gently."

Thayer only hesitates for a second before he loses the fight and circles his finger around my nipple, following the outline of the piercing. "Yeah, you're not so innocent, are you, baby?" he teases. The throbbing between my legs intensifies and my mouth falls open as he repeats the motion to the other side. My hands fly to his shoulders, needing something to hold on to, but he captures both my wrists in his left hand, pinning them above my head.

"Yes," I breathe, rocking into him as my inhibitions fly out the window along with my pride. I shouldn't let him touch me like this after the things he's said and done, but here I am practically pleading for it.

He shoves my shirt up my chest and I tense, halting my movements. "They're still healing," I explain. No matter how much I want his hands and mouth on me without the barrier of my shirt, I won't risk it. I'm already pushing my luck letting it go this far.

"I'm just going to look."

I bite down on my lower lip, suddenly feeling nervous, but I nod anyway. Slowly, he lifts my shirt, exposing my bare tits to the cold air. I shiver and he sucks in a breath at the sight. He dips his head, still holding my hands above my head.

"Thayer," I warn, squirming beneath him.

"You have everyone fooled, don't you?" he murmurs, bringing his lips to the underside of my breast, kissing the sensitive flesh. "They don't know about this side of you," he continues, grinding into me at the same time. "So innocent. So *pure*. But they don't know what you like to do with your stepbrother in the dark."

The pulsing between my legs intensifies in spite of his words, or maybe because of them, and I speed up my movements, close to the edge. He gives one last lick to the swell of my breast before moving to the other side, his free hand snaking around my waist, making me arch into him.

"Oh God," I whisper as he grinds into me, his breath hot on my skin. All I can feel and smell and think is Thayer, and having him touch me like this is overwhelming me both physically and emotionally. I tremble beneath him, and I don't know if I'm going to cry or come first, but I know I don't want him to stop.

His open mouth ghosts across my nipple, barely grazing the tip, and when his piercing nudges mine, I tense up, falling over the edge. Thayer hooks a hand under my knee to lift my leg, slowly working me back down to Earth, and when I finally open my eyes, he's hovering over me, still fully clothed in his hoodie and all, peering down at me with an inscrutable expression.

Reality crashes into me all too soon and I suddenly feel vulnerable and exposed and I hate it.

How can you simultaneously love and hate how a person makes you feel?

Without a single word, Thayer captures the key in his fist before yanking it from my neck. I gasp, not expecting it, and then he's pocketing the string and pulling away from me to stand.

"Don't lie to me again."

TEN

Thayer

FUCK. GODDAMMIT. I SLAM THE FRONT DOOR, BYPASSING HOLDEN and Christian groping some chicks on the couch in the family room, and head straight to my room upstairs. An image of Shayne lying shell-shocked and half-naked plays in my mind. I shouldn't have allowed myself to be alone with her. I underestimated the effect she still has on me. She's been fucking with my head since the moment she came back. She's the only thing that gives me a distraction from this past year, but I can't let myself forget that she played a part. Maybe. Fuck, I don't know anymore. When she was gone, everything was so clear, and now? Now I don't know which way is up. I don't know what's real. All I know is that I can't let it happen again.

A knock on my door pulls me from my thoughts, followed by Holden's voice. "You good, man?"

"Fine," I snap, not wanting any company when my dick is still half-hard, but he opens the door anyway, letting himself in. Christian trails in behind him, sitting in the chair at my desk while Holden opts for the edge of my bed.

"What's good?" Holden asks.

"Not shit. Go back to your party."

"We got rid of them," Christian supplies, leaning forward to rest his elbows on his knees.

I nod, then lace my fingers together behind my head and blow out a breath. "It's almost been a year."

Holden shakes his head, staring off blankly, while Christian's eyes are fixed on his shoes.

"A whole fucking year, and we still don't have answers."

"Maybe there aren't any," Holden says, still not looking at me. "Maybe he really just fucking fell."

"You said he was acting cagey the day before," I remind him. "So was Dad." I wouldn't know. I was too wrapped up in a pretty blonde distraction with the face of an angel to notice anything else.

Holden scratches the back of his neck. "I don't know, man. When isn't Dad being weird as fuck?"

I look over at my cousin. "What about you? You think I'm trippin', too?"

"I didn't say that," Christian answers.

"Our family has connections. Your dad is a fucking judge, for fuck's sake, and we were denied a police report because the investigation is ongoing, but no one's investigating. Why is that?"

"They didn't find shit, T," Christian says. "That's why."

"Or they're covering something up." The question is why.

"I agree that it's fishy as fuck," Holden chimes in.

"And if we find out someone did it?" I ask, just to be sure we're on the same page.

Holden looks up at me without a trace of humor in his expression. "Then we get our payback."

"Even if it's Grey?"

He shrugs. "Doesn't matter who it is. But for what it's worth, I don't think Shayne knows anything."

Holden's always had a soft spot for Shayne, but I'm starting to suspect the same thing. She seemed clueless when we questioned her, and it could be an act, but my gut tells me that it isn't.

It doesn't change the fact that there's a good chance her brother killed mine.

ELEVEN

Shayne

"H**ATE** M**E**" **BY** E**LLIE** G**OULDING PLAYS FROM MY CAR** speakers on my drive home from Valen's. It's been three weeks since the barn incident. My days have consisted of nothing but school and volleyball. Besides the occasional dirty look and snide comment from Taylor, everything has been…normal. Holden still tries to talk to me every day. He even sat with Valen and me at lunch the other day after I once again declined to sit at his table, which, in turn, ended up causing even more of a scene.

Thayer, on the other hand, hasn't made an appearance once. It's a good thing. It's what I wanted. There's no way I could face him after that night in the barn, anyway. He ripped the key from my neck, then left me lying there, feeling like an idiot for letting him touch me. So why do I feel rejected, and worse than that…disappointed?

Something darts in front of my car, jerking me from my thoughts, and I slam on my brakes to avoid hitting it, squeezing my eyes shut. I peel one eye open, heart pounding, to see a man in a black hoodie, both hands braced on the hood of my car.

"Holden?" I ask, incredulous. I narrow my eyes, taking in his disheveled state and the blood coming from his hand. He's looking behind him, as if waiting for someone to come charging after him. I push the button to roll my window down. "Holden!" I snap, finally getting his attention. When he realizes it's me, I can see the relief set in.

"Thank fuck." He rounds the car, coming for the passenger side door and yanks the handle. "Come on, Shayne. Let me in."

I squint, assessing his glassy eyes and the way he sways on his feet. He's either really drunk or really hurt. Either way, he's fucked up.

Headlights appear in my rearview mirror, coming up way too fast. I snap into action, hitting the unlock button. Holden stumbles into my passenger seat, filling my car with the scent of alcohol, and quickly closes the door. "Go!" he shouts.

I slam on the gas, my tires screeching against the pavement. Once the car's no longer visible in my rearview mirror, I reach behind my seat, fishing my extra shirt out of my volleyball bag. "Here." I toss it at Holden, and he wraps it around his hand.

"Drunk or hurt?"

"Both. The former more than the latter." He chuckles.

I shake my head. "I don't even want to know."

"Probably for the best," he agrees, reclining the seat to lie back. "Wake me up when we get home."

Home.

His house. As in Whittemore. Where Thayer lives. I haven't stepped foot inside in nearly a year. My stomach turns at the prospect of seeing Thayer, my hands tightening around the wheel. Then again, I haven't seen him in weeks. He's probably at some college party, anyway. The odds of him being home on a Friday night are slim to none.

"You better not bleed on my seat," I mutter. Technically, it's my mom's old car, but she drives my grandmother's car now, so I use this one when I need to. It's not flashy. A little white Nissan that gets me from point A to point B. But that's all I need.

I don't expect him to actually pass out in the short five-minute drive to his property, but when I pull up to his open gate and reach over to shake his shoulder, he mumbles something intelligible before promptly falling back asleep.

"Great."

I follow the long, winding driveway that leads to the house, dread creeping in when I notice all the cars lining both sides. Dozens of them. Daddy Dearest must be out of town. That's the only time the boys decide to throw a party. Not that it's exactly a rare occasion—he's gone more often than not, staying at his apartment in the city most nights—and he doesn't give a shit, so long as they clean up their mess. I follow the road up to the circular driveway and around the old brick water fountain surrounded by wildflowers that sits in the center, then throw my car into park.

"We're here," I say, shaking his shoulder. He doesn't budge. "Holden!" I snap. "Wake. Up."

He finally rouses, looking over at me as if he has no idea how he got here.

"You're home," I say, gesturing toward the front door. He scans his surroundings, taking in the clusters of people drinking on the steps and scattered across the lawn.

"Thanks, little sister," he slurs, reaching for the handle. He falls out of the car, landing on the pavement, and a groan follows.

Dammit. I throw my door open and hurry over to help him up. All two hundred pounds of drunk, sweaty, dead weight. I wrap one arm around his waist while his goes around my shoulders. I hold his arm in place, walking him toward the front door.

Some girl bites down on her lip when she sees us approach, giving a little wave. "Hey, Holden."

Is she kidding? Does she not realize he's barely conscious?

"Make yourself useful and open the door. You can try again tomorrow when he's not comatose."

She blinks twice before quickly opening the front door and holding it for us. "Is he okay?" she calls out after us. I don't bother responding.

"Hot Girl Bummer" blasts from the sound system, and there are people drinking, dancing, and making out in every corner. "You owe me for this," I mutter under my breath, ignoring the curious eyes, and head straight for the stairs. Holden holds his own weight surprisingly well all the way up. When we get to the top, I cast a glance toward the black door that leads to Thayer's room, the one right across from where I used to sleep, and it's just my luck that even in his drunken state Holden catches it.

"He's different now," he says, out of nowhere.

"We all are." I clear my throat. "Come on. Almost there."

We amble down the hallway lined with old photos of the estate in various states dating back to the 1800s. It burned down in the early 1900s, but my favorite photos have always been the ones before the fire. This place has so much history, and it's always fascinated me.

Holden's feet somehow get tangled up with mine, knocking me off balance. We both go down, him taking the brunt of the fall, me landing on top of him. His arms come around my waist, holding me to him when I try to get up.

"Oh my God, get off of me," I whine, trying to wiggle out of his hold.

"You're warm and you smell pretty and I miss you." I don't know if it's the alcohol talking, or if there's any truth to it, but he sounds sincere, and it breaks my heart a little. Sometimes, I forget there's a boy with feelings under all that bravado and sarcasm. We didn't just lose Danny. We all lost each other. "We all do, even Thayer."

I purse my lips. *Even* Thayer. Right. "Come on," I say, patting his chest. "Let's get you to bed."

"What the fuck?" a voice booms from behind us. Holden's chest shakes with laughter and I whip my head around to see Thayer standing there, a murderous expression on his face. I roll my eyes, pushing off Holden, and this time he lets me up.

Holden takes my outstretched hands, and I try to pull his heavy ass up.

"A little help would be nice," I snap over my shoulder.

Thayer frowns, looking between the two of us before he prowls toward us and pulls Holden's arm around his neck to hoist him up. "The fuck happened?"

"I don't know. I found him like this."

"Where?"

"Arrowhead Trail. I was driving home and he was just there. Like this," I say, gesturing to his bloody state.

"Thayer?" a feminine voice calls out. My stomach drops when I see a beautiful, leggy brunette clad in only a bra and cut-off shorts standing in Thayer's doorway. "What's taking so long?" She cocks her head to the side, twirling her hair around her finger.

"You can handle it from here," I say, quickly turning to leave. I know there have been other girls. I'm not dumb enough to think he hadn't moved on. But knowing and seeing are two completely different things. I tuck my hair behind my ear, making my way down the steps as fast as I can without actually running away.

"Whoa, girl, where you going in such a hurry?" Aiden catches me by my shoulders when I hit the bottom step, pulling me in for a hug.

"Ew, what is she even doing here?" Taylor asks, holding out a cup that matches the shade of her lips in my direction as she saunters in from the other room. "You do realize you don't live here anymore, right?"

"I was just leaving," I tell Aiden, ignoring Taylor's comment. She's drunk and feels threatened by the fact that I just came from upstairs, so nothing I can say will piss her off more than what's inevitably going through her head. Let her come to her own conclusions.

"Have a beer with me before you go." Aiden's gorgeous in that hot jock kind of way with his square jaw and thick, dark, tight curls. His honey eyes against tawny skin. Full lips.

Unfortunately for me, only broody assholes with lip rings seem to do it for me these days.

"My car's running." I hitch a thumb over my shoulder. "I'll see you later?"

"Want me to walk you out?" he asks.

"She's a big girl, Aiden," Taylor snaps.

I glance back up to the top of the stairs to find Thayer looking down at me, leaning forward with his hands braced on the rail. I force myself to look away, needing to get out of here.

"I'll see you Monday," I mutter, turning for the door. I step around a kid smoking on the stairs, then jump into my car. I'm half-surprised no one fucked with it. I drive straight home, being as quiet as possible when I slip inside.

"Shayne, honey, is that you?" my mom calls from her room.

"It's me," I call back.

"Don't forget to lock up."

I breathe a sigh of relief that she doesn't plan on carrying on a conversation. "Okay. Night!" I go straight for my bathroom, stripping off my clothes and tennis shoes before stepping into the shower. I close my eyes and stand under the stream of hot water, letting it wash over me.

What the hell was Holden involved in earlier? The fact that Thayer seemed to know about as much as I did doesn't sit right. Thayer and Holden have always moved as a unit, always in sync. Was he doing something he didn't want Thayer to find out about? Or just decided to fuck shit up on a whim? The latter seems more likely.

I reach for my body wash and squirt it onto a washcloth

that has replaced my loofahs for the time being and bring it to my chest, careful to avoid my piercings. After Thayer played with them, they were sore for a couple days, but I was lucky that was all that happened. *And God, was it worth it.* I've never felt anything like it. I was on sensory overload, and I think at that point, a heavy breeze would've sent me over the edge.

I shake the thoughts out of my head. He's probably fucking that girl six ways from Sunday while I'm in here reliving some heavy petting like an idiot. I throw the washcloth down and it lands on the tub floor with a wet smack, then I crank the knob none too gently, turning the water off. Stepping onto the cushy mat, I pluck the towel off the hook on the back of the door and wrap it around myself.

Standing in front of the foggy mirror, I swipe my hand across it, just enough to see my face in the reflection. How did everything get so messed up? And what the hell was Holden up to?

After brushing my teeth and throwing on last year's oversized volleyball shirt, I shoot a quick text to Grey.

I miss you. Call me.

When ten minutes go by without a response, I know I won't hear from him tonight, if at all. I crawl into bed in a room that still doesn't feel like mine and dream of a boy who never really was.

TWELVE

Shayne

S CHOOL DRAGS ON SLOW AS EVER, BUT I MANAGE TO MAKE IT
through without incident. It's the end of the day, and
since we have a game tonight, we had to wear our
warm-ups to school. Black track pants with the snaps down
the side and our maroon and black uniform shirts, donning
our new mascot. Opening my locker, I shove my backpack
inside, taking only my calculus book and a pencil.

"Are you avoiding me, little sister?"

I close my locker to see Holden standing there with his
arm propped against the locker next to mine, looking no
worse for wear. You'd never guess that he looked like the living dead two nights ago.

"Let me guess. You had sex with the wrong guy's daughter," I deadpan, hitching my bag onto my shoulder before
walking away. Holden falls into step with me.

"*Wife*," he corrects, and I snort, knowing that there's a
very real possibility that he's not joking. When we walk into
class together, Taylor is already there, shooting daggers at me
with her eyes.

"Better go. Your little girlfriend doesn't look too happy,"

I tease him, sliding into a desk at the opposite side of the room.

"She'll live." He smirks, taking the desk next to mine, but then he focuses on something behind me, and his smile falters. I frown, looking over my shoulder to see two police officers making their way into the room. Everyone in class exchanges confused looks while they speak in hushed whispers with Mr. Turner.

"Listen up," Mr. Turner says in a voice more serious than the one he usually uses. "These officers would like to talk to you about an incident that occurred over the weekend."

One of the officers with dark, slicked-back hair moves toward the front of the class to address us. "As he said, an incident occurred on Friday night involving one of our officer's houses. The perpetrator is believed to be a student here, so if anyone knows anything, or maybe saw something, now is the time to speak up."

No one says a word as the officers survey the class with expectant expressions. I swallow hard, looking at Holden out of the corner of my eye. He flicks a pencil between his thumb and forefinger, appearing bored, but I know it's an act. The all-black getup. The bloody nose. It was him. It wasn't some pissed-off husband he was running from. It was the police, and by letting him in my car, I unknowingly became an accomplice.

I sit back, folding my arms across my chest, pissed that he dragged me into this.

When it's clear that no one is going to talk, he speaks again. "All right, well, if anyone has any information, I'll leave our card with your teacher." He turns to Mr. Turner. "Thanks for letting us interrupt."

Mr. Turner nods, shaking the officer's hand. Everyone breaks out in chatter about what could've possibly happened and who it could be. As the officers near my desk, one narrows his eyes, regarding me warily. He pauses next to me, tapping two knuckles on my desk.

"Shayne Courtland?" he asks, and my eyes lift to meet his.

"Yeah?" My stomach drops, anxiety making my heart rate double.

"Mind if we have a word with you in the hall for a second?"

"Um." I look around, not knowing what to say.

"It'll only take a minute," he says, assuring me. I nod, pushing out of my desk. I chance a glance at Holden, and I can tell he's nervous by the way his jaw tenses.

"Are they even allowed to do that?" some girl I don't know asks in a hushed tone.

"It's not like they're interrogating anyone," a kid named Jason replies. "They don't need permission to talk to us."

"He's right. It's at the school's discretion," Mr. Turner explains. "Now let's get back to work."

I fold my arms over my chest as I follow them out of the classroom. As soon as we're in the hall and the door is closed, they don't waste any time getting to the point. "There was a car stopped on Arrowhead Trail at the same time of the incident that matches your vehicle's description."

I blink, surprised. "How do you know what car I drive?" How do they know *me* at all?

"Small town," the second officer supplies after they exchange a look. "We were actually about to call you up to the front. Did you happen to see anything?"

I shake my head. "No."

"So, why were you stopped in the middle of the road?" Suspicious eyes narrow at me.

The question catches me off guard. I should tell the truth. I don't owe Holden a thing, and this kind of trouble is the last thing I need. Arms still folded, I turn my head toward the window in the door, seeking him out. He's watching me intently, his expression unreadable.

"It was a deer," I say, peeling my eyes away from Holden.

"A deer," he repeats, skepticism lacing his tone.

I bob my head. "Yeah. It shot out of the woods," I swipe the air with my arm, "and ran right in front of my car."

Officer number one looks over at the other one, the two of them having a silent conversation. It's not like it's an unlikely story. It happens all the time.

"Did you hit it?"

"No. I slammed on the brakes in time, but it spooked me. I took a minute to collect myself, and then I drove home."

Officer number two pulls out a notepad, writing something down.

"Did I do something wrong? Do I need to call my mom?" I frown, giving them my best wide-eyed innocent look, pushing my lips into a pout.

"No, no," officer number one is quick to reassure me. "We're about done here. You didn't happen to see anyone on your way home?"

I mash my lips together, pretending to think it over. "No, not that I can recall."

"Okay." He sighs. "If you happen to remember anything that might be useful…" he trails off, stretching out his hand to offer me his card. I take it from between his two fingers, nodding as I read the information.

Edward Wood
Officer- Badge #580
Sawyer Point Police Department
Underneath that are his email, phone, and fax number.
"Thanks."

"Have a good one," he says while the other guy dips his chin before turning to leave. "And watch out for deer."

The tension leaves my shoulders and I breathe out a sigh of relief while walking back into class. I ignore Holden for the rest of class, even though I can feel his eyes on me, and when the bell rings, I'm the first one out the door. Holden catches up to me and captures my elbow, spinning me around to face him.

"Thank you." His eyes that remind me so much of Thayer's don't hold their usual mirth. He's being sincere, letting the mask slip just a little.

"Whatever you're doing, leave me out of it."

"What's your problem?" he asks, frowning, as if he genuinely doesn't understand.

"My problem? We could go to jail," I whisper-yell through clenched teeth, glancing around to make sure no one is listening.

Holden scoffs, a smile tugging at his lips. "Relax, no one is going to jail."

"I realize that you're essentially above the law, but we normal people don't have the luxury of having families with deep pockets."

"You really think I'd let you go out like that?"

"What am I supposed to think? A couple weeks of playing nice don't change the past year."

Something like hurt flashes in his eyes, but he hides it almost as quickly as it came. "Fair enough." He looks me up and down, as if seeing me in a new light, taking a couple backwards steps away from me.

"Holden—"

"Nah. I get it." He turns his back to me, and I sigh.

"What was that about?" Valen asks, sidling up to me.

"I think I just hurt his feelings."

"He has feelings?" She mock gasps.

"Apparently so."

"Interesting." She tilts her head, looking after his retreating form as he disappears into the crowd of students milling around for a second before turning back to me. "Are you, like, so ready for the big game tonight?" she asks in a ridiculous Valley Girl accent.

"Totally. Are you coming?"

"That depends. Are you coming out with me this weekend?"

I press my lips together, unimpressed. "Sure."

"Then it's a date."

When we turn to leave, her for the parking lot and me for the gym, I spot Ms. Thomas heading our way.

"Haven't seen you in a while, Shayne," she says, subtle as ever as she passes by. "Stop by this week?" she phrases it as a question, but we both know it's a warning.

I nod my answer and she gives me a thumbs-up before turning the corner. I've been distracted, and honestly, with Thayer taking away my access to the barn, I haven't felt like writing.

"I gotta go," I tell Valen. Coach decided we should have some *team bonding* beforehand, so instead of going home, I get to go out for ice cream with the team. *Yay*. And to make matters worse, as varsity players, we have to sit through the freshmen and JV games to show our support before we play.

"Good luck, buttercup." Valen slaps my butt. "Break a leg or whatever."

We won the game.

I'm hot, sweaty, and still on an adrenaline high as I walk out of the gym toward the parking lot. I didn't realize how much I missed this feeling until tonight. I can't even complain about the team-bonding trip. With Coach there, Taylor didn't pull any of her shit, and hanging out with some of my old teammates felt good. Valen left right after the game, knowing it would be a while before I could break away from the team, and with Mom on another overnight trip, I'm all alone, but even that's not enough to get me down.

That is, until I see my car. Flat on the ground with the tires—all four by the looks of it—slashed. *You have got to be shitting me*. Anger burns a hole in the pit of my stomach, my fingernails leaving half-moon indents on the insides of my palms. The fact that they're still doing this to me even after I've gone out of my way not only to help Holden, but also to keep him out of trouble is unbelievable.

"Oh my God," a soft, high-pitched voice says behind me. I turn around to see Ashley, one of the girls from my team. "Who would do that?"

"Oh, I know exactly who." I clench my fists, wanting to scream. But instead, I take a deep breath to compose myself before speaking again. "Hey, do you think you could give me a ride home?" I'm not going to roll over and play dead anymore.

"Yeah, of course," she says, looking at me with pity in her eyes. "I'm right here." She points to a little silver sports car.

"Thanks." I follow her to the car, getting in on the passenger side before pulling my seatbelt over my chest. "Do you know where I live?"

She starts the car with a push of the button. "Not unless you're still living at Whittemore." Her voice holds a hint of an apology.

"Actually, that's exactly where I want you to take me."

FOURTEEN

Thayer

"THINK THEY KNOW IT WAS YOU?" I ASK MY DUMB FUCK OF a brother. Holden shakes his head.

"Nah. They went class to class asking everyone."

"They came to mine, too," Christian says, slouched back in his chair. "They don't know shit."

"What the fuck were you thinking?" I ask Holden for the tenth time since the other night. His impulsiveness isn't anything new, but this shit is on another level. When I left a few weeks ago, he seemed like he was ready to let it go.

"I told you. I was drunk as shit. Seemed like a good idea at the time."

"Yeah, well. Next time you decide to go all mission impossible and bash the fuck out of a detective's vehicle, fill us in first."

He twirls a beer cap on the tabletop, a weird look on his face.

"What?" I ask.

"Our girl had my back. Again."

My eyebrows shoot up to my hairline, ignoring that he referred to Shayne as *our girl*. "How so?"

"She was sitting right next to me when those cops came in our class. They pulled her out of class to question her. She had the chance to rat my ass out, but she didn't."

"Yet," Christian tacks on.

Holden shrugs. "It's possible. I don't know, man. I trust her."

Once again, Shayne manages to fuck with my head, and I don't know which version of her is the real one.

The sound of the front door flying open and hitting the wall has all three of us jumping up, ready for a fight. What I don't expect is to see Shayne storming into the kitchen in her volleyball uniform looking both fine as fuck and deadly. When she sees that we're all here, she falters for half a second before pulling it together.

"Which one of you assholes did it?"

Her hair is in a messy ponytail, cheeks flushed, and she's wearing those spandex shorts that leave nothing to the imagination, knee pads still around her legs. My dick jumps in my pants at the sight of her.

"You're going to have to be more specific than that," I tell her, crossing my arms over my chest. The other night, she couldn't get out of here fast enough, and now she's practically breaking the door down like she owns the place?

"My car," she says through clenched teeth. "You slashed my tires."

I turn to look at Holden and Christian, eyebrows raised in question. Both of them hold their hands up, proclaiming their innocence.

"I'm done. I've put up with your pranks, I've let you push me around out of, I don't know, *guilt*," she rambles. "I've saved your ass, kept your secrets." She points at Holden. "And this is how you repay me?"

He steps to her, closing the distance between them. "It wasn't me. But you made it clear earlier that you want to think the worst of me, so I guess I shouldn't be surprised."

"No." She shakes her head, stubbing a finger into his chest. "You don't get to do that. You don't get to manipulate me and make me feel guilty for being honest."

I don't know what they're talking about now, but it's clear that I've missed something, and I don't like the way it makes me feel. Like they're in on something I'm not.

"It wasn't us," he says again, throwing up his arms. He shakes his head, frustrated, and sits back down at the table.

Shayne looks over at me in question.

"I'd like to think I'm a little more creative than that."

"You mean like the cockroaches?" she throws back. "That was pretty clever."

I move toward her, crowding her space. "I'm getting real sick of being accused of shit I didn't do." She tries to hold her ground, but the way her throat moves when she swallows hard gives away her nerves. "You seem to think I spend a lot more time thinking about you than I do. Don't flatter yourself." It's a flat-out fucking lie that she hasn't occupied every one of my thoughts since she's been back, and even before that if I'm being honest with myself. But she doesn't have to know that.

"Right. And it wasn't you who threw me into your car against my will either, I'm sure. Just some other guy wearing your face."

Touché.

"Boys," I hear my father holler from the foyer. "Were you raised by wolves? Why is the front door wide open?"

At the sound of his voice, Shayne's expression morphs from anger to fear in record time. I think about sneaking her out the back, not wanting my father involved in any of this, but it's too late, because two sets of footsteps grow louder, about to walk in at any moment.

Both my father and grandfather appear wearing matching uncertain expressions. "Shayne," my father says, trying—and failing—to sound pleasant. "Well, I must say this is a surprise."

"Hi...Mr. Ames," she stumbles on her words, not knowing

how to refer to him anymore. Not that she ever called him *Dad*. Her wide eyes dart to mine, begging me to save her.

He appraises her for a moment, and unease pricks my spine. They haven't seen each other in nearly a year, and I have no idea how he's going to react to her being here in the house. "Don't be ridiculous. You know you can call me August." He smiles. "I've been meaning to check in since I heard you were back."

"I was just taking her home," I cut in before she can respond, angling my body in front of hers.

"Of course," he says easily, his eyes shifting between the two of us, but the moment we walk out that door, I know he's going to demand answers. And I can only hope that Holden and Christian will come up with something halfway believable. "Give Elena my condolences."

He's doing his best to be polite, but my grandfather, on the other hand, doesn't seem to have the same idea. He eyes her with such disdain that it catches me off guard. Seems I'm not the only one harboring a grudge. Even more surprising is the fact that my need to protect her is still alive and well, buried underneath all the resentment. Talk about fucked up.

"Sure." Shayne nods, a frown tugging at her pretty features.

I shoot Holden a look telling him to do damage control and he gives me an almost imperceptible nod to let me know he's got it, and then I'm walking out of the house with Shayne right behind me.

FIFTEEN

Shayne

WHAT WAS I THINKING? I CANNOT BELIEVE I JUST BARGED into Whittemore like a psycho. Going over there was a half-baked plan at best. I didn't know if anyone would be home, but I definitely didn't expect to see August. He's *never* home. Even when we lived there, I could count how many times I interacted with him on both hands. If I thought Thayer was cold, August was ice. But the two of them have nothing on his grandfather.

He's old money and has that air of superiority thing down pat. He clearly hasn't forgotten our last encounter at the funeral, if the way he was looking at me is anything to go on. It was as if he was trying to see inside my soul and figure out my motive.

Thayer walks ahead of me, heading for his matte black Challenger Hellcat. Even his vehicle manages to look sinister. I ignore the way my stomach flips at the idea of being inside it again. He unlocks the door, and I slip into the smooth leather seat, pulling my seatbelt over my chest.

"Where's your car?" Thayer asks, looking straight ahead at the dark driveway. He pushes the ignition button, and the engine roars to life, the seat vibrating beneath me. A thrill shoots up my spine remembering how it felt to fly down the back roads at night with Thayer's hand cupping my thigh.

"Shayne. Your car. Where is it?" Thayer repeats.

I scoff. "Like you don't know."

His nostrils flare, clearly losing patience as he looks over at me.

"Okay, fine. You didn't do it," I concede, crossing my arms and sitting back in my seat. "It's in the student parking lot. Came out after my game and found it like that." But if he didn't do it, then who did? Taylor wouldn't have had the time. She was with me for the better part of the day, anyway. Unease creeps in, and I find myself wishing it had been Thayer. Better the devil you know than the devil you don't.

We spend the remainder of the short drive home in silence as "What It Is to Burn" plays softly. So many things run through my mind, and I want to take advantage of this rare display of human decency by asking him everything he's avoided telling me. Why did he go cold on me that night in the barn? What happened after I left? Why doesn't he seem to ever go to school? But my pride won't let me ask any of those things.

"Your mom gone?" he asks, and I can hear the judgment in his tone. He dips his head to look out of the windshield at my house. No lights. No cars. No movement.

"Out of town for work," I say shortly.

"She do that often?"

I snort out a laugh. "You mean *work*? Yeah. She doesn't have the luxury of staying home." My tone is snotty and defensive, but I've seen how people in this town have treated her. I've heard the whispers. But for it to come from Thayer, when his dad is the one who left her high and dry, it's a low blow.

"Thanks for the ride." I push the door open, and by the time I get out and close it behind me, Thayer's out of the car, rounding the hood of his Challenger.

"Is there something you're trying to say?" he asks, coming to a stop in front of his lit headlights.

"Not all of us were born with a silver spoon in our mouth."

He chuckles darkly, closing the distance between us. I take a step back, the backs of my thighs hitting the front bumper. "Is that what this is about?" he asks, tucking a wayward strand of hair behind my ear, and I fight the shiver that threatens to roll through me. It's not fair for his touch to be so sweet when his words cut like a knife. It's not fair that he still has this effect on me. He widens his stance, making our height difference less apparent. "Because you didn't seem to care about that when you were begging me to fuck you."

My breath catches and I shove his shoulder, but he barely budges. He looks down at his shoulder with a smirk, as if he barely felt it.

"Tell me why," I demand. "Why do you hate me so much?" I finally spit out the question that's plagued my thoughts for almost an entire year.

I see the muscle beneath his jaw twitch, his nostrils flaring, and I know I've struck a nerve. "Because I have to."

"Then why do you keep coming back?" The hushed words are out of my mouth before I can stop them.

"Because I have to." His thumb swipes over the pulse that jumps in my neck at his admission. Maybe I'm not the only one who can't seem to sever this connection. Maybe it's killing him as much as it's killing me.

Slowly, he angles his face toward mine, his lips grazing my cheek on their way to my mouth. My eyes fall shut, heart lodged in my throat as I wait for him to make his move. I push up onto my toes the slightest bit, and that's all it takes. His hand fists my hair and his tongue licks the seal of my lips, seeking entrance. I let him in, feeling his tongue slide against mine, and a moan slips free. *He's kissing me.* After all this time, he's kissing me, and I almost forgot how it felt. My hands find his hoodie, clenching the material in my fists to stay upright.

Thayer's hands wrap around my waist and he jerks me onto the hood, not breaking the kiss. He plants himself between my thighs, and I lie back onto the cool metal, yanking on the front of his sweatshirt to bring him with me. Planting my feet flat on the hood and bending my knees, I flick my tongue across his piercing, earning a growl from him. Then he's sliding a hand down my stomach, stopping between my thighs. My head falls back onto the hood with a thud as his fingers rub me through my shorts. This is crazy. We shouldn't be doing this, especially out in the open like this. But I've never been able to see reason where Thayer is concerned.

His lips find my neck, sucking and biting as brings me closer to the edge, but in the worst timing, visions of the girl in his room cut through the fog of lust. When he pulls away and the tips of his fingers dip into the waistband of my shorts, I grab his wrist, stopping him.

"You were with another girl the other night." The words seem so juvenile out loud, but I'm not a homewrecker.

Thayer laughs darkly against my neck, sending a chill down my spine. "You think this makes you my girlfriend or something?" he asks, then scrapes his teeth across my neck.

"I hate you." Even as I say the words, I'm arching into him, needing more.

"Tell me another lie." His hand flattens against my stomach and slides beneath my shorts and underwear. My grip on his wrist is loose, hardly a protest. "Tell me more pretty little lies from these pretty little lips." His fingers part me and I gasp, squeezing his wrist, and he groans appreciatively. "This doesn't feel like hate."

My knees fall open, some sick part of me getting off on his taunts, and he pushes a finger inside. It doesn't escape me that I had a game earlier and I could use a shower. I don't even want to know what I look like, messy hair, still in my uniform—knee pads and all—getting finger fucked on the hood of a car. Any hope of keeping my pride intact flies out the window when I urge him to speed up his movements by guiding his wrist to move faster.

"Fuck," Thayer groans, his free hand jerking my shorts down to give him better access. He pumps his hand faster, and I tug at the hem of his sweatshirt, wanting to feel his skin, but he stops me. I give a frustrated growl and he answers by pushing my shirt up my chest and scraping his teeth over my piercing through my white sports bra. The orgasm I don't see coming hits me hard and fast, and I clench around his fingers, mouth falling open in a silent scream.

When I come back down to Earth, I open my eyes to find Thayer's attention locked onto where he slowly slides his fingers in and out of me, seeming dazed. I lick my lips that are dry from the cool air, still shuddering with aftershocks. Thayer pulls his fingers from me, giving my pussy two pats, and I flinch, still sensitive.

"Welcome home, Shayne."

SIXTEEN

Shayne

I HATE THAYER AMES.

At least that's what I tell myself every time my thoughts drift back to him and how he left me on the hood of his car with my shorts still around my thighs. Reaching an entirely unprecedented level of asshole, he walked away, got into his car, started the engine, and held my forgotten backpack from his window, dangling it from two fingers, while he waited for me to pull myself together. I pulled my shorts back into place and peeled myself—along with my dignity—off the hood before storming into the house without a backwards glance.

Just when I think he's finally showing me a glimpse of something real, he has to ruin it by being an asshole. And I'm the idiot who fell for it. Again.

To make matters worse, I still don't know what I'm going to tell my mom about my car. If it was one tire, I could make up some story about getting a flat or running over a nail or something. But four of them sliced open at the wall? There's no denying that it was intentional, and that will lead to her worrying about me and how I'm…reacclimating.

Not to mention the financial burden. I can't even begin to accurately guess how much it will cost to replace four tires. Eight-hundred bucks? A thousand? She won't talk money with me—says that's not a kid's business to worry about finances—but I know we're struggling. Grey is going to one of the best colleges in the country, and it's not like he has a scholarship. Living in Sawyer Point isn't exactly cheap either.

"All right, ladies," Coach calls out, bringing me out of my thoughts. "That's it for today. Once again, good job last night. Let's carry that same energy through the season. Enjoy your day off tomorrow, then we have a game against Mountain View on Thursday."

I throw my ball into the bin, and when I turn around, I see Holden sitting on the bleachers on the other side of the gym. What the hell is he doing here? Has he been there this whole time? I roll my eyes when I notice Taylor spot him at the same time, a flirty grin spreading over her face as she saunters toward him. He stands, walking toward her.

"Hey, sexy," she says coyly, once she's a few feet away.

Holden notices her, seemingly for the first time, and barely acknowledges her with a flick of his chin before he walks right past her. Taylor's face is beet-red with what I'm sure is a mixture of anger and embarrassment. The only thing worse than rejection for a girl like that is *public* rejection. Because her little friends, along with the entire team, just witnessed the whole thing.

"Hey, baby sister."

"For the last time—" I say, glaring at him.

"Yeah, yeah, you're not my sister. The sound of it just gets me hot, what can I say?" He takes my bag, then puts a hand on the small of my back as we walk through the gym.

"What the hell are you doing?" I whisper.

"Thayer said you'd need a ride."

I snort. How gallant. "Not from you."

"I thought we were past this," he says, sounding bored.

"You don't even realize what you just did, do you?"

"What?" His eyebrows pull together, genuinely confused, and I shake my head, amused at how oblivious he can be.

"As if I wasn't already on her shit list, *that* just made me an even bigger target."

"Who, Taylor?" he asks, glancing behind us to see her standing there, seething. "Fuck her. She's not my girlfriend. We fucked like two times."

Wow. These Ames boys sure know how to treat a girl. Not that it's news to me. Holden has never had an exclusive relationship in all the time that I've known him.

"Okay, first of all, gross. Second of all, it doesn't matter. She thinks *I'm* what's standing in her way."

"And you care because?"

I stop to look at him. I...I don't know. Why *do* I care? It's not like I'm afraid of her. I just prefer to avoid her if I can help it. "I *don't* care. It seems to be her mission in life to make my life hell, so I'd rather not hand her the ammunition." *And she slept with your brother on the night of the funeral.* Not that I can really fault her for it. It's not like she knew about Thayer and me. Still, Taylor has always been a mean girl through and through.

"I'll fix it," he promises.

"No—"

"I'll fix it," he cuts me off, his voice firmer this time, then he takes my hand in his. "Come on."

Reluctantly, I drop it, even though I know his idea of *fixing it* will no doubt make it worse. It's like when the nerdy kid's mom calls the school to tell them they're being picked on, and they only end up getting it ten times worse. That's just how bullies operate.

Once we're outside, I stop dead in my tracks, noticing my car is gone. Valen picked me up for school this morning, and it was still parked when we got there.

"Dammit!"

"What's the problem?" Holden frowns.

"My car got towed."

He shrugs, probably not understanding why I'm upset. And why would he? Money isn't an issue for him. But all I can think is how that's going to be another hundred or two added to the list of expenses.

Holden unlocks the doors, and I climb into the passenger seat. The song "Drowning" starts blasting when he starts the car, but he quickly turns it off. We both sit there in silence for a beat, and I know we're both thinking about Danny.

"I miss him, too," I admit, feeling weird talking about Danny out loud. He's been the elephant in the room ever since I got back, but maybe it's time we start talking about him. Maybe this is how they—how *we*—heal.

Holden clenches his jaw, throwing the car into drive. *Okay, so maybe he's not there yet.*

"Have you heard anything from the police?" I ask, deciding a subject change is probably for the best.

He visibly relaxes. "Not shit."

"That's good. What were you doing there, anyway?"

One hand on the wheel, he glances over at me, a grim expression on his face. "Blowing off some steam."

I narrow my eyes at him, not following.

"Can I trust you?"

I snort out a bitter laugh. "Can *you* trust *me*? I'm not the one who's done anything to have you questioning my loyalty."

"I'm not fucking around," he says, his voice holding an unusually serious tone. "No one can know. Not my dad, not your mom. No one."

I nod, apprehension swirling in my stomach.

"Something's off, Shayne." His hand tightens around the steering wheel. "Someone knows something, and they're covering it up."

I shake my head, confused. "But why would anyone want to do that?"

"That's what we're going to find out."

I rack my brain for answers. None of it makes sense. The car slows, and I look out the window, noticing we're close to my house. "Hey, pull over," I say, unbuckling.

"What, here?"

"Yeah. I'll walk the rest of the way."

"It's dark."

I raise my eyebrows. "And? My driveway is right there," I say, gesturing to the gravel path that leads to my house. "My mom is home and I'm stalling." I need all the extra time I can get to figure out how the hell to explain my tire situation. Plus, I'd rather not answer questions about why Thayer was in my room a couple weeks ago, and now Holden's dropping me off. She's been a little intense lately.

"Thanks for the ride." I jump down from the car and swing my bag over my shoulder. The chilly night air has me rubbing my arms as I make my way up to the house. Unfortunately, I don't think there's any getting out of telling my mom the truth. I'll just have to convince her that it was random. That I'm not the target. Everything is fine. I'm fine.

I stop short when I notice my car. In my driveway. With four brand new tires. As if nothing ever happened.

"What the hell?" I circle the car, giving it a quick once-over. How did she already take care of it? I wonder if the school called her. Or, more likely, the towing company. Bracing myself for the third degree, I walk up the porch and open the front door. I follow the rustling sound coming from the kitchen and find my mom standing at the counter with a plethora of takeout boxes.

"Just in time," she says, reaching for some plates from the cabinet above her head. "I ordered Chinese. Figured you'd have a late night." She scoops some noodles onto a plate. "How was the game last night? I'm sorry I couldn't make it."

I stand there watching her load my plate up with the chicken and vegetables, waiting for her to mention the car.

She rounds the counter, setting the plate down in front of me before pulling me in for a hug. "What, you didn't miss your mom?" she asks when I don't return her hug right away.

"Sorry," I say, snapping out of it and wrapping my arms around her. "Long day. I'm out of it."

She pulls back, assessing. "Why didn't you drive today?"

"Hmm?" I look up at her. "Oh, I rode with Valen."

She nods, not questioning the lie, then goes to make a plate for herself. A thought occurs to me, and I bend down, fishing my keys out of the front pocket of my backpack. But they're not there. Unzipping the main compartment, I tip it over, dumping out all the contents. No keys.

What the hell? I know they were in here. I threw them in after locking my car up when Ashley gave me a ride. I stand abruptly, speed walking toward the front door.

"Where are you going?"

"I forgot something in my car," I throw over my shoulder. I jerk the door open, running down the porch and to my car. Pulling on the handle, I find it unlocked, my keys sitting in the driver's seat. My brain is about to short circuit wondering who's fucking with me now, waiting for the punch line, when something dangling from the rearview mirror catches my attention.

The key from the barn. *Thayer.* I unhook the key from the mirror, feeling the cold, rusted metal in my palm. He did this? Why? Why would he go out of his way to help me? And why return the key? If sending mixed signals were an Olympic sport, he would be a gold medalist.

Maybe it's a trick. Maybe it means nothing at all. But I can't help wondering if this is the old Thayer coming back to me little by little.

SEVENTEEN

Shayne

"I CAN'T BELIEVE I'M HERE OF MY OWN FREE WILL," I say, bringing the red plastic cup of beer to my lips. Valen and I already had some drinks while we got ready at my house, and I realize I'm not as uncomfortable as I thought I'd be. Holden begged us to come by tonight, and I've actually started to let my guard down with him a little bit. I said no at first, but then Valen talked me into it because Liam canceled his visit this weekend, and she wanted a distraction.

"Is it weird being back?" Valen asks, scanning the crowd of people. The house is bursting at the seams, and somehow, that makes me feel better. Everyone's too preoccupied with getting trashed and finding someone to hook up with, making it easier for me to blend. "I mean, since you used to live here?"

Nodding, I lick the excess beer from my lips. "Yep," I say, the word popping from my mouth. I spot Holden coming our way from the other room, making his way through the throng of drunk people. I think everyone in town between the ages of seventeen and twenty-five is here. That's nothing new, though. With the Ames boys all being different ages, their parties have always been a mix of both high school and college. But they're usually more selective of who and how many people they let in. This…this is on another level.

"Well, look who didn't puss out!" Holden yells, holding out his arms. When he bends his knees and wraps his arms around my waist, I let out a surprised squeal, holding my beer out as he spins me around.

"Holden, my butt!"

He sets me down and tugs my dress back down from where it rode up, and I slap his hands away.

"Damn, Shayne," he remarks, looking me up and down, taking in my houndstooth print mini dress with spaghetti straps. It's a little too short and a little too tight, but I paired it with black Converse instead of heels to make it more casual.

"Shut up," I say, rolling my eyes, but the tips of my ears smolder under his attention. "Stop looking at me like that."

I spend most days in spandex shorts and baggy t-shirts with volleyball, and I felt like getting dressed for once. So sue me. I won't lie and say that the possibility of seeing Thayer here didn't factor into my decision, which is all kinds of messed up, considering how we left things. Or rather, how he left me. Near naked. On top of his car.

"Thayer's gonna love this," he says, snapping me out of my thoughts.

"What?" I snap, taken aback. No one knows about us, so the off-handed comment catches me off guard along with the news that Thayer is here somewhere. I wasn't sure he would be with the disappearing act he likes to pull.

"Nothing." He turns to Valen, greeting her with the flick of his chin. "'Sup, Valentina?"

She gives him a bratty smile, hating that he used her full name. "Not much, Holden Cock."

"Always so pleasant." Holden laughs, scraping his teeth over his bottom lip. "But if you want to hold *my* cock, all you have to do is say the word."

Valen shakes her head, but a smile pulls at her lips.

"Come on, let's go see what's up out back."

Holden grabs my hand, pulling me through the crowd, and Valen follows, latching onto my shoulder. Holden stops in the kitchen to grab another cup, and we refill ours. Drinks in hand, we head out back where clusters of people are grouped off in various parts of the yard. To the left, an obnoxiously loud game of beer pong takes place, and to the right, tucked into the corner, sits a fire pit with only a few people. Christian, Baker, Taylor, Alexis, and Aiden. Christian and Baker exchange a look that I don't care to decode, and the girls look annoyed that female competition is encroaching on their territory.

"Why is she here?" Taylor asks, nodding in my direction, a sense of déjà vu creeping in.

"Because she's fucking family, and she has more of a right to be here than you ever will," Holden shocks me—along with everyone else by the looks of it—by saying. "And if your insecure, petty ass can't handle it, you can get the fuck out."

No one speaks. Alexis averts her eyes, taking a sip of her drink, but I swear I see a flash of a smile. Aiden smirks, sitting back in his chair, and Taylor looks around for support, finding none. Valen, of course, is the one to break the silence by snorting out a laugh, and I elbow her side.

"Great," Holden says, lifting his cup. "Now that that's settled, let's get fucked up."

Everyone falls back into their conversations with the exception of Taylor who looks to be plotting my demise. I know Holden thinks he's helping, but once again, he only poked the bear. I decide here and now that I'm done caring about Taylor. What is she going to do? Start another nasty rumor about me? Sling insults at me in the halls? *How will I ever survive?* Note the sarcasm.

Holden takes a seat around the fire between Christian and Baker, and Valen takes the remaining one next to Aiden, while I stand here still stunned, wondering what the fuck just happened.

"Hey, Blondie."

I look to my left to see Aiden slouched back in his Adirondack chair wearing a hoodie pulled over his head with the strings tied in a bow, matching sweatpants, and white kicks. He's so hot, he manages to make even loungewear look both stylish and expensive.

"You get all dressed up for me?" he asks, eyes roaming me head to toe, but somehow, it doesn't come across in a salacious way.

I tilt my head, eyebrow raised. "Obviously," I tease. Aiden is tempting, but dark, broody eyes pop into my mind, unbidden, and I know it wouldn't be fair to lead him on when I'm hung up on someone else.

He pats his lap. "Have a seat."

"Sorry," I say, pushing my lips into a pout. "I'm here with my boyfriend."

The confusion on his face morphs into amusement as I reach a hand toward Valen, and she pulls me onto her lap.

"It's true. I'm her daddy."

I snort out a laugh and she wiggles back into the chair, making room for me to sit in between her legs.

"I saw a porn that started like this once," Holden says, rubbing his hands together.

"Just once?" Christian gibes.

Taylor rolls her eyes. "Pretending to be lesbians for attention. *How original.*"

Holden cuts her a warning glare and she throws up her manicured hands in mock surrender. "Sorry." She shrugs in a way that says she's not sorry at all. "Old habits die hard."

"It's called a joke. You should try it sometime," I say. She's always so busy trying to be the prettiest, the richest, the smartest, the most athletic, that I don't think she'd know what fun was if it bit her in the ass.

She gives me a bratty smile and then averts her eyes, effectively ending the conversation. I don't know how I was ever friends with her. I mean, we were frenemies at best, but even being friendly with Taylor seems impossible at this point.

"I think summer is officially over." I shiver, glad for the fire. I should've brought a jacket.

"Drink more. It'll warm you up," Valen teases, guiding my cup to my mouth with the palm of her hand. Usually when we go out, one of us will limit ourselves to a drink or two if the other plans on getting drunk, but since I live right across the woods, we can both partake.

The guys fall into some conversation about basketball, and Valen rolls her eyes, completely uninterested. At first, I'm tense, still not completely at ease here, but then we all fall into conversation, and I start to loosen up. Taylor still looks put out, as if my mere presence offends her, but she doesn't make any additional snide comments. The more I drink, the more I relax. I'm feeling warm from both the fire and the alcohol, leaning back on Valen, with my feet perched on the edge of the brick fire pit.

"Up," Valen says, smacking the tops of my thighs. "We need more beer."

I stand too fast and stumble a little, feeling tipsier than I thought I was. Aiden stands and his hands steady me at my waist.

"You good?" he asks quietly.

"I'm *so* good." I laugh. I haven't let my guard down like this in over a year, and it feels like a weight has started to lift from my chest. Not fully, but enough to notice. Enough to breathe a little easier.

A giggle rings out into the night air, and I look up to see Thayer standing on the balcony above us, hands braced on the ledge, staring daggers at me. A small group of people are up there with him, and a girl named Lissa whispers something into his ear, pressing her tits into the side of his arm. Lissa graduated last year, but it seems she still hasn't given up on getting Thayer to notice her. I frown, looking away.

"Take care of her," Valen says, pointing a threatening finger at Aiden. "I'll be right back."

"I need a re-up, too." Holden stands, and the two of them walk inside together. Once they're gone, Taylor takes the opportunity to sidle up to me, and I can tell by the look on her face that she's way too excited about whatever bomb she's about to drop on me.

"Since you like jokes so much, want to hear a funny one?" she asks, tilting her head to the side with a fake-innocent expression on her face.

"Let's hear it," I deadpan. She's going to say it either way.

"Okay, it's a good one." She claps her hands under her chin. "Are you ready?"

When I don't respond, she continues, cupping her hands around her mouth in a mock whisper. "It's you. You're the joke."

I poke out my bottom lip, patting the top of her head. "We'll work on it. You'll get better with practice."

"Oh, that's not all," she says when I start to turn around. I pause, waiting for her to finish. "The only reason you're here right now is because Thayer told Holden to get close to you. But it's super cute that you actually thought they were your friends."

What? I falter, not expecting that.

"What the fuck, Taylor? Chill," Aiden chimes in.

"What? You don't believe me? Just ask him."

"Tay!" Christian snaps, and the look on his face is all I need to know it's true. The way Holden flip-flopped so suddenly and basically forced me to be his friend again. The way he's always there, whether it be at lunch, in between classes, or picking me up from practice.

My stomach churns, feeling stupid, but not exactly surprised.

"Enjoy it while it lasts, because your time here," she lowers her voice, moving close enough to tower over me, "is almost up."

"Thanks for the warning," I manage to force sarcasm into my tone.

"Anytime." She smiles.

I turn to the side yard, knowing there's a gate over there I can leave through so I don't have to walk back through the house.

"Shayne," Aiden calls out, but I wave him off.

"I'm fine. I'll be back in a minute."

I hear bickering break out among Christian, Baker, and Taylor, but I keep going. I make it to the perimeter of the yard, outside the clusters of people, eyes glued to my Chucks as I follow the fence down toward the gate. Using my free hand, I pull my phone from the purse at my hip and open Valen's text thread to let her know I'll be out front.

"Where you going in such a hurry?" an unfamiliar voice asks, or slurs, rather. "I remember you."

I stop short just as Ryan...*something* approaches, beer in hand. I don't know much about him, other than he used to play basketball with my brother and graduated last year. "It's me," I deadpan. Not in the mood for small talk or reunions, I move around him. Ryan sidesteps, blocking my way, and his beer jostles with the movement, spilling down my chest. I gasp, holding my arms out to shake off the excess beer before pinching the wet fabric of my dress and pulling it away from my chest.

"Shit, my bad. Let me take care of that for you."

Before I can blink, his cup falls to the ground, forgotten, and he wraps his arms around the small of my back, bringing his mouth to my chest with all the desperation of a newly turned vampire needing to feed.

"Gross, get the hell off me," I grunt, shoving him away before he's able to make contact. I try to move past him, and he blocks me once again, pissed at the rejection. Just when I'm poised to knee him between the legs, a fist shoots out, hitting the side of his face, making his head snap to the side.

EIGHTEEN

Shayne

I JUMP BACK, WIDE-EYED, AS THAYER FISTS THE COLLAR OF RYAN'S shirt before he's recovered from the hit, then throws him to the ground.

"Hold up," Ryan shouts, cupping his jaw, looking up at Thayer from the grass, blood dripping from his lip. "I didn't know she was your girl. My bad, man."

Thayer lunges for him, but I pull on his shirt, holding him back. "Stop!"

Ryan flinches, holding up his arms to protect his face, but to my surprise, Thayer listens to me, stopping at the last second. Instead, he spits on the ground next to him.

"Oh, that's lovely," I say drily. "And I had it handled."

"The fuck you did."

Holden and Aiden must have heard the commotion, because they're running up to us wearing matching confused expressions.

"What the hell happened?" Holden barks, looking from Thayer to Ryan's form lying in the grass.

"I'm leaving," I snap. "That's what happened." I head for the side gate.

"Get rid of him," I hear Thayer order, and then I'm being picked up and thrown over his shoulder. Again.

"Put me down, Thayer," I demand, squirming in his hold.

"You're drunk."

"And you're an asshole!"

Thayer doesn't answer, but I think I hear him chuckle as he prowls back toward the house. My hair hangs in my face, and I'm glad for the barrier it creates between me and everyone who's gawking at us. I feel a tug on my dress at my thighs, followed by the warmth of Thayer's palm over my ass, shielding me from prying eyes. *How chivalrous.*

All the blood rushes to my head, and hanging upside down doesn't do anything to help the dizzying drunk feeling. As soon as Thayer steps inside, people part like the Red Sea, making way for him. I hear a mixture of whistles, laughter, and cheers, and I try once again to get down to no avail.

"Shayne, what the hell?!" I hear Valen's voice shout. I brace my hands against Thayer's lower back to push myself up, seeking her out. "Two minutes! I leave you for two minutes!" She abandons her drink, then rushes after us, but Holden intercepts her, his hand flattening against her stomach. I catch the scathing look she gives him before Thayer rounds the corner, then starts up the stairs. Once we're down the long hallway, he pivots right, throwing his door open.

He's taking me to his room? My stomach flips, and not because of the alcohol. It's been a long time since I've been in here, and I'm not sure I want to be now. Thayer kicks the door shut behind him, then stalks to the center of his room and tosses me onto the bed.

I yelp, bouncing onto his mattress, throwing my arms out behind me out of reflex. Thayer's eyes flit down my body, landing on my exposed underwear, and I quickly jerk my dress down, clamping my legs shut around my hand.

"What is *wrong* with you? You just hauled me up here like a jealous boyfriend! Do you realize what this looks like?"

"Why should I give a fuck what they think? I just saved your ass."

"Saved me?" I snort, incredulous. "Or was it just a part of your grand scheme to *get close to me*?" I use air quotes to drive my point home, but Thayer doesn't react like I thought he would. He doesn't seem like he's been caught. I push to my feet, closing the distance between us. "It wasn't real, was it?"

"What wasn't?"

"Any of it. You fixing my car. Giving me the key to the barn. Holden," I tick off. "You made him pretend to be my friend. And for what?" What did he hope to accomplish?

"I told him to *watch* you," he clarifies. "Big deal."

"Like that's so much better."

"I'm not sorry, Shayne."

"Of course you're not."

"I needed to know if I could trust you."

"And?" I ask, raising an eyebrow, challenging.

"Jury's still out."

"Great talk. Don't you have to get back to Lissa?" I realize my mistake the moment the words leave my lips. Thayer scrapes his teeth across his bottom lip, capturing his piercing.

"Now look who's jealous," he accuses, moving in on me.

"Just an observation."

He hooks a finger underneath the strap on my shoulder, sliding it back and forth under the thin material, teasing. I slap his hand away, not wanting him to see how he affects me, even when he's acting like an irrational, unbearable asshole.

Pounding at the door has both our heads snapping toward the sound. "Shayne, are you okay?" Valen's voice calls out, a mixture of irritation and worry.

"Make her leave," he says, low enough so only I can hear.

"Why should I?"

"Because this doesn't involve her."

"What is *this*?" I ask. I feel like everyone around me is in on something I'm not.

"You have questions?"

I nod.

"Get rid of her and I'll tell you what you need to know."

"She didn't drive here. We walked from my house. I'm not letting her leave alone."

"We'll get her home safe."

"You'll answer my questions?"

"I said I'll tell you what you need to know."

I purse my lips, looking into his stormy eyes. "No deal."

Valen pounds again. "I'm two seconds from calling the police."

"No, she's not!" Holden yells, amusement clear in his voice.

"Give that back!"

The sounds of them tussling on the other side of the door tells me that he took her phone.

Thayer narrows his eyes. "Fine. I'll answer your questions."

I smile, victorious. "I'm fine!"

"Not good enough. I want to see that you're okay," Valen's muffled voice calls out.

My heart swells and my chest fills with pride. I've subjected her to enough horror stories for her to walk away without seeing for herself. Not that Thayer's capable of any of those things. But rule number one? You never truly know anyone. Rule number two? Never, under any circumstance, leave your friend alone in a potentially dangerous situation.

I move past Thayer and pull the door open. Valen's eyes are full of suspicion as she glances between us, then pushes the door open to scan the room.

"I'm fine, I promise."

"You're soaking wet," she points out.

"Don't look at me like that. Ryan Matthews doused her with beer, then tried to stick his tongue down her throat," Thayer explains.

Valen raises her eyebrows, looking at me for confirmation. I roll my eyes, then nod. "I'll explain everything tomorrow, okay?"

She crosses her arms, seeming to mull it over. "Better be one hell of an explanation," she relents.

"Where's Christian?" Thayer asks Holden.

"He and Baker are getting rid of Ryan."

"Kick everyone out, then take her home."

"Gladly." He grins, handing Valen's phone back to her. She jerks it from his hand, giving him a scathing look.

"No thanks. I'd rather crawl home."

Holden's eyes flash with a wicked gleam. "That could be arranged."

"Valen, please let him take you." Holden isn't a threat. Conniving and manipulative, sure, but not dangerous. She knows that, too. She's just being stubborn—not that I blame her.

"Fine." She turns for the stairs, making it halfway down before she turns back around. "Well? Are you coming?"

"With any luck," Holden mumbles under his breath.

"Tell Christian to stick around. Meet back here when you're done with her?"

Holden nods before following Valen down.

Thayer reaches an arm around me to slam the door shut and I flinch, turning to face him with a glare. "Start talking."

"Not yet."

I shake my head, irritated with these games. "Fine. I need to get cleaned up," I say, gesturing to my wet dress that sticks to me like a second skin. I smell like beer and I feel like a drowned rat. If we're going to have some sort of powwow, I'm not going to sit through it like this.

Thayer jerks his chin toward the hall bathroom. "You know where the shower is. I'll leave some clothes on the sink."

"Great," I clip out, turning for the door. I pull it open and step into the hall, hesitating at my old bedroom door directly across from Thayer's. Curiosity has my hand reaching out, hovering over the lever, but I drop it at the last second. That's not my room anymore. This isn't my house, and this isn't my family.

"It's empty," Thayer answers my unspoken question, his voice much closer than I thought he was. A pile of clothes appears in front of me on top of his outstretched palm.

I swallow hard. *Of course* it's empty. What did I expect, that they'd keep it for me, just in case? Without a word, I take the clothes and turn for the door to the left of my old one, then shut it behind me. I flip the lock, then toss the clothes onto the marble countertop. I brace my hands on the edge of it, taking in the white vessel sink, the ceiling showerheads that pour onto you like rain, and the separate oversized bathtub off to the side, separated by only a glass partition. My grandmother's house is no shack, but it doesn't compare to the luxury of the Ames' estate.

I toe off my wet Chucks, then shrug out of my straps, pushing my dress down my body, letting it fall to the floor. I look in the mirror with fresh eyes, as if I didn't spend an hour in front of it earlier, trying to see what Thayer sees. My cheeks are red, same with the tip of my nose. My eyes are glassy, and my mascara is smudged a little under my right eye. One side of my curls has gone flat, thanks to Ryan's beer. I'm a mess, and for once, my appearance reflects exactly how I'm feeling on the inside.

I reach for the faucet on the stone wall, flipping it on. I push my underwear down my hips, then kick them over to my join my dress and shoes before I step underneath the large, rectangular showerhead. I close my eyes, letting the hot water fall onto me for long seconds, allowing myself to enjoy it for just a minute. After my minute is up, I make quick work of scrubbing my body with some men's body wash I find on the built-in shelf and wash my hair with some fancy shampoo and conditioner that I can't even pronounce the name of, trying in vain not to notice how much it smells like Thayer.

I pluck a clean towel folded on the rack, then wrap the plush material around me and knot it at my chest, relishing in how much softer it is than my towels. It's the little, insignificant things like this that you don't realize you miss until you have them again. Padding over toward the vanity, I pluck my clothes off the counter, taking stock of what Thayer gave me. A plain white t-shirt and a tiny pair of black shorts. I frown, holding the shorts in my palm. Are these…mine?

Throwing open the door, I storm across the hall and back into Thayer's room. He's standing there, head bent, doing something on his phone. Bored eyes lift to mine, but I don't miss the flash of hunger in them before he conceals it. I throw the shorts at him and they hit his face before he snatches them.

"Why did you keep those?" I demand. Beads of water roll off my hair and down my legs, leaving a puddle at my feet. I look and feel like a crazy person, but I'm past caring.

"Don't flatter yourself. They've been here since you left them."

Left them? My cheeks burn when I realize what night he's referring to. I pad across the floor, closing the distance between us. "For a year?" I ask skeptically.

He shrugs. "I've always loved your ass in spandex."

"God, Thayer, why are you so confusing?" My eyes search his for answers I know I won't find. "You tell me to leave you alone, and then you seek me out." My voice lowers to a whisper. "You touch me and then you leave me…"

"Does it make you mad?" he asks, his voice sounding like gravel. "That your brain wants to hate me, but your body… your body fucking loves me." He rubs a thumb across my cheek, capturing a bead of water. "But you let me touch you anyway because you can't resist me, can you? And you can't fucking stand that about yourself."

His smug tone infuriates me. Even more so because there's a grain of truth to it. But I straighten my shoulders, deciding to gain the upper hand.

"I could say the same about you," I start, toying with the knot in my towel with my fingers. His eyes follow the movement as he scrapes his teeth over his bottom lip, the two piercings glinting with the motion. "You can't seem to stay away from me, and you hate yourself for it, don't you?" His eyes tighten at the corners, and I know I'm getting to him.

"You're playing with fire, Shayne," he warns, taking a step back, but I continue anyway.

"The only difference is I'm the one having my needs met without having to give anything in return." Summoning confidence I don't feel, I drop my towel, letting it fall to the floor with a *whoosh*.

Thayer's throat bobs when he swallows, and he loses the fight to keep his gaze from falling to my chest. The cold air has my nipples tightening almost painfully as I watch his hungry eyes roam my body.

I hear the door slam downstairs, and I know I have less than a minute to wrap this up before they come barging in.

"It seems to me that you're the one getting the short end of the stick in this scenario." I try to snatch the shorts from his grip, but he holds them out of reach, high above his head. I lunge for them and his free arm bands around my waist, spinning me around before he tackles me to the bed. He settles in between my legs, his chest against mine.

"First of all," he starts, pushing his groin into me. "Who's to say my needs aren't being met by someone else?"

I practically growl, shoving him away, but he pins my arms above my head. "Second, you're going to pay for that later."

My chest heaves as he holds my gaze, his mouth lowering to place a gentle kiss on the tip of my nipple. I shiver, feeling wetness pool between my legs, but two sets of footsteps on the stairs hit me like a bucket of cold water. Thayer smirks knowingly before he pushes off me, then he's throwing my clothes at me. I catch them as they land on my chest and scowl up at him.

"Get dressed and meet us in the poolroom."

Just as his doorknob turns, he blocks their entrance and steps out, shutting the door behind him.

I groan, swiping the clothes from my chest. How the hell does he always win?

NINETEEN

Thayer

I ADJUST MY JEANS, TRYING TO CONCEAL MY DICK THAT'S TRYING TO burst through my zipper. Fuck. I'm losing control. The lines are starting to blur, and I'm getting sloppy. I don't know what the fuck I was thinking bringing her up to my room in front of everyone, fueling the rumors that have surrounded Shayne since she moved in with us, but it's getting harder to stay away from her. It's like a compulsion. Getting under her skin, igniting that temper, feeling her hot little breaths on my skin when I make her come. It's an addiction. A sick, toxic addiction.

I tell myself that there's no harm in touching her, as long as I don't let it go any further than that, but even I know I'm playing a dangerous game. Being with Shayne is a slippery slope, and it's impossible to not want more.

She's changed, too. She's always been a good girl at her core, but the side of her she keeps locked up tight, the little spitfire that only I was able to catch glimpses of before, is clawing its way to the surface. And that stunt she just pulled? I didn't see that coming. When she walked in, dripping wet, face free of makeup, I wanted to push up her towel, bend her over, and slide into her from behind. And when she dropped her towel, her long, blonde hair curving around her perky tits, the tiny metal bars through her nipples, I almost did just that. It took the restraint of a thousand saints not to fuck her right then and there.

"What's all this about?" Holden asks from his place on the couch. Christian sits on the loveseat, while I stand in front of the TV that stretches across the wall of the billiard room, arms crossed over my chest.

"I want answers, and so does she. But before she gets down here… Someone's fucking with Shayne. Was it either one of you?" They both shake their heads.

"I told you, man. It wasn't me. My money's on Taylor. She's always had it out for Shayne, even when they were *friends*," he says, using air quotes. It's true. Taylor doesn't play nice with others, but she didn't really have a choice before. Being with us offered a certain amount of protection. It made Shayne untouchable. Off limits. Taylor seems to think fucking with Shayne is fair game now that our parents split, and I'm betting that school of thought isn't limited to Taylor.

"It's just mean girl shit. I put her in check tonight, so she won't be a problem," Holden says dismissively.

I rake a hand through my hair, nodding. It makes sense, but something tells me that there's more to it.

"What's up with you two? You suddenly give a shit again?" This comes from Christian. I can't say I blame him for not understanding when I can't make sense of it myself.

Before I can answer, Shayne clears her throat, standing in the doorway. Her wet hair falls over one shoulder, my t-shirt hanging almost down to her knees, giving her the illusion of being naked underneath.

"Hey." She gives an awkward wave.

Holden pats the cushion next to him. "Come sit, baby sister."

She cuts him a look, but doesn't comment as she pads across the room, arms folded over her chest, still distrustful. I can tell that being here again makes her uncomfortable by her body language alone. She takes a seat on the opposite side of the couch, leaving a healthy distance between her and Holden, taking up as little space as possible.

"Why am I here?"

"That's what I'd like to know," Christian says.

"Bro, what the fuck," Holden chimes in.

"No, it's fine. He's the only one who's making any sense to me," Shayne says.

"You want answers. So do we."

"So let's get this shit out on the table then," Holden suggests, slouching back against the couch and kicking his feet up onto the table in front of him.

"Okay," Shayne drawls, skepticism lacing her tone as she looks at me. "Why did you tell Holden to get close to me?"

I glare at Holden and his big ass mouth.

"First of all, I never faked it with you," he says, tossing her a wink, and Shayne blinks, unamused before she stands like she's going to leave.

"All right, hold up," he says, blowing out a breath, looking at me. I nod, giving him silent permission to be real with her. It's been a year, and we still don't have answers. Our way isn't working. Might as well try a different tactic.

"A few months ago, we started looking into the day that Danny…" he trails off, still not able to say the words, and clears his throat before he looks up at the ceiling, his head leaning on the back of the couch, knees bouncing. "Something didn't feel right. We've fucked around in these woods and up at the falls our whole lives. There's no way he fell. And he sure as fuck didn't kill himself."

"Even if he wanted to take his life, he wouldn't do it there," I point out. "How many times have we all jumped off that cliff? It's not a deadly fall." It can be, but it's far from a sure thing. We've jumped off that same cliff since we were twelve. If I were going to take myself out, it would be foolproof.

Shayne nods, her eyes shining with empathy that almost fucking hurts to look at.

"So we start digging into it, right?" Holden says, lifting his head to look at her. "Tried to find the nine-one-one-call. The police report...something. But we don't get anywhere. Shit's locked up tighter than Fort Knox."

Her lips tug into a frown, her eyebrows pinching together. "I thought emergency calls were public record."

"They're supposed to be," I say, impressed that she knew that, but not altogether surprised. "Someone's going out of their way to make sure it's sealed."

"That's…"

"Suspicious as fuck?" Holden offers.

"Yeah." She nods her head slowly, seeming slightly dazed by the information. "Is this related to the cops who were looking for you?" she asks, looking over at Holden.

He nods. "We aren't allowed to get a copy of the police report because it's supposedly ongoing, but the detective hasn't done shit. I bashed the fuck out of his car with a baseball bat. Not my finest moment."

Fucking dumbass.

"Wait, you didn't have a bat when I picked you up."

"Dropped it in the woods."

"Are you kidding? You left a bat behind, probably with your blood on it, after you fled a crime scene. You might as well have left your name and number, Holden. What were you thinking?"

"I was thinking *I'm very drunk and I miss my fucking brother and want answers*. Next time I'll call a professional," he says pointedly. "We don't all have extensive knowledge about serial killers and how to not get caught."

Shayne rolls her eyes, but her face softens at his words. "But that still doesn't answer my question. What do I have to do with any of this? Why don't you trust me?"

Holden hesitates, not knowing how to go about this one, and Christian remains quiet.

"Because we think we know who did it. Danny had an argument with someone the day before," I say, leaning back onto the entertainment center that spans the length of the wall and cross my arms, watching her closely for her reaction.

"Okay, and?"

"It was Grey."

TWENTY

Shayne

"I T WAS GREY."

"What?" I breathe out the word. Needing to sit down, I drop back onto the couch, trying to make sense of everything I've learned in the past few minutes. He never mentioned an argument. "No." I shake my head. "You don't understand. Grey was wrecked after Danny... He's *still* wrecked." I lock eyes with Thayer, willing him to believe me. "You have no idea how much it messed him up. He barely speaks to me. He won't even come home."

The three of them exchange looks, and I can almost hear their unspoken thoughts. They think Grey's behavior is coming from a place of guilt.

"I know my brother," I say defensively. "And even if they did argue, so what? They were best friends. *Brothers*," I grind out. "Just because we're not blood..."

"Relax." Thayer holds up his palms, approaching me as if I'm a wounded animal.

"We don't have the facts. This is why we're trying to fill in the blanks here," Holden adds. "We need to know what else happened."

"So you thought I was covering for Grey," I say, still trying to piece things together. That's why they turned on me. On all of us.

"Would it be that crazy to assume you'd be loyal to your family?" Thayer asks, coming to a stop in front of me.

"You are my family!" I blurt out, frustrated, before realizing my mistake. "Or...were. Back then."

"We're still family," Holden says, looking over at me with those puppy dog eyes.

A bitter laugh leaves my mouth. "You both treated me like shit." Christian wasn't ever particularly vocal about how he felt about me. I got the feeling that he stayed out of it, and as long as he wasn't going out of his way to make me miserable, that was good enough for me, regardless of how he felt about me. Thayer and Holden, on the other hand...they hurt me. Because I cared for both of them in a way I didn't care about many other people in my life.

"Families fight." He shrugs.

Thayer doesn't echo Holden's sentiments, but he comes to sit between us on the oversized sofa. I lean my back against the armrest to face them both, wrapping my arms around my bent knees.

"I do have another question," I say, changing the subject. I have a lot of other questions, but most of them are for Thayer, and I'm sure he made this little family meeting on purpose, knowing I wouldn't ask him anything about us. "Why did our parents call off the engagement?" One day, things were fine— or as fine as things could be, all things considered. The next, I was told to pack my things.

Holden and Thayer exchange a knowing look.

"What?" I ask, looking between the two of them, feeling slightly on edge. "Tell me."

"Word on the street is that your mom was having an affair," Holden says.

I laugh, actually laugh out loud. "Word on the *street*?"

That's ridiculous. "Which jealous housewife started that rumor?"

"My dad," Thayer says.

"What?" I frown, not believing that for a second. But then I remember the night I saw her with another man. Was that him? But why wouldn't she say anything? If she was having a year-long affair, you'd think I'd have been introduced to the guy—or at the very least, aware of his existence. Is this what she's been hiding?

"Don't hurt yourself thinking so hard," Holden quips.

"I'm gonna go pass out," Christian announces with a yawn, standing. He's been so silent that I almost forgot he was here.

"What, no sleepover with your boyfriend, Baker?" Holden taunts.

Christian gives him a mocking laugh and moves his wrist, miming jerking off, and then he's heading upstairs, leaving Holden and Thayer chuckling behind him.

"I should get home." I stretch my arms above my head, suddenly feeling exhausted. My earlier buzz is long gone, and there's nothing I want more than to fall into my bed.

"I'll take you in the morning," Thayer says. "You can crash here."

"Uh, I don't think that's a good idea."

"Why not?"

"Because I don't live here anymore, because it's weird, because our parents would probably lose their shit…" I tick off the reasons. "Take your pick."

"Who cares, no, it's not, and they won't find out," Holden argues each point. "Come on, we'll put on a movie and have a sleepover in here like old times."

I narrow my eyes. "We never once did that."

"Then it's about time we start." He jumps up, grabbing some blankets from the back of the sofa and tossing them at me, grabs the remote, then he sprawls out on the blanket that Christian was occupying a minute ago.

I look over at Thayer, trying to read his thoughts. Unsurprisingly, he gives nothing away. "You'll take me home first thing in the morning?" It's not like I can't walk home if it came down to it. I could technically walk home now, if I was up for a twenty-minute, late-night stroll through the woods. Alone.

Thayer gives me a nod, and I sigh loudly. I don't even know what time it is. When Thayer left me upstairs to get dressed, I collected my shoes and wet clothes from the bathroom floor, rinsed my dress in the sink, then folded and stacked them in the corner of the bathroom, making sure to stash my underwear inside of my dress. After I called Valen to make sure she got home safe and promised to fill her in tomorrow, I tossed my phone on top of my clothes, then walked my half-embarrassed, half-still-turned-on ass in here.

Too tired to argue, I slump back against the cushions, pulling the cream-colored cashmere throw blanket over me, with my knees tucked into my chest.

"Atta girl," Holden praises, and I detect a hint of excitement in his voice. Like he's genuinely happy to have me here.

"I can't promise I'll stay awake," I warn.

"Then you won't mind if I put this on?"

Porn categories fill the screen, and Holden uses his phone to scroll through the options. He's literally streaming porn from his phone to the TV. I didn't know that was possible. He clicks on one titled *Stepsister Fucked by Horny Brother While Parents are Away.*

"Really?" I roll my eyes at his selection.

"I mean, unless you're too much of a prude…"

I shrug, trying my best to appear unfazed, hoping Thayer will be the one to shut it down. Holden chuckles, taking that as permission granted, then folds his hands behind his head, crosses his ankles, and focuses his attention on the scene playing out on the TV.

"Promise you won't tell Mom and Dad I snuck out?" the pretty, young brunette coos, pushing her lips into a pout as she opens her legs in invitation, her tiny dress bunched up high on her hips. Her "stepbrother" moves toward the bed, putting his hands on her spread knees.

"That depends. Are you going to finally let me fuck this tight little pussy?"

She plants a foot on his chest when he tries to move in. "One time," she says firmly. "I'll let you fuck me once, if you promise not to tell."

"Deal."

It's cheesy. And so obviously scripted. But my pulse quickens, and the arousal I was feeling earlier returns with a vengeance. I feel my nipples tighten painfully underneath Thayer's shirt, and my breath catches when the guy on the screen shoves his boxers down before he slides into her without preamble. They both groan as he moves inside her, and after only a few short seconds, he's flipping her onto her stomach and pushing into her from behind. I bite down on my lip, squeezing my thighs together.

Closing my eyes, I will myself to think about anything other than what's on the screen, but all my stupid brain manages to do is picture Thayer inside me, his lips on my neck and his hands on my hips as I straddle him.

"Turn it off," Thayer's angry voice breaks into my fantasy. My eyes snap open to find him watching me with his fists clenched at his side and a noticeable bulge in his jeans.

My cheeks burn and I avert my gaze. Holden chuckles knowingly, exiting out of the app. Stephen King's *It*—the new one—replaces the porno. *Much better*. My heartrate returns to normal after a few minutes, and my eyes start to grow heavy. I inch down enough to lay my head flat on the cushion, keeping my legs curled up tight, away from Thayer, but then I feel his hand on my ankle right before he pulls my legs to rest on top of his lap, one at a time. I'm even more surprised when he doesn't release me. His right hand stays wrapped around my ankle.

"Thanks," I mutter, returning my attention to the movie, even though I can't focus on anything other than the feeling of his warm fingers on my ankle. His thumb glides back and forth, but his eyes are locked on the TV, making me wonder if he's even aware he's doing it. When his fingertips ghost over my calves and up to the insides of my thighs and back down again under the blanket, I know it's intentional. Goosebumps break out over my skin, but I don't make a move to stop him.

For what seems like forever, his fingers continue their path up and down my legs, inching a little higher with each pass, teasing. When he finally reaches the seam of my shorts, I'm practically shaking with need. My eyes shoot over to make sure Holden isn't aware of what's happening right next to him. I can't see his face, but his hand hangs limply off the side of the sofa, telling me he's passed out. Thayer's thumb presses against my clit through the thin fabric of my shorts, and my eyes fall shut at the sensation. He only applies the faintest amount of pressure, rubbing slow circles, and I part my legs, encouraging him to give me more even though I shouldn't let this happen. I *should* be stopping this.

Thayer groans, then both of his hands are at my hips, pulling my shorts down. Panicked, I cover his hands with mine, stopping him. I look over at Holden once again, but he's still in the same position, asleep and oblivious.

"Remember when I said you'd pay for that little show later?" he asks, his voice low and gravelly. "It's later."

I gnaw on my lip, nervous, but I slowly release my grip on his hands, unable to resist temptation. My heart slams against my ribs as Thayer slides my shorts down my legs, stuffing them in between the cushions. His warm palm skims up my left leg, pushing my knee up under the blanket, then he repeats the motion with the other one. Reaching over, he drags his thumb against my bottom lip. When my mouth parts, his middle finger dips past my lips.

"Suck," he instructs. I close my lips around his finger, sucking lightly as he slides it in and out. His eyes blaze as he watches my mouth, then he pulls it out, replacing it with a different finger. "Again."

I do as he says. Once he's satisfied, his hand moves under the blanket, finding the heat between my legs. His two middle fingers flatten against me, rubbing up and down before he curls them to push inside me.

"Fuck, that's tight," Thayer murmurs.

His words spur me on, but I cast a nervous glance toward Holden's sleeping form once more.

"Relax. He can't see anything."

His words do little to calm me. The blanket covers what we're doing, but that doesn't mean he doesn't have ears. Luckily, the movie is loud, because I'm way too turned on to stop whatever it is that we're doing. Holden could wake up at any moment, but I think the added element of fear somehow adds to the intensity.

"Show me those perfect little tits," he says, curling his fingers, hitting a spot inside me I didn't know existed. I tense up, arching off the couch with a moan.

"Shayne," he all but growls. "Lift your shirt."

I pull the hem of my shirt up, keeping my arms pressed to my sides to push my chest together for his benefit.

"Fuck, that's good." Thayer's eyes darken as he lifts the side of the blanket up and dips his head to see underneath, watching his fingers pump into me. He licks his lips and then he's disappearing beneath the blanket. Before I know what's happening, I feel his hot, wet tongue dart out to taste me. I gasp, my hips jerking off the couch. Thayer's free hand snakes up my stomach and covers my mouth as his tongue continues its ministrations.

I let my thighs fall open, drunk off the feeling. He fucks me with his fingers as he sucks and licks, and it isn't long before I'm trembling beneath him. I can hear how wet I am with each pump of his hand, and when I start to clench around his fingers, he picks up the pace while simultaneously sucking my clit into his mouth.

I cry out, unable to hold back, and Thayer presses his palm

harder against my mouth. I bite down on it, chest heaving, as he brings me back down to Earth with soft strokes with the flat of his tongue.

Holy shit.

My hair clings to my damp forehead, my ears still buzzing. That was hands-down, the most intense orgasm I've ever had. I'm still catching my breath when Thayer's head appears from under the blanket before he crawls on top of me, kissing me hard. I moan into his mouth when his jeans press into my still sensitive center, unable to keep from rubbing against him. Rough hands grip my thighs and then he's lifting me from the couch.

"What are you doing?" I whisper-yell, my arms wrapping around his neck out of reflex as he walks away, his hands moving to knead my ass. Holden could wake up. Christian could still be awake, for all I know. Yet Thayer's carrying me through his house half-naked.

"We're not done yet."

TWENTY-ONE

Thayer

I DON'T KNOW WHAT THE FUCK I'M THINKING. SHAYNE HAS A WAY of getting inside my head and making me want things I know I can't have. Things I don't deserve. The more time I spend with her, the more conflicted I feel. My misery doesn't just want company. It wants Shayne. And for some fucked-up reason, she wants me, too.

She thinks I don't care about her. She thinks I like to fuck with her body, her mind, and her emotions for the fun of it. What she doesn't know is I'm fighting myself every goddamn day. Guilt for wanting her like I do. Guilt for stringing her along. Guilt for finding some sliver of fucking happiness in her when Danny is rotting six feet under. I'm drawn to her for the same reason I hate her.

She makes me feel.

I could've killed Holden when he streamed that fucking porn. I let it play out, just to see Shayne's reaction, expecting her to protest. Instead, I watched her while she watched them fuck on screen, her lips parting slightly, a flush crawling up her neck. She liked it. Maybe even wished it was her. Her breathing changed, coming out in shallow, little pants, and the lust in her eyes mirrored my own. To say it backfired would be putting it mildly. I was hard as fuck, needing to touch her. To taste her. To be so far inside her that we both forgot about our families, our tragedies, our fucked-up lives, and everything that's keeping us apart.

Since the day she wandered into the barn, there was something between us. We were all close—Holden, Grey, Danny, Shayne, and me. But Shayne was mine. And as I carry her tight little body down the hall to my bedroom, I know she still is.

Walking into my room, I kick the door shut behind me, then prowl over to my bed, dropping Shayne onto my sheets. She lands with a squeal, her light blonde hair a stark contrast against my black sheets. She frowns, sitting up and pulling my T-shirt down to cover herself.

"What?" I ask, my patience wearing thin. My cock is about to burst through my zipper.

Her little nose scrunches up, eyeing my sheets with disdain. *She has a possessive streak.* And it only gets me harder.

"No one's been in here for a long time," I say, crawling over her, my palms braced on either side of her head.

"That's a lie."

Oh, right. The chick from the night Holden decided to go rogue. I don't even know her name. All I know is that while I was minding my own fucking business, she snuck into my room. When I told her to get the fuck out, she dropped to her knees, her fingers undoing the button of my jeans in record time. For a brief moment, I considered letting her suck me off. I figured she might be a nice distraction from the little devil underneath me. But she felt all wrong. Her tits were too big. Her hair the wrong color. In short, she wasn't Shayne. And as it turns out, my dick didn't want anything to do with her. No sooner had I zipped up my pants and told her to leave than I heard the commotion out in the hall.

"She tried it. I wasn't interested."

Shayne narrows her eyes at me, searching for signs of

deception. She won't find any. "If I let you touch me again, are you going to turn cold and leave me right after?"

"Probably," I answer truthfully. Disappointment and maybe even hurt flash in her eyes and I feel a stab of regret for putting it there. "Unless…"

"Unless what?" she asks, her eyes locked onto my chest, avoiding my gaze. Her little fingers toy with the strings of my hoodie as she waits for my response.

"Unless you want to stay."

What the fuck am I saying?

Hopeful blue eyes meet mine, and it's *that* look right there that tells me what I already know. I shouldn't have said that. It's only going to make things more difficult when this thing, whatever it is, inevitably blows up in both our faces. Even if she didn't know about Grey, her brother is still responsible for the death of mine. That's something you don't move on from.

"In here?" she asks, her tone slightly defensive. Guarded. She doesn't trust me. I don't trust her. And until that changes, the walls we've stacked up high over the past year will stay firmly in place.

I nod silently, dipping my head to kiss her collarbone. She arches her neck in invitation, turning her head to the side. She smells so fucking good, a combination of my shampoo and something uniquely Shayne. I slip my hand between her thighs, feeling her pussy still slick with the evidence of her orgasm. I tease her clit with the tip of my finger, working her up all over again.

"Are you going to sleep in my bed, Shayne?" I ask before catching her earlobe between my teeth, tugging. "Because I think it's time that I get something out of this." I throw her earlier words back at her.

Shayne shivers beneath me as she rocks into my hand, but she doesn't give me the words I want to hear.

"Yes or no?" I ask, slipping a finger inside her. Her hands come up to grip my biceps and squeeze.

"Yes," she breathes. "But we're going to talk first."

I groan, knowing that was coming, but my finger doesn't stop pumping. "You can talk. I'll do this."

"You fixed my tires," she says, trying to keep her voice normal.

"You helped Holden," I say by way of explanation.

"You slept with Taylor," she accuses, the hurt in her voice evident.

I pause my movements, looking down into her pools of blue. I pull my fingers from her, my hand curling around her hip. "I never fucked her. As soon as I saw your face, I made her leave."

Her eyes widen in surprise, and the relief I see in them does something to me. I knew she thought I fucked Taylor, and I let her think that. I *wanted* her to. But now...now I feel like a dick.

"My turn. Aiden wants you."

"I don't want him."

"I don't want anyone else touching you."

"Same goes for you."

"Deal."

"Thayer?"

"Yeah?"

"Touch me."

"Gladly." Pulling back, I tear off my jacket before returning to my position with my arms caging her in beneath me, palms flat on my mattress.

Shayne looks up at me, wide-eyed and innocent. "I want to touch you this time."

Her words go straight to my cock. "Then do it," I say, my voice strangled.

Her eyes flit down between us as tentative fingers reach out to unbutton my jeans. She tugs on the zipper, eyes widening as if she's opening a present on Christmas morning, and then she's pushing my jeans down.

I help her out, standing to get rid of them before I'm back between her warm thighs. "Lift your shirt." I want to see all of her. Shayne does one better, pulling it up and over her head before tossing it onto the floor. Her tits are flawless. Two perfect handfuls, slightly fuller on the bottom, and tiny pink nipples decorated with those piercings. I still can't believe she followed through with it, but I'm glad she did, because it's the hottest thing I've ever seen in my life.

Her fingers are warm when they dip inside my boxers, and my abs tighten when they wrap around me.

"Oh, fuck." I reach down to pull my shirt up so I can see everything happening between us. "Take me out."

One hand tugs my boxers down while the other stays wrapped around me, then she looks up at me, as if waiting for further instruction. It didn't dawn on me until this very second that she might not have much experience. She lived with us from the time she was fourteen until she turned seventeen, and most of that last year was spent with me. I just assumed that when she went away, she'd find some new guy to give all her firsts to.

"Have you done this before?"

"Of course," she says with a defensive edge to her tone, like the question embarrasses her, but I don't care either way.

"Squeeze harder."

She tightens her grip around me, and I groan, closing my eyes. Slowly, she starts to work my length, moving her fist up and down, and it feels so fucking good. After a few strokes, she releases me, but then I look up to see her bringing her hand to her mouth. Her tongue slips past her lips to lick her palm, and then she's wrapping it around me again.

Damn, that was hot. I don't know if it was the move itself or the fact that it's Shayne. My bet is on the latter, because everything she does turns me on. Her eyes are glued to where she fists me as she starts to move faster, making my hips jerk. My arms are starting to strain from holding myself up, but

Shayne has her hand on my dick for the first time, and I'm not doing anything to fuck this up.

I dip my head to nip at the swell of her tits before I bring my lips up to ghost across her nipples. My lip rings bump into her piercing and she moans, so I do it again. I don't know how tender they are, but she doesn't stop me, so I continue, dragging my lips over the hardened tip over and over before switching to the other side. Her breathing grows ragged, and the more worked up I get her, the faster her hand moves.

Shayne moans, arching her chest off the mattress, and I pull back, sitting on my heels between her bent knees.

"Rub your clit."

Hesitant, lust-filled eyes meet mine, and she wets her lips in a nervous gesture, bringing her knees back together. I shove my shirt up, pinning it between my chin and my chest before I wrap my fist around my cock. Shayne's lips part as she watches me. I use my free hand to grip her knee, slowly opening her legs. She lets her thighs fall apart, and then two fingers snake in between her legs, rubbing her little clit.

She's perfect down there, too. Completely smooth and bare. And I know firsthand that she tastes as good as she looks.

I start to fuck myself with my fist as I watch her rub tiny circles, watching in fascination as her pussy grows slick. Her left hand kneads her tit, and the sight of her touching herself like this is almost enough to make me come. Just when I think it can't possibly get any better, her hand darts out to grip my cock, pulling me to her warm, wet pussy. I fall forward, my left fist pressed into the mattress above her shoulder.

"Fuck, Shayne," I groan, dropping my hand to let her take control.

She presses my tip against her clit, getting herself off while her hand works my shaft. She slides me through her wetness, her hips bucking against me. It'd be so easy to slip inside her right now. I'm about to blow, and I can tell she is, too, so I push two fingers into her without warning at the same time I flick my tongue against her nipple.

Shayne moans loud as fuck as her body tenses up, and then she's spasming around my fingers over and over. Her hand keeps moving, milking my orgasm from me.

"Goddamn," I grind out, watching the way my cum coats her clit. Shayne's body goes limp, her hand loosening as she slowly glides my tip through our combined mess. Not wanting to take any chances, I roll off her, pulling my boxers back into place, and pluck her discarded shirt off the floor. I bring it between her legs to clean her up and she flinches, still sensitive. Her cheeks are pink, and her eyes are glazed over, a satisfied look in them. She blinks slowly, and I realize how tired she must be.

She looks good in my bed. Too good. And this feeling right here is exactly why I didn't let myself go any further with her before. I knew I wouldn't want to stop. Neither one of us speaks as the reality of what we just did hits us.

Shayne pulls my sheet up around her, and I see her wall starting to slide back in place, so I thow some sweatpants on, turn off my light, and crawl into bed with her, tugging her naked, boneless body back into my chest. She's tense at first, but then she starts to relax, and her breathing evens out, telling me that she's fallen asleep.

I push away the hint of guilt that tries to break though, allowing myself the temporary comfort of having Shayne back in my bed. I don't know what this means for us, but I'll worry about the fallout tomorrow.

TWENTY-TWO

Shayne

THAYER'S HEAVY ARM IS LOCKED AROUND ME, HIS BREATHING coming out in steady breaths behind me. I don't know what woke me. All I know is that I have the sudden urge to bolt. Sleeping here, being here like this with him… it's a bad idea. It makes me want things I know I can't have. After last night's revelations, I feel like we turned a corner, but everyone knows words said in the heat of the moment are to be taken with a grain of salt. I don't want to see the disappointment in his eyes that always seems to come after we give in to temptation. And I definitely don't want to risk doing the walk of shame and getting busted by Christian or Holden.

I give myself thirty seconds. Thirty seconds to soak in the feeling of Thayer's arm wrapped around the curve of my hip, his hand gripping my boob, even in sleep. I imagine what it would be like if he was just a boy and I was just a girl and our parents hadn't ever met. I wonder how things would be by now if Danny hadn't died. When my thirty seconds are up, I slip out from his hold, trying my best not to wake him. He groans in his sleep, rolling onto his back as I sit on the edge of his bed, wearing nothing but his scent and the bruises his mouth left on my skin, and I miss his warmth immediately. His shirt has risen enough to expose the V lines that lead below his low-slung sweatpants and I chew on my thumbnail, having to talk myself out of crawling back into bed.

But our story isn't a fairytale. More like a Shakespearean tragedy. Allowing myself to believe otherwise is pathetic, and allowing this thing to go any further than it already has is reckless. Because when everything comes crumbling down, I'm going to be the one left feeling empty and alone. Again. I stand, using one arm to band across my bare chest, and push my wild hair out of my face, looking for my clothes.

Shit. Where are my shorts? I replay last night's events in my mind, trying to remember what I did with them, when I realize they must still be downstairs. I'll have to throw my dress from last night on. Tiptoeing over to my pile of soiled clothes, my hopes are dashed when I pick up the cold, still wet fabric. I consider putting it on anyway, but then I spot Thayer's discarded hoodie on the floor next to the bed.

Good enough.

Bending over, I pluck it off the floor then slide my arms through the sleeves before zipping it up. I consider stealing a pair of his boxers, too, but his dresser is on the other side of the room, and I don't want to risk getting caught. Luckily, his hoodie hits mid-thigh, so I slip on my Converse, tuck my wet underwear inside my pocket, and decide to abandon the dress entirely. I don't care if I ever see it again, but I'm not going to leave my underwear on Thayer's floor. Picking up my purse, I sling it over my head, the strap lying across my chest, and with one last look at Thayer's sleeping form, I leave.

I shut the door behind me, slowly releasing the doorknob so as to not make a sound. I make my way down the stairs, cringing when one of the steps creaks beneath my foot. Tiptoeing the rest of the way down, I take in the unholy number of empty cups and bottles left on every surface. It'll no doubt be gone in a couple hours once Holden calls their cleaners over to cover up the evidence.

Once I'm at the bottom of the stairs with the front door in sight, I breathe out a sigh of relief. That is, until it opens, revealing August. I freeze, rooted to the bottom step, heart racing. The shock on his face matches my own as his eyes roam over my bare legs, making their way up to my sex hair. He scowls at me, his expression troubled and angry. He calmly sets his briefcase down on the entryway table, closing the door behind him. His eyes drift past me, noticing the mess, but he doesn't seem to care one way or another.

"Which one?" he asks.

"Excuse me?" I tilt my head, not understanding his meaning.

"Whose bed did you just crawl out of?" He raises a questioning eyebrow, his voice stern.

I frown, my stomach rolling with nerves. What kind of question is that? Never mind the fact that I did, in fact, just crawl out of Thayer's bed. "No one's," I lie.

"I'm sure you've realized that you no longer have a bedroom here." Dark hazel green eyes that remind me so much of Thayer's bore into me.

"I'm aware. I fell asleep on the sofa in the poolroom."

"Ah," he says knowingly. "Over imbibe, did we?" He's giving me an out, but I can tell he doesn't believe me.

"Yeah." I lick my dry lips, casting a glance upstairs. I was so hell-bent on getting out of here undetected just minutes ago, but now I'd give anything for Holden or Thayer to wake up and save me from this awkward encounter. "I'm not much of a drinker, so I decided to play it safe and sleep here."

He nods, sliding his hands into his pockets. "Is Thayer awake?"

This feels like a trick question, and the fact that he knew to ask about Thayer specifically has me feeling even more on edge. Maybe we haven't been as careful as I thought. I shrug, playing it off. "I'm not sure. I just woke up and I'm supposed to be meeting a friend."

Another nod. When he doesn't speak, I take that as my cue to leave. I step down from the last step, moving past him, but his hand darts out, catching my arm. I stop short, giving a pointed look at his where he grips me, apprehension snaking its way up my spine. He notices my discomfort and releases his hold immediately, taking a step back.

"How's Greyson doing?"

I feel my eyebrows tug together, confused by the sudden change in subject.

"I haven't seen him in town at all," he elaborates when he notices my confusion. "Just making sure everything's okay." It sounds more like a question than a statement. Is it possible that August still cares for my mom?

"He's okay," I lie again. "School is keeping him busy, so we don't see him as much as we'd like."

Something genuine flashes in his eyes, but he conceals it before I'm able to place it. "And you? I was worried you and the boys wouldn't get along, but I see that concern was unfounded."

"I'm fine." I leave it at that. He's clearly fishing for information, and I'm not taking the bait. I don't get the sudden interest in our lives. If he gives a shit, then where has he been for the past year? I think back to what Holden said about my mom having an affair but dismiss the possibility. Why is it when something goes wrong, their first reaction is to blame my family?

"Well, I'll let you get to your plans," he says, dismissing me as he loosens the tie around his neck. I head for the door once more, and this time, he doesn't stop me.

I practically ran home through the woods. The sun was just starting to rise, barely peeking through the trees, telling me it was still before seven. If I hadn't been in such a hurry, it would've been the perfect morning to hang out at the barn. I've never been a morning person, but there's a certain peacefulness in the early hours. Thayer told me once that he could tell what time it was based on which birds were chirping, but the chirping left with the warm weather. This time of year, it's calm and quiet, the air crisp. The only sound was my shoes running through the fallen leaves.

I managed to sneak into my house undetected. I grabbed a banana from the fruit rack, needing something to coat my empty stomach, then slipped off my shoes and quickly headed upstairs to my room. I finished half of my banana before giving up, threw my dead phone on the charger, then promptly passed back out in the comfort of my own bed. I didn't bother to shower or even change my clothes.

I wake up to Valen standing over me, a mixture of disgust and concern screwing up her features. "What—and I cannot stress this enough—the fuck."

"What?" I grumble, half-awake.

"I've been calling you all morning." She looks over to the table beside my bed and plucks my phone from it, showing me the missed calls and texts before tossing it down onto the bed. "You owe me answers. And a shower." She pulls up the corner of my blanket, looking underneath. "Are you even wearing pants?"

I jerk the blanket back down and Valen climbs onto my bed, crossing her long legs. I sit up and stumble out of bed to lock my bedroom door.

"Ohhh, she locked the door. That means it's juicy." Valen wiggles her brows.

"You have no idea," I mutter, padding back toward her.

"Whose jacket is that?" She tugs at the hem as I crawl back into my bed, pulling the blanket over my lap.

"I don't even know where to start." Taking the hair tie off my wrist, I throw my hair into a messy bun on top of my head.

"Let's start with the fact that Thayer carried you off like a caveman in front of the entire town."

I rack my brain for the right thing to say. I don't know why I'm having such a hard time spitting it out. For so long, we met in secret, knowing it was wrong, but unable to stay away from each other. We knew it could ruin our family, that we ran the risk of being separated if anyone found out. So we took to stolen moments when no one was looking, and spending nearly all of our time in the barn. We had to hide for so long that I got used to lying to everyone around me. It became automatic. But we didn't tell anyone, and things didn't just fall apart. They shattered.

It's not that I don't trust Valen. We tell each other everything. But Thayer was different. I wanted our secret to stay safely tucked away inside our barn without anyone else's opinions or judgment interfering. I felt like if I said it out loud, it would jinx it. But there's no harm in telling her now that there's nothing left to protect, and I could use someone to talk to.

"Before Danny died, Thayer and I were…*together*." Sort of.

"I knew it!" she exclaims, slapping the mattress. "You fucked your stepbrother, didn't you?"

I widen my eyes at her, gesturing toward the door. This is one conversation I don't want my mom overhearing. "Be a little louder, why don't you."

Valen mimes zipping her lips and throwing away an invisible key. "Proceed," she whispers.

Taking a fortifying breath, I decide to tell her everything. I tell her about the night of the funeral, when I nearly gave him my virginity. I tell her how I told him I loved him, and he told me to leave. I tell her about seeing Taylor there in his room later that night. I tell her about the suspicions surrounding Danny's death, about Grey's weird behavior, and how

Holden and Thayer think he might have something to do with it. Everything I've been holding in spills out of me like an overflowing bathtub, but I can't stop.

Valen goes through every emotion as I spew my verbal diarrhea, and when I'm done, all she does is pull me into a hug.

"I've made Valentina Solorio speechless." I half-laugh into her sweater.

"You should've told me."

"I know."

"But I get why you didn't."

I hear Valen's muffled laughter and I pull back, looking at her with my eyebrows raised in question.

"I'm sorry," she says, shaking her head. "This just makes my petty heart so happy. Taylor is going to *die* when she finds out."

"Valen! Did you not hear anything I just said? She's not going to find out. There's nothing *to* find out."

"Why? It's not like he's your stepbrother anymore. And even if he was…" she trails off, a devilish gleam in her eyes.

I roll my eyes, flopping back onto my pillow. "It's complicated."

"Then uncomplicate it," she says simply.

"I don't know if it's possible." I wish it was. I wish we could let go of the lies, secrets, and hurt between us. I wish we could lay down our swords and give us a chance. But that kind of optimism belonged to the girl who confessed her love for the boy in the barn, only to have her heart broken. That girl learned her lesson.

Valen huffs out a sigh, falling back to my pillow beside me. We both stare at the ceiling, lost in thought.

"Let's talk about something else," I say.

"I think Liam's going to break up with me." Her tone is casual, betraying the sadness I know she must feel.

"What?" I ask, rolling onto my side to face her. "Why would you even think that?"

She keeps her eyes focused on the ceiling. "I don't know. It's just a feeling, you know? We're drifting apart. We barely talk on the phone anymore. He hasn't come down to see me for the past two weekends."

"Maybe he's just busy," I offer. "He's crazy about you."

"Or maybe he's surrounded by hot college girls and I'm not cutting it anymore."

I snort out a laugh. "You're joking, right? There isn't a man between the age of twelve and two hundred who wouldn't want you."

"Yeah, for a night."

When I realize she's serious, the smile falls from my face. Valen is gorgeous and confident and strong and she knows it. It's unlike her to let a boy get inside her head like this. Her sudden display of insecurity catches me off guard, but it also comforts me in some weird way. We all have our own shit.

"So go to him. Surprise him and spend the weekend with him. Show him what he's missing."

Valen bites down on her lip, considering it before she turns her head to look at me, a smile spreading across her face. "I do have some new lingerie that I've been waiting to put to use."

"Not exactly where I was going with that, but that works, too." I laugh.

"Okay. Enough feeling sorry for ourselves." Valen sits up, pulling on my arm to bring me with her. "You're going to shower. I'm going to order pizza, and then we're going to watch that serial killer documentary you've been trying to force on me."

"Who needs boyfriends when your best friend knows the way to your heart?" I jump down from the bed and she smacks my ass on my way out.

"Really sad that this is your idea of a good time. But you're welcome."

TWENTY-THREE

Shayne

I JOG DOWN THE STAIRS, STOPPING IN THE KITCHEN TO GRAB A muffin before I leave for school. My mom is at the counter with her back to me, coffee mug in one hand and the phone to her ear, speaking in a hushed voice. I slow my steps, trying not to alert her to my presence.

"It's not the right time," she says, sounding exasperated. "They've had a rough year. They all have. They're just now finding their new normal."

Who is she talking to? She pauses and my heartrate picks up in pace at her cryptic words, as if it has information that I'm not yet privy to.

"It's not only up to you."

Another pause.

"What do you expect me to do? Lock her in her room?" she whispers. "She's a teenage girl, August."

August? *Great.* He's probably ratting me out for the other night. I roll my eyes. What a pal.

"Mom, I'm leaving!" I call out as I pluck a blueberry muffin out of the plastic container on the counter. She whips around to face me, and I give her a quick wave before turning to leave. She hurries off the phone, telling August they'll continue their conversation later, and then she's calling my name.

"Shayne, wait!"

My shoulders tense as I slowly turn back around, ready for the lecture that's sure to come.

"I know you've got a lot going on with school and volleyball, but I could use your help cleaning out some of the rooms upstairs."

I was not expecting that. "Okay."

"The sooner we can get this place cleaned up, the sooner I can sell it."

That gives me pause. "Sell it? Why would you sell it?"

"Why wouldn't I?" she asks, as if that's been her plan all along. "Grey's on his own. You're going off to college soon." She glances around. "This place is too big and too much responsibility for just me."

"That's what you want?" I know my mom's relationship with her parents was rough, but this is her childhood home. She has to have some attachment to it. This house doesn't hold any sentimental value to me, but this town does, and the prospect of not having a reason to come back has my stomach twisting in knots.

She shrugs. "It's really my only option, Shayne. I'll sell the house to some rich jerk, put you through college, and buy myself a nice little three-bedroom home somewhere between you and Grey."

I nod. "Okay. Well, I'm gonna be late," I say, hitching a thumb over my shoulder. "Talk later?"

"Go, go," she says, pasting a smile on her face. "I'll be at your game tonight."

I almost forgot I had a game.

"There is a game, right?" She looks down at her phone, tapping at the screen. "I could've sworn it said today."

"No, it's today. I'll see you tonight then."

Her phone rings again, and she gives me a wave before

turning back for the kitchen. I walk to my car, hop inside, and start the engine, my mind going in twenty-seven directions. On a whim, I try to call Grey again as I'm backing out of the driveway. Maybe he'll pick up this time.

Unsurprisingly, he doesn't.

"Asshole," I mutter, tossing my phone to the passenger seat.

I start driving, fingers tapping on my steering wheel. I don't want to go school today. I want answers.

Fuck it.

I turn left instead of right and pull onto the highway.

One stop for gas, a coffee run, and an hour and thirteen minutes later, I made it to Grey's campus. I've only been here once with my mom to help Grey move in, so I wasn't sure I'd remember how to find his dorm, but low and behold, I found it.

I stand in front of his door, suddenly nervous. I shake my head, internally chastising myself. *This is your brother, idiot.* The one who learned to braid my hair for volleyball when my mom was out of town for work. The one who always gave me an extra scoop of brown sugar in my oatmeal because he knew I loved it. The one who always stuck up for me, no matter the circumstances.

Taking a deep breath, I bring my fist up to knock on the door. I don't hear anything, so I knock again, louder this time, leaning in to listen.

"Coming, fuck," my brother's voice calls out, sounding less than pleased. I hear him shuffling around, and then the knob is turning. "I told you to stop leaving your key here—oh." He stops short when he realizes it's me and not his roommate.

He looks like he just crawled out of bed. His hair is messy, the stubble on his jaw longer than I've ever seen it before.

"Surprise," I say weakly, ducking under his arm that holds the door open.

He follows me into his dorm, kicking the door shut behind him. "Aren't you supposed to be in class?"

"Aren't you?" I toss back.

"Touché." He scratches his jaw, uncomfortable. "What are you doing here, Shayne?" He ambles back over to his bed and plops down onto the edge of it. Beer bottles and food containers litter the floor and every surface on his side of the room. On the other side of the room is a matching bed and some storage containers with wheels underneath, a desk that must be for both of them, and not much else.

I walk over, standing in front of him, arms folded over my chest. "I've been calling you. A lot."

"I've been busy."

"Yeah, so you've mentioned. What's going on with you?"

"There's nothing—"

"I swear to God, Grey, if you lie to me one more time. You don't take my calls, you barely respond to texts, and you haven't set foot in Sawyer Point in almost a year." Even before we moved back to Sawyer Point, he rarely visited us.

"Why would I? There's nothing left in that town for me."

Ouch. "Thanks."

"Dammit, Shayne, that's not what I meant."

"Then what did you mean? Because you bailed on me when I needed you the most."

Grey's eyes are full of concern when he looks up at me. "What do you mean?" He stands. "What's wrong?"

In the weeks that followed Danny's death, Grey had already checked out, both physically and mentally before we even moved out of Whittemore. He went back to school, so he has no idea what happened during that time.

"Danny died, Mom and August split, and then you left. And now…"

"Now, what?"

"Now I'm just…alone." It sounds pathetic even to my own ears, but I keep going. "Mom is hiding something. You never talk to me anymore. Everyone's keeping secrets. I had to move back to the town where all my old friends hate me."

"Back up. What's up with Mom?"

I roll my eyes. Of course that's the part of the story he'd focus on. "I don't know. You know that weird sniff thing she does when she's lying?"

He nods.

"She does it a lot. And I saw her with some random guy a few weeks back, looking pretty cozy. Just this morning, she was whispering on the phone with August."

His brows furrow together in thought as he swipes a discarded t-shirt from the floor and pulls it on over his head. "I don't see how that's exactly a case for the FBI, Shayne."

"It's not only that," I say, feeling frustrated. Grey moves around the room, swiping some deodorant under his arms, then grabs his hat from the small table next to his bed. "I can't explain it. I just get the feeling that there's something going on that we don't know about."

Grey keeps moving around the room, looking anywhere but my direction as he collects his keys and wallet. His cagey behavior is starting to make me feel on edge.

"Did you have a fight with Danny?" I ask point-blank. Grey tenses, and an uneasy feeling creeps up my spine. "The night he died," I clarify.

"Where did you hear that?" he asks, his tone defensive, his hazel eyes finally meeting mine.

"Thayer mentioned—"

"You're still talking to Thayer?" His eyebrows shoot up.

"Why wouldn't I?"

"I don't want you around him. Or any of them."

I huff out a bitter laugh. "That's rich coming from someone who can't even bother to return a phone call." They've been there for me more than he has this past year, which is really something considering we were enemies only three seconds ago.

"I'm sorry, okay?" he yells. "I was going through my own shit, stuck in my head, and I didn't realize you'd be going through it, too."

"Just tell me what happened that night."

"I can't."

I shake my head, disappointment rolling off me in waves. "Tell me you didn't have anything to do with it."

"What?" he barks, his head snapping up to meet my eyes, and I see the realization set in. "Is that why you're here? You think *I* killed Danny?"

"No," I say, considering my words and how much to tell him. I decide to come out and just say it, because it's been nearly a year of secrecy, and everyone knows that secrets can only hide out in the dark. It's time to shed some light. "But someone did."

"Explain."

"Thayer and Holden think someone pushed Danny. And that the person is trying to cover it up."

"What makes them think that?" he hedges, running a hand through his light brown hair.

"Something wasn't adding up, so they tried to get a copy of the nine-one-one call, and it's sealed. They won't give them the police report either."

My brother's eyes widen, and he blows out a breath, dropping back down to sit on the edge of his bed. "We did have an argument," he admits. "But it wasn't anything serious."

"So why didn't you just say that?"

"The last time we talked, we were fighting, and then he was just…gone. Do you know how much I wish that I could go back and change things?"

Before I can respond, his door flies open, startling us both.

"Shit, my bad," a guy says, and I assume it's his roommate. "I'll give you some privacy."

"Gross, bro. This is my sister. Shayne, that's Jace. Jace, my sister."

"Hey," I say with a wave, barely sparing him a glance before turning back to my brother. "I have to get back. I have a game tonight. But you should call Mom. She misses you."

I turn to leave, walking past his roommate on my way to the door. The void between my brother and me feels bigger than ever, but his voice stops me. I turn back around, waiting for him to continue.

"I didn't do it."

I nod, wanting so badly to believe him, but I know he's not telling me something. I came here for answers. Instead, I'm leaving feeling even more confused than ever.

TWENTY-FOUR

Thayer

I'M DOING SOMETHING I NEVER THOUGHT I'D DO AGAIN. ALL BECAUSE of a little blonde girl who's driving me fucking crazy. After last night, she left me sometime before I woke up. *She* left *me*. I'd be offended if I wasn't so amused at her attempt to gain the upper hand. And a little turned on. I was prepared to back off, to let her come back to me, but then Holden mentioned she wasn't at school today. Curiosity got the best of me, so I went by her house, but her car wasn't there. Shayne hasn't ditched a day in her life, so what was so important that she started today?

So here I am, in my old high school's gym, practically stalking her like some lovesick puppy. The logo on the floor has changed to a tiger, but everything else is the same. The people, the championship banners lining the walls, the smell.

"You expect me to believe she isn't the reason for your delayed sense of school spirit?" Holden says, nodding toward the group of volleyball players huddled up in a circle around their coach with their arms wrapped around each other's waists. I spot Shayne quickly thanks to the fact that she's shorter than the rest of the team, unable to tear my eyes away from the way her ass looks in those shorts.

They break apart, taking their places on the court. Shayne goes for the middle, bending over to adjust her knee pads, and Holden inhales sharply. "All that cake and it's not even my birthday." His eyes are glued to Shayne's ass and those toned, thick thighs that I had my face between last night.

I swallow hard, forcing myself not to react when all I want to do is knock his ass out for even looking at her. He's testing me, watching me for a reaction, so I give him none. I didn't ask why he wanted to come to a girls' volleyball game, and he didn't ask why I offered to come with him. As long as he's not trying to shoot his shot with Shayne, I don't give a fuck what his reason is.

"Come on." I shove my hands into my front pockets, walking over to an empty row toward the back of the bleachers, avoiding the stares and whispers as we pass the group of cheerleaders sitting together at the front, probably passing time before the football game. Coming here was a bad idea for more than one reason. It's not hard for someone to put two and two together, especially when I can't peel my eyes off Shayne for more than two seconds at a time.

It's loud as fuck, but I drown out the sound of whistles being blown, people cheering, the coach barking orders, and sneakers screeching against the gym floor as I watch Shayne do her thing. I always knew she must have been good for how much she played, but I've never seen her in action before now.

The chick from the other team serves the ball and it comes at Shayne fast. She sticks her arms out, palms together, but it's too late. The ball hits her right in her collarbone, knocking her on her ass. The whistle blows and her teammates rush to help her to her feet. She waves them off, getting back into position with her hands braced on her bent knees. Her eyes narrow, as if challenging the girl from the other team, and she stretches her neck from side to side. The ball comes fast again, but this time, Shayne's ready. She gets the ball up to the setter who pushes it to another girl who then spikes it for a point. Then Shayne's back on it, covering in case of a block.

She smirks, a look that radiates superiority on her face as she high-fives her teammates.

My dick jumps in my pants. Fuck, that was hot. I'm not looking forward to sitting here with my dick half-hard.

Eventually, they win the game. The cheerleaders stand from their spot, gathering their pom-poms, and then Holden slaps a hand on my shoulder.

"Meet you back at the house," he says, hopping up before jogging down the bleachers. He heads straight for the cheerleaders, all of whom are thrilled to see him. Except for one. Valen scrunches up her nose when he says something to her, and then she holds up her middle finger before walking away. *Good luck with that one.*

The volleyball team disperses to find their family or friends after talking to their coach. Shayne bites down on her lip, pressing up on her toes to scan the bleachers. I see the minute she realizes her mom isn't here, her shoulders sagging. Some of the excitement drains from her eyes, but she masks her disappointment in record time. She glances around, as if to make sure no one catches the flash of vulnerability, but I'm the only one who sees her. I'm probably the only one who's ever seen her. The version of her that matters, anyway. Something gnaws at my conscience seeing the whole thing play out, but I shove it away.

Shayne heads for the lobby so I follow suit, staying far enough away that she doesn't notice my presence. When she goes into the girls' locker room, I hang back, waiting for everyone to clear out. After a solid ten minutes pass without anyone going in or out, I survey my surroundings to make sure I'm alone before ducking inside.

I spot Shayne standing in front of a locker with her back to me, wrapped in a towel. Her hair is piled on top of her head, wet strands sticking to her neck, but the rest is dry. Tossing the towel inside her locker, she bends over to pull a pair of white underwear up her legs. My dick jumps at the sight as I eat up the distance between us without making a sound. Once she's within arm's length, I pull her into me, wrapping my arms around her waist from behind. She squeals, trying to jerk out of my hold, and I cover her mouth with my palm.

"Shh," I whisper, and Shayne's body loses some of its tension once she realizes it's me. I bring my lips to her neck, sucking the tender skin into my mouth before licking away the sting. She shivers, leaning her head to the side to give me better access. "You've been avoiding me."

She peels my hand away from her mouth. "You missed me," she accuses.

I spin her around, reaching down to grab a handful of her ass cheek, gripping it hard. "I missed *this*."

Her bare tits are pressed against my stomach as she looks up at me with suspicious eyes. "What are you doing here?"

"I watched you play," I say, avoiding her question mostly because I don't know how the fuck to respond. I don't even know the answer myself.

"You did?" Her eyebrows pull together in confusion.

I nod. "You're kind of a badass."

Her smug expression quickly gives way to surprise as I lift her up and pin her against the locker. Her legs wrap around my waist as her arms circle my neck.

"I was hard the whole time," I say, pushing my hips into her to illustrate my point.

Shayne lets out a tiny moan, her eyes falling to my mouth. She wants to kiss me. And I should walk the fuck away right now, to end this before shit gets messier than it already has. Instead, I'm leaning in closer, bracing one hand on the locker above her head. Her tongue darts out to wet her lips as her fingers slide up into my hair, pulling me closer. Her full lips ghost across mine, and then I feel her tongue flick against my piercings at the corner of my lips. I groan, pushing into her heat, wanting to pull her panties to the side and fuck her right here and now.

Shayne's mouth moves against mine, her tongue slipping inside tentatively at first, but then her arms tighten around my neck, her thighs squeezing me as she deepens the kiss. I snap into action, kissing her hard but slow as she grinds her pussy against the bulge in my pants.

Hooking my hands underneath her thighs, I walk her over to straddle the bench between the rows of lockers, bringing her on top of me. She doesn't miss a beat, bringing her palms to either side of my face as her mouth moves against me, her hips shifting forward. Her movements are confident and it's hot as fuck to see her like this, taking what she needs from me, but if she doesn't stop soon, I'm going to blow my fucking load like a middle schooler getting his first hand job.

Suddenly, the sound of the door opening then slamming shut echoes through the locker room, causing us both to freeze, Shayne's eyes widen with panic. When we don't hear anything else for a few seconds, I lift her off me, then stand from the bench.

"What if someone saw us?" she whispers.

This right here is why I should stay away from her. No matter how much I want to hate her, no matter how much I want to blame her, my need for her is stronger. Always.

"It's fine."

"It's fine?" she repeats, incredulous, reaching into her locker to pull a shirt over her head. "It's fine that someone might've just seen me naked on top of my ex-stepbrother?"

"I'll take care of it."

She scoffs, pulling a pair of sweatpants and a jacket from the bag inside her locker.

"Did you take my jacket?" I ask, remembering that it went missing the morning she snuck out of my bed.

She flings her locker door shut, turning to meet my eyes. "I didn't have much of a choice," she says defensively.

"I need it back."

"Fine."

TWENTY-FIVE

Shayne

"**I**S EVERYTHING OKAY?" MS. THOMAS ASKS, EYEING MY LATEST entries as if she's reading the manifesto of a man who planned to blow up an entire city instead of the angsty teenage ramblings that they are.

"Fine," I say with false cheeriness. I've had a lot to say lately. So sue me. Her eyes linger a little too long on an X-rated page, so I impatiently stick out my palm, clearing my throat.

"Right," she says, blinking rapidly. *So much for not reading my personal thoughts.* Gently, she drops the composition book into my hand, and I snatch it back, feeling exposed. "Let's switch gears," she suggests.

"Please."

"College."

"Or maybe not."

"Shayne," she chides, tilting her head. "You have options."

"I know," I assure her before she launches into her spiel about scholarships and financial aid that I know I won't even be eligible for. Everyone here, guidance counselor included, knows I'm not like the rest of the kids at Sawyer Point High. My mom might've come from money, but she doesn't get a dime from her parents. "I'm actually going to tour campuses with my team next week."

Her eyebrows shoot up, surprised. "Perfect. Anything else you want to talk about?"

"Nope."

"Then I'll see you in two weeks."

I stuff my journal into my bag, then shrug it over my shoulder as I walk out into the hall. Our meeting ran a little late, so most of the students have already gone back to class after lunch, but as I turn the corner, I see Christian and Baker arguing in hushed tones. I take a step back, peeking around the wall. Christian fists Baker's collar, shoving him up against a locker. For a second, I think he's going to hit him, but then he releases him, taking a step back. Baker shoves him away, straightening his shirt.

"Don't forget who made you who you are," Christian threatens. "You were fucking *nothing*. I can take you down just as quick."

"Back at you," Baker sneers.

All of a sudden, a class door slams behind me, drawing both their attention. Two sets of angry eyes lock onto mine, and I know I'm caught. I don't bother pretending otherwise. Christian works his jaw, glaring in my direction, and then he's storming off in the opposite direction. Baker hesitates, pinning me with a look I can't decode before disappearing into the classroom to the right of the lockers.

What the hell was that about? Their friendship has never made sense to me, and this only adds to my confusion.

I hurry to my last period, quietly slipping into class and taking the empty desk next to Holden, who tosses me a wink. I wonder if he's in on whatever's going on with Christian and Baker, or if he's in the dark like I am. I make a mental note to ask him about it later.

An hour later, the bell rings, and Holden and I walk out of class together. Valen has a cheer thing, and I won't see her tonight, so we head straight for the student parking lot.

"Oh, I almost forgot," Holden says, stopping short. I stop with him, looking at him expectantly. He reaches into his pocket before producing a small bundle of black fabric, then he's dangling it from his index finger. "I think these belong to you."

My cheeks burn when I realize he's holding my shorts from the other night and my hand shoots out to snatch them from him. "What the hell!" I stuff them into my backpack, looking around to make sure no one else just saw Holden Ames returning what will surely appear to be my underwear to onlookers.

"What?" he asks with mock sincerity. "I found these bad boys stuffed in the couch cushion. Thought you might want them back."

I flatten my lips, speed walking toward my car, and I hear his chuckle behind me.

"Come on, Shayne." He laughs, catching up to me.

"You're an asshole."

"It's funny, though. I don't recall you taking your clothes off on my couch. Seems like something I'd remember." He arches one dark eyebrow, his eyes roaming my body. "Could it be that a certain movie got you all worked up?"

I snort. "You wish."

"I mean, I get it. It got me hot, too, but next time don't wait for me to pass out before you take care of it. I'm more than happy to lend my services."

"God, you're gross," I say, rolling my eyes, both relieved and embarrassed that he thinks I masturbated on his couch while he was asleep rather than hooking up with his brother.

"It's part of my charm," he says, gripping his chest.

He has a point.

"On a serious note..." he says as I hop into the driver's seat. He stands between me and the door, one hand braced on the top of my car. "Next week."

It's all he has to say. Next week is the one-year anniversary of Danny's death. Sometimes it feels like a lifetime has passed, and other times only seconds. I nod in understanding, waiting for him to continue.

"The school's planning some memorial tribute thing for Danny. I don't know if you have a game or whatever—"

"Don't be an idiot, Holden. Of course I'll be there." I jerk on his shirt, pulling him in for a hug. He locks both arms around my head, holding me to his chest, the scent of his cologne and deodorant smothering me.

"Okay, okay," I say, shoving him off me, and then he's mussing up my hair with his heavy palm before throwing my door shut and walking away.

Maybe it's Danny's anniversary. Maybe it's the fact that for the first time in a long time I feel like I have a piece of my family back, but instead of being happy or content, I feel...like I'm waiting for the other shoe to drop. Like it's all going to be taken from me again. It's only a matter of when.

TWENTY-SIX

Thayer

"**S**O, SHOULD I JUST EXPECT YOU HERE ALL THE TIME NOW?" my dad asks as I'm walking through the front door, before I've even had the chance to put my keys down.

"Something on your mind, old man?" I'm not in the mood for this shit. I run a hand through my hair, shaking the rain out of it.

He pours two fingers of whiskey into a tumbler, setting the bottle down with a loud thud against the countertop. I take one look at his bloodshot eyes and know he's had a few more before that one. He wasn't ever around much to begin with, and I preferred it that way, but since Danny's death, here's here even less. On the rare occasion he is around, he's hammered—not that I blame him. His wife abandoned him and his kids, and then his favorite son died. That's not including countless failed relationships and one failed engagement. Life hasn't exactly been a picnic for him.

"Just that you're home an awful lot lately for someone who's going to school on my dime."

"I've got it under control." I keep it short, knowing this

could easily turn into a blowout that I don't have the energy for, then turn for the stairs.

"Do you, though?"

I stop in my tracks, looking at him over my shoulder. "If you're trying to say something, say it. I don't have all night."

He moves around the counter, advancing on me. "I'm saying you're not going to continue to throw your life away under my roof. Starting after the memorial, you're gone. You go to class. You get your shit together."

"And if I don't?" I challenge.

"Then consider yourself cut off."

A slow smile spreads across my face. "If you think money is what motivates me, you clearly don't fucking know me at all." Not giving him a chance to respond, I turn on my heels, heading for the door.

"Where are you going?"

"You want me gone? I'm gone."

His shocked expression is the last thing I see before I slam the door behind me, prowling out into the rain. He really thought he could use money to get his way? Why the fuck does he suddenly have an issue with my being here, anyway? Money isn't a factor. I know that much. My tuition is chump change for him. Maybe he knows more about Danny than he's letting on, and he doesn't want me sniffing around. Who the fuck knows?

Thunder rumbles in the distance, and I know where I want to be. Before I can think better of it, I bypass my car, walking into the woods instead. The Hellcat is loud as fuck, and I don't want to wake her mom. I pull out my phone, using it to light my way through the pitch-black trees, past the lightning tree, past the barn, and finally, to the edge of the property where her grandmother's house sits.

Both Shayne's car and her mom's Jeep are in the driveway, so I go for Shayne's window on the side of the house. I shove my phone into my pocket, then curl my fingers around the cool metal edges of the wet screen, popping it off easily. Hoisting myself up, I swing my leg through her open window and stand, my wet boots leaving a puddle on her floor. The moonlight barely peeks through the trees enough for me to make out her sleeping form. Her back is to me, and she has one bare, tanned leg hooked over the top of her blankets.

Without thinking of the consequences, I kick off my boots and strip down until I'm in nothing but my boxers. Trying to keep my steps light, I slide into bed behind her, curling my arm around her waist.

"Thayer," she says my name on a sleepy moan. The fact that she knows me, even in sleep, is enough to give me a semi. I pull her closer until her back is flush to my front, her hot skin warming my cold chest. She gasps at the feeling, fully awake now, her body tensing against me.

"It's me," I say quickly, not wanting her to scream and wake her mom.

"Thayer?" she asks, her voice raspy with sleep as she rolls over to face me. "What are you doing here?" She sits up and the blanket falls away, revealing her body. She's wearing nothing but a ribbed, white tank top and underwear. Even in the dark, I can see the outline of her nipple piercings.

"I don't know," I say, giving her the honest answer.

"Are you okay?" Her brows furrow and she runs a hand through her wild hair to push it out of her face.

I don't respond. I curl my hand behind her thigh, prompting her to lift her knee to straddle me. I roll onto my back, smoothing my hands up the tops of her thighs, watching her nipples harden beneath the thin fabric. I can feel the warmth of her pussy through her underwear as she grinds against me ever so slightly, but I squeeze her thighs, stopping her movements.

She pouts, looking down at me in question.

"Come here," I say, my voice suddenly thick. She repositions herself, her legs straight between mine, her face inches above me. I slide my hand into her hair, bringing her mouth to mine. Shayne's lips part on a moan, her tongue sliding against mine. Her hands come up to cup my face, one leg hitching up onto my hip in an effort to get closer. I grip her hips that rock against me, trying hard to ignore that I could be inside her with a few quick adjustments. My thumbs rub the exposed skin above the waistband of her underwear, and she sucks on my tongue, making my dick swell even more.

"Stop," I say, breaking away from the kiss, demonstrating self-control I didn't know I possessed. Shayne pulls back, confusion shining in her eyes. "I didn't come for this."

"Then what did you come for?" she whispers.

I don't know. I don't know how to tell her that I just wanted to be near her, to fucking feel her. To be selfish for one night before we go back to our game of cat and mouse. Instead of saying any of that, I shift out from beneath her, then roll onto my side, bringing her back to my front again. I shove my right arm under the pillow beneath my head, then flatten my left hand against her stomach, holding her close. I can feel her heart beating, her breathing still ragged, but slowly, I feel the tension leave her body, her breathing returning to normal.

I lazily drag my lip piercings back and forth across her skin from her neck to the tip of her bare shoulder, loving the way she shivers and melts into me.

"How did you know my window would be open?" she murmurs, her voice telling me she's on the brink of falling asleep.

"It's raining. You always leave your window open when it rains."

TWENTY-SEVEN

Shayne

I STARE DOWN AT MY PHONE, WILLING IT TO LIGHT UP WITH A response from Grey. I texted him about Danny's memorial ceremony, and he said he'd think about it. I really thought he'd show, and I think Thayer and Holden are using his presence, or lack thereof, to determine whether he's hiding something or not. If he's guilty of something, he wouldn't dare show his face. On the flip side, if he isn't, he wouldn't miss it. *Would he?* I know my brother. I know he wouldn't hurt anyone, let alone Danny, but what if he *knows* something? His suspicious behavior is getting harder and harder to justify, not only to Thayer and Holden, but to myself. And the fact that I'm even doubting him is, in turn, making *me* feel guilty.

"Still nothing?" Valen asks, looking over my shoulder at my phone.

I shake my head, stuffing my phone into my jacket pocket as August makes his way to the podium at the top of the stairs outside the school entrance. Thayer, Holden, and William are seated behind the podium, along with Christian and his parents, Samuel and Elyse. I've only met Samuel a handful of times at various family gatherings, but I don't think we've ever had an actual conversation. He's tall and imposing, like the rest of the Ames men, but he seems more approachable than August and William. Maybe it's due to the fact that he actually smiles. The people of Sawyer Point must love him, seeing as how he's an elected official.

I feel a sprinkle on the back of my hand, but the scent of impending rain tipped me off twenty minutes ago. The Ames family is protected by the awning, but the rest of the town huddles together, sharing umbrellas with the people who came prepared. The school's orchestra plays some sad classical piece as a couple of students pass out white candlesticks for everyone to hold.

I look up at Thayer, who manages to look both lethal and elegant in his peacoat with a dress shirt and tie underneath, then back down at my oversized tan Sherpa jacket, black leggings, and Adidas, feeling underdressed. I wish I would've worn something more appropriate for the occasion. Always a bit of a rebel, his hair is still disheveled, mussed in that perfectly imperfect way, and he kept his piercings in. His face is blank, void of emotion, but his sad eyes give him away.

As if he can hear my thoughts, his eyes scan the crowd, seeking me out. He holds my gaze and I attempt to give him a reassuring smile. I know he's not looking forward to this. If there are two things Thayer hates, it's being in the spotlight and emotions. Add in the reason for this gathering and it's the perfect shit storm.

Valen's outstretched arm appears in front of me, handing me a lit candle with a paper around the bottom to catch the wax, pulling my attention away from Thayer.

"Thanks."

I turn around, searching for Grey once more, but deep down, I know he's not coming. I do, however, spot my mom on the perimeter, and she holds up her hand, giving me a discrete wave of her fingers, still in her flight attendant getup. She had a quick flight today, but she leaves tomorrow morning for a long trip, so I doubt she'll stick around long. It has to be un-comfortable for her to show her face around these people, but Danny was practically her stepson, and splitting from August doesn't change that.

The music comes to an end as August's voice fills the air. "Thank you to the Sawyer Point orchestra," he says before clearing his throat. "It's hard to believe it's been a year since my son was taken from me—from all of you—from this earth. Daniel was a light in this community. He loved his family and friends, he loved his school, he loved the game, and most of all, he loved his brothers."

Thayer's hands tighten into fists on top of his thighs.

"Our family aren't the only ones who suffered a loss," August continues. "The entire town mourned with us. Prayed with us. And ultimately, it was your love and support that got us through it."

He's really laying it on thick. Thayer must think so, too, if the way he rolls his eyes is anything to go by. I slide my gaze over to Holden to find a similar reaction. He bounces his knee, appearing antsy already and it's only just started. Christian looks down at the ground, twisting his fingers.

"In his honor, we've started the Daniel Ames Memorial Scholarship Fund. Each year, two students will receive a twenty-thousand-dollar scholarship."

Everyone applauds, but I fight an eyeroll. The people of Sawyer Point aren't exactly in need of assistance. August holds up a hand, silencing.

"Daniel's college experience was cut short. It is my hope that out of this tragedy can come something good. We'll be able to make a difference in the lives of young people for years to come and keep Daniel's memory alive."

Another round of soft applause.

"I think Coach Shaw has something else he'd like to announce."

The basketball coach joins them at the stop of the steps.

He shakes August's hand before August returns to the empty seat between Holden and William, then takes the podium.

"It's starting to come down," he starts, gesturing to the rain. "So, I'll keep this short.

Danny, as we called him, was an exceptionally talented player, and an even better kid. I was lucky to have him on my team, and lucky to know him. As most of you know, last year a lot of you petitioned to have Danny's number retired."

Coach looks back at Christian and Holden, and they take that as their cue to stand. They walk behind the row of seats to retrieve something out of a large box, then make their way up to the podium, each of them holding a side. They prop it up on the stand, then remove the black fabric to reveal a large shadow box that holds Daniel's jersey, with the number sixteen below his last name. A couple of pictures line the side of the frame, along with what appears to be a quote that I'm unable to read from where I'm standing.

"I'm happy to announce that we've made that happen. This will hang in the gymnasium lobby. That way a piece of Danny will always be with us here at Sawyer Point High."

People clap, and some guy—presumably from the basketball team—cheers loudly before a couple of his friends join in. Holden and Christian bring the jersey back to the box behind the chairs before returning to their seats. Once the noise dies down, a projector screen to the left lights up. "Forever Young" by Bob Dylan plays as a picture of Danny as a baby fills the screen, then one as a toddler holding a basketball, one of him and Thayer on the beach at maybe four and five years old, another one of all three brothers opening presents on Christmas morning.

When he reaches middle school, it becomes a timeline of all of his awards and achievements, everything from sports to academics. As the song winds down, the pictures become more recent. A shot of him during a basketball game after scoring the winning point with his hands in the air as his team runs to bombard him, one of him in his cap and gown at graduation. His senior photo. And the last one is of Danny, Thayer, Holden, and Christian at the falls, of all places, standing in a line with their arms over each other's shoulders. I remember that day. It was one of the last good ones we had all together.

My chin starts to tremble as the tears I'm trying so hard to keep from falling finally spill over, and Valen puts her arm around me, pulling me into her. She sniffs, and I know she's crying, too, as I wrap my arms around her middle, careful to hold the candle away from her. My shoulders start to shake, and I turn my head into her chest to hide my face. The only thing worse than crying is crying in public. Not that anyone would fault me. There isn't a dry eye in sight. Still, I feel like I'm under a microscope, like everyone reads into every little thing I do.

A loud sound coming from the top of the steps has me pulling back to see Thayer storming away, his chair tipped over behind him. The crowd parts as he cuts through it. I want to follow him, to make sure he's okay, but people are already suspecting something as it is. I can't risk raising his dad's suspicion. As he's passing me, I catch his palm in mine. He doesn't look at me, keeping his gaze forward, but his thumb glides over my wrist, caressing the faint scar there. The entire thing happens in less than two seconds, and then he's prowling toward the parking lot.

Holden stands to go after him, but William stops him with a hand on his shoulder. He says something in his ear, and Holden's nostrils flare, his jaw set tight as he reluctantly takes his seat. The slideshow ends, and August thanks everyone for coming.

When the crowd starts to disperse, I blow out my candle, then hand it over to Valen. "I'm going to talk to Holden."

She nods. "Go. Call me later."

I pull her in for a hug, seeing Holden and Christian walking away behind her. But they're not going for the parking lot.

They're going around the school, I'm assuming for the student parking lot, while August and Samuel are distracted by people giving their condolences and commending their generosity. I start in their direction, but my mom calls my name, stopping me in my tracks.

Shit. I forgot she was here.

"Where are you going?" she asks, concern etched into her features. Her eyes are glassy from crying, but she still looks like a million bucks.

"Oh," I hesitate, trying to think of something. "I need to grab something from my locker before they lock up for the night," I say, hitching a thumb over my shoulder.

"Okay. Want me to wait for you?"

"No, that's okay. I'm supposed to meet up with Valen. If that's okay with you…"

She twists her lips, considering, and every second feels like an hour because I just want to find Thayer. But first, I need to talk to Holden.

"Fine." She sighs, pulling me in for a hug. "I'll be gone by the time you wake up, so tell me you love me." She pats my hair as she holds on to me.

"I love you," I assure her. "Have a safe trip."

When she leaves, I sprint up the stairs and toward the school. Thankfully, the doors are still unlocked, so I decide to go through the hall and out the back entrance instead of around the perimeter to shave off time. My wet shoes squeak against the hall floor as I jog down the hall, and when I push the back doors open, I spot Holden's Rover pulling out of the lot.

"Shit," I hiss.

I pull out my phone to text him, but I catch movement to my left in my peripheral vision, and I look over to see Christian and his dad, Samuel, having what appears to be a heated discussion next to Samuel's Mercedes. I slip behind a pillar to keep from being seen. Samuel's face is centimeters from Christian's, and although I can't hear what he's saying, I know they're not discussing the weather. Christian's hands are balled into fists at his side, his spine ramrod straight, as if it's taking everything in him to not react.

Samuel's hands shoot out to fist Christian's collar, and then he's throwing him up against the side of the car. *Jesus.* I wasn't expecting that. Apparently, he isn't as genial as he seems. Christian says something, and suddenly, Samuel's fist cocks back and smashes into the side of his face. I gasp, slapping a hand over my mouth, stomach churning. He does it again and again, and when Christian slides down the side of the car, landing in a puddle on the ground, Samuel kicks him in the stomach, causing him to groan in pain.

I don't think. I just react. I charge toward them without considering the consequences. All I know is that if I don't step in, Christian could get seriously injured. Christian spots me first, his eyes widening as if warning me to stay out of sight. Even if I wanted to listen, it's too late, because Samuel takes notice, turning to look at me over his shoulder with a crazed look in his eyes. He takes a step back from Christian, smoothing out his suit jacket and schooling his features as I drop to my knees to help him up.

"Get away from me," Christian grumbles, clutching his stomach.

I frown, trying to pull him to his feet anyway, but he jerks out of my grasp and stands on his own. Blood drips from his lip and he swipes the back of his hand across his mouth. Rising to my feet, I look between them. Adrenaline has my heart pounding in my ears, apprehension creeping up my spine at the way Samuel's looking at me.

"Look what you've done," Samuel says to Christian before turning back for me. He advances on me, and instinctively, I take a step back. Suddenly, I'm not feeling so brave.

"Dad," Christian says, but he ignores it, closing the distance between us.

"As you can imagine, it's been a bit of an emotional night." His voice is calm but deadly, and I slip my hand into my jacket pocket, gripping my self-defense keychain in the shape of kitty ears that Grey gave me a couple years back. "It would be a shame if you had the wrong impression of me."

I shake my head, slipping my fingers through the holes of the keychain, ready to use it if need be, but hoping like hell that it doesn't come to that.

"This is family business, and I'm sure I don't have to tell you how imperative it is that it stays that way."

I look over at Christian whose eyes beg me to back down, but I straighten my shoulders, steeling my voice. "Just leave him alone and I won't say anything."

Samuel's eyebrows shoot up his forehead as he chuckles, looking back at Christian. When he turns back to face me, the amusement is gone, replaced with barely contained rage. "Pretty bold of you to tell me how to handle my son."

I swallow hard as he takes another threatening step toward me.

"Dad!" Christian yells, and this time his voice is firmer. Samuel pauses. "She won't tell anyone. I'll handle it."

Samuel runs a hand through his hair to smooth it back in place before turning back around for his car. "Clean up your own mess this time," he spits, stubbing a finger into Christian's chest. Without another word from either of them, he's gone, leaving Christian and me alone in the parking lot.

"Are you okay?" he asks.

"Are *you*?"

"I'm fine. Listen, Thayer and Holden…" he trails off, shoving his hands into his pants pockets.

"They don't know," I guess, finishing his sentence. He nods. I start to wonder how something like this can go unnoticed, but then I realize that I never once suspected anything either and I practically lived with the guy. Christian stays at Whittemore so often he has his own room there, and I never noticed any bruises or injuries.

Maybe this is why he doesn't like to stay with his own parents.

"How long has this—"

Christian shakes his head, cutting me off. "I don't want to talk about it. You looking for Thayer?"

"I was trying to catch a ride with Holden. I came with Valen."

"Let's go," he says, nodding toward his Black BMW in the spot next to where Samuel was parked. He digs his keys out of his pocket, wincing with the movement.

"Do you want me to drive?"

"I've got it," he says, his tone clipped.

Once we're inside the car, he starts the engine and I pull the seatbelt across my chest. Neither one of us speaks as he pulls out of the lot, heading toward Whittemore.

"What are you going to tell them?" I ask, referring to his bruised and bloody state.

"I'll handle it." His hands tighten around the steering wheel.

"Okay."

TWENTY-EIGHT

Shayne

WHEN WE PULL UP TO WHITTEMORE, THE FIRST THING I notice is that Thayer's Hellcat isn't here. A sinking feeling hits my gut as Christian pulls the car around the fountain, coming to a stop right at the steps. Unbuckling, I open the door and hop out, but I stop when I notice Christian doesn't make any move to get up.

"You're not coming in?" I brace one hand on the top of the door, bending over to see inside the car.

"I gotta go clean up," he says, gesturing to his face. *Oh, right.* "Tell Holden I'll hit him up later."

I gnaw on my lip, stuck between wanting to say something supportive and not wanting to make him feel uncomfortable at the same time. I end up settling with, "Thanks for the ride." I straighten, turning for the steps, hearing music before I've even opened the front door. I have my hand on the handle when Christian's voice stops me.

"Shayne."

I glance at him over my shoulder, but he doesn't speak, a conflicted expression on his face.

"I won't say anything," I assure him.

He gives a sharp nod, his jaw set tight.

"But you should tell them."

He drives off without responding, and I push the door open, the music growing louder. I tiptoe upstairs, following the sound of "Go Fuck Yourself" into the second floor living room. I don't know if August is around here somewhere, so I peek around the corner, finding Holden with two near-naked girls kneeling in front of him and a bottle to his lips. His stance is wide, pants around his ankles. His tie is loosened, and his dress shirt hangs open but still clings to his shoulders. One of the girls works his length with her hand and her mouth, while the other one pays attention to his balls.

I cringe, but I'm unable to look away, caught somewhere between disgusted and intrigued.

"Hey, baby sister. You're just in time for the party."

The girl sucking on him pulls back, releasing him with a pop, but she doesn't seem embarrassed by my presence. A scathing response is on the tip of my tongue, but then I notice the sadness in his eyes, and the way he sways on his feet, just a little. He didn't seem drunk at the memorial. Did he manage to drink that much within the twenty or so minutes it took to get here?

"Where's your brother?" I ask, crossing my arms like I'm not affected in the least by the scene before me.

He gives a bitter laugh. "Six feet under."

Jesus, Holden.

The girls exchange looks, clearly uncomfortable with the awkward turn of events.

"Oh, you mean Thayer? Probably doing the same thing as me, with any luck." His smile is wide, but his eyes betray him. He's testing me, watching for a reaction. And maybe even trying to hurt me.

He holds my gaze, but I break contact, shaking my head, disappointed, then turn to leave without another word. If it were any other day, I would've told him to fuck off. If it were any other day, I'd say screw all of these Ames boys. But to-night, they're grieving. *Tonight*, they don't have anyone look-ing out for them—evidently, not even each other. Christian's being secretly abused by his father, Holden's self-medicating with booze and threesomes, and Thayer's most likely self-de-structing, God knows where.

These brooding assholes in peacoats are going to be the death of me.

TWENTY-NINE

Thayer

I COULDN'T TAKE ANOTHER FUCKING SECOND. I COULDN'T SIT there while my dad played the part of the grieving father of the golden boy, reducing Danny's entire life to a collection of accomplishments. As if he was merely an extension of my father, and not his own person. Fake. Every goddamn thing about that bullshit ceremony was fake, right down to the people who cried for him.

Except Shayne.

The look on her face reflected everything I was feeling inside, and seeing her cry tonight did something to me. It's confusing as fuck to want to protect and punish someone at the same time, but I couldn't do either one, even if I wanted to. All I could do was sit there on display, like a fucking lion in a zoo.

"Thayer?" Shayne's voice calls out for me. I should've known she'd find me. Might even be the reason I subconsciously chose this place. But I'm too raw, too fucked up to be around her right now. I stand with my head bowed, hands braced in the back of the old leather couch I commandeered for the barn when I started coming here a few years back.

She walks up next to me, and I feel her warmth against my side, but I don't lift my gaze.

"I thought you could use a friend."

"I don't want to be your fucking friend," I snap.

"Then what do you want?" she whispers.

"What do I want?" I repeat, swiveling my head to look up at her. "What I want is for you to leave."

"Why?" she grits out through clenched teeth.

"Because even as you stand there with tears in your eyes, all I want to do is bend you over and fuck you until I don't feel anything other than your tight ass pussy squeezing my dick. So, unless you want to finish what we started in this barn a year ago, I suggest you leave."

I fully expect her to walk away. Maybe even cry. What I don't expect is for her to push up on the tips of her toes, bringing those full pink lips to my ear.

"Then do it," Shayne dares, her tits pressing into me.

I give a bitter laugh, taking a step back. "No."

"Why not?"

"Because you couldn't handle it."

"Try me," she says, lifting her chin defiantly.

I clench my jaw so tight I'm surprised my teeth don't crack under the pressure. I'm trying to do the right thing, but my willpower is fading fast. If she wants to play this game, I won't be the one to back down. I drop down onto the couch, bringing my hands behind my head as if I'm a paying customer.

"Take off your clothes."

Once again, she does the unexpected. Her hands shake as she unzips her jacket, then lets it fall to the floor. Her white t-shirt is next, revealing two black, mesh triangles that do nothing to hide the perfect tits underneath. Those piercings I love so much are visible through the fabric, making my dick even harder. The old Shayne was so concerned with what other people thought that she wasn't true to herself. The piercings, the black polish on the tips of her fingers, her smart mouth...

all proof that she's running out of fucks to give. And I've never wanted her more.

She swallows hard, hooking her thumbs into the waistband of her pants before pushing them down her legs and kicking off her shoes. She steps forward in only her bra and matching underwear, away from the pile of discarded clothes. She's almost close enough to touch. I bite down on my bottom lip, my eyes roaming her sweet little body as she lifts one hand to pull out her hair tie, thick blonde hair falling down around her shoulders. It takes every ounce of self-control to keep my hands behind my head.

Shayne nudges my knee with hers, waiting for further instruction.

"All of it."

She glares at me, even as she reaches behind her to unclasp her bra, one hand holding it to her chest. For a second, I think she's going to forfeit this dangerous game we're playing, but then her hand falls away, letting her bra drop to the floor between us.

Fuck. I slide a hand down to squeeze my dick through my pants and Shayne smirks, knowing she's winning. Her underwear is the last to go, then she's taking another small step toward me, completely naked now. I finally break, my hands shooting out to grip the back of her thighs. I pull her to my face as I spread her legs from behind. Shayne gasps, her hands flying out to clutch my head for balance as I part her lower lips with my tongue and her gasp turns into a moan as I take one long lick. Her knees almost buckle, but I hold her steady, sucking her clit into my mouth.

"No," she breathes, tugging me back by my hair. I wipe my mouth with the back of my hand, cocking my head to the side in question. She can't be stopping this now.

"Your turn," Shayne says, giving me a pointed look.

I clench my jaw and hold her stare as I undo the buttons of my shirt, one by one. I must not be fast enough, because then Shayne's dropping to her knees in front of me, impatient fingers tugging at my belt. I lift up enough to let her pull my pants and boxers down my legs, throwing them behind her. Her eyes lock onto my cock, standing thick and hard. I grip the base, holding it out for her.

"Sit on me."

She doesn't hesitate, straddling me, one knee on each side. My hands find the dip in her waist as she pushes my shirt over my shoulders, shoving it down my arms. I hold my breath, waiting for her reaction.

"Thayer," she breathes out in surprise, her eyebrows pulling together as tentative fingers reach out to trace the lines of ink that run from my shoulder down to my wrist where the lightning hit me. When the marks first started to fade, I decided I wanted to keep them, so I had my scars tattooed over. Showing her felt like admitting I kept a piece of her with me. A piece I wasn't willing to let go of.

"When? *Why?*"

I bring my mouth to her chest, ignoring her questions as my lips ghost across her nipple while my fingers find her clit. I stroke her until her eyes fall shut, her hands squeezing my shoulders. She's so fucking wet already.

Suddenly, she's jerking my hand out of the way, lowering herself onto me. As soon as her wet, warm pussy makes contact with the tip of my cock, she freezes, looking into my eyes.

"Thayer." Her voice holds a hint of panic, as if she just realized what we're about to do.

I should stop her. I should walk away for good. But instead, I say, "Slide down, baby. I've got you."

Shayne

"Slide down, baby. I've got you."

Thayer keeps one hand at my waist and slides the other one through my hair, gripping the back of my neck. I nod wordlessly, and then I'm slowly pushing down on him. His stomach tenses as his thick tip breaches my entrance and the pain is sharp enough to steal my breath. I pause to adjust to the feeling, my wide eyes finding his. This is really happening. Thayer's finally inside me, and there's no going back now, even if I wanted to. I lick my lips, and he pulls my mouth to his. My lips part on a moan and he takes the opportunity to slide his tongue inside. The more he kisses me, the more I relax. After a few seconds, I start to inch down little by little, stretching around him until he's fully inside of me, my ass hitting the top of his thighs.

"Shayne," he says my name, his strangled voice laced with suspicion.

"Don't move," I say, my voice shaky. My fingers clutch his shoulders, holding on for dear life. Thayer's dark eyes snap up to mine.

"This is your first time." He states it as a fact, not a question.

I nod, and his eyes flash with something I can't pinpoint before they squeeze shut.

"I want this," I assure him, starting to move my hips in small circles.

Thayer pulls back, looking down between us with a groan. "Fuck."

I feel impossibly full in the best way. Thayer hasn't even moved, and this is already better than anything I've ever experienced before. I shouldn't be surprised. This is Thayer. Everything with him is just…more. *We* are more.

"I need you to move, Shayne," he grits out, his hands squeezing my ass.

Bracing my hands on his thighs behind me, I ride him slowly, fascinated with watching his length slide in and out of me. Thayer's eyes are glued to where we connect, watching intently. His palms smooth up my stomach, and when he brushes his thumbs across my nipples, I close my eyes, my head falling back.

Soon, I feel the urge to move faster, so I sit forward, using his shoulders for leverage as I lift up, then slowly slide back down, then repeat the motion.

"Just like that," Thayer praises, his hands guiding my movements. "Good girl." His words spur me on, and I start to move faster, needing more as pain gives way to pleasure. I brace my hands on his shoulders, keeping him close as I roll my hips. His hard stomach presses against my clit, giving me the friction that I need, and when his tongue flicks out against my nipple, I feel myself clench around him, eliciting a groan from him. They've always been sensitive, but now they're even more so. I could orgasm from his mouth on me alone.

"You keep doing that and I'm not going to last long," he warns.

"Neither am I," I confess, leaning forward to bring my nipple to his lips again. This time, his teeth scrape over my piercing and then he's pulling it deep into his mouth, sucking hard. It sends a jolt straight down to my core and I feel myself tightening around him again.

"Oh my God," I whine. I don't even recognize my own voice. I don't sound like me. I sound like some sex-crazed, needy version of myself, but I'm past caring. Thayer sucks harder and a rush of heat floods me as I feel myself grow even slicker.

"Fuck this," Thayer curses, flipping me over, then he's sliding back into me. I gasp, my hips lifting off the couch as he pumps into me. "Listen to how wet you are." He hooks my ankles over his shoulders, one of his knees on the ground and one pressing into the cushion as he fucks me, like he's trying to get deeper. As if he's not already imbedded in the deepest parts of me.

"Thayer," I warn. I can feel it building. His hair is wet with sweat, and his neck is corded with exertion. My hands smooth up his back to curl over his muscular shoulders, pulling him close to me.

"Do it," he says, already knowing. "Come all over me."

He slips a hand between us to stroke my clit and that's all it takes. My head swims and my entire body tingles as I cry out, my nails digging into his damp skin before raking down his back. Thayer sucks in a breath and I quickly let go, thinking I hurt him, but then he takes one of my hands, putting it back where it was. I drag my nails down his back again and his mouth falls open, eyes squeezing shut. Using my free hand, I pull his face to mine, sucking on the twin piercings in the corner of his lip. Thayer tenses up before he slams into me once, twice, three times, and then he's pulling out, his fist pumping his length, the muscles in his stomach flexing as his release spills onto my thigh.

He collapses onto me, his breathing ragged. His cheek presses against my chest and he's still halfway off the couch as we both attempt to catch our breath, the weight of what we just did finally creeping in. Eventually, he scoops me up, then flips our positions so I'm lying on top of him. He reaches an arm up to snatch the blanket off the back of the couch, spreading it over us. It's only big enough to cover our feet up to my lower back, but Thayer is like a furnace beneath me, so it doesn't matter.

"Did I hurt you?"

"No." *Yes.*

"Are you okay?"

"Yes." *No.*

To be honest, I don't know what I'm feeling. So many emotions overwhelm me at once, making it hard to settle on one. If I had to pick an adjective, I'd go with…nervous. I've been waiting for this moment for three years, and it was better than anything I've ever been able to conjure up in my imagination, but what now? Is this where Thayer turns cold and leaves me again?

But then I feel his finger trace my spine up and down then back again, sending a shiver through me as goosebumps prick my skin. I relax a little, melting into him.

I follow the branch-like design that crawls down his arm with the tips of my fingers. That night was one of the worst in my life—it had to be up there for him, too—so why would he want a permanent reminder? I can't deny that it's beautiful. Somehow it makes me feel closer to him, to have this memory, this connection, that no one else can touch.

"Why did you get this?" I finally ask.

Thayer doesn't answer. Instead, he brings my wrist to his mouth, pressing his lips against the matching mark.

"I'll walk you home."

The brief moment of tenderness is gone, his mask back in place, and suddenly, I feel cold. I huff out a bitter laugh, peeling myself away from his warmth. I'm not surprised. I'd be stupid to think this would change anything. I stand, quickly pulling my underwear up my legs.

"Shayne."

I don't respond, searching the ground for the rest of my clothes. I throw my t-shirt over my head before shrugging my jacket on.

"Shayne."

Tucking my hair behind my ear, I glance around the dimly lit space to make sure I'm not forgetting anything when I see my bra. Stuffing it into my jacket pocket, I walk over to where I left my shoes and slip them on.

"Shayne, fucking stop for a minute!"

I finally face him, finding him in his dress pants, his chest heaving, eyes conflicted.

"It's late. You should probably go check on Holden," I dismiss him, keeping my tone light in an attempt to appear unaffected.

He frowns, and the crease between his eyes growing deeper is the last thing I see before I walk away.

THIRTY

Shayne

I T'S BEEN A WEEK SINCE I HANDED MY VIRGINITY TO THAYER ON A silver platter, and I haven't seen or heard from him once. I spent my weekend doing homework and helping my mom clean out some of the cluttered bedrooms on the second floor, but I was too distracted to focus on either one. My thoughts vacillated between what happened in the barn and stumbling upon Christian's secret. I feel guilty keeping it from Thayer, but I promised Christian I wouldn't say anything. I just don't know how long I can keep that promise. It doesn't feel right to keep something like this a secret. I still can't wrap my mind around it. If I hadn't seen it with my own eyes, I'd never believe it. I guess monsters come in all different forms, even charismatic family men with friendly smiles. Christian's prickly demeanor makes sense to me now.

When Monday rolled around, Holden acted as if Friday night never happened, and I was happy to play along. Christian avoided me entirely, which wasn't unexpected. I wanted to talk to him, to make sure he was okay, but the only time I saw him was at lunch in front of everyone, and even then, he left early. Seeing him made me feel slightly better because he didn't seem to be in pain, and I wondered if that was because he wasn't hurting, or if he was simply good at hiding it.

Baker was noticeably absent, too. I thought back to their fight in the hall, knowing it's somehow related. All these pieces to the puzzle, but I can't seem to figure out how to make them all fit. I don't even know if they're from the same puzzle.

"Shayne!" Valen snaps her fingers in front of my face, jerking me from my thoughts.

"Sorry." I shake my head, focusing my attention on her as we walk to our cars. "What'd you say?"

"What's up with you?" She narrows her eyes at me. "You've been distracted all day."

"I didn't get much sleep last night."

Valen wiggles her brows. "Wouldn't have anything to do with that sexy stepbrother of yours, would it?"

I roll my eyes. "He's *not* my stepbrother." I feel like I should get it tattooed on my forehead at this point.

"Shayne Elizabeth Courtland, did you fuck him?" Her eyes widen, and she stops short, facing me.

"No!" I snap, looking around to make sure we don't have an audience. How would she even begin to guess that based off that response? "I mean *yes*, but no," I whisper.

Her eyes shift back and forth, confused. "I'm not following."

"I'll call you later," I promise, not wanting to have this conversation here, pulling her in for a hug before heading for my car.

"You're an asshole!" she singsongs as I walk away.

When I open the door, I find a hoodie folded up in my front seat. I scan the parking lot, searching for Thayer's Challenger. It's just a plain black hoodie, but I know it's his. I've seen him wear it a thousand times. I bite down on my lip to keep from smiling, fighting the urge to do something stupid, like bring it to my nose and see if it smells like him.

No. Don't swoon, you idiot. You should be mad. He doesn't get to give you emotional whiplash.

Tossing it onto the passenger seat, I climb in, drop my phone into my lap, then stick my key into the ignition. Before I can back out of my spot, my phone buzzes between my thighs.

Keep your window open tonight.

The number is one I don't recognize, but there's only one person it could be. Nerves and excitement tangle together at the promise of seeing him. *Ugh.* I've never met someone so hot and cold in my life, not to mention infuriating, impossible, and entitled.

Try telling that to the butterflies in my stomach.

The rest of the night dragged on mercilessly slow. I'm sure it didn't have anything to do with the fact that I spent every agonizing second anticipating whatever Thayer was up to. Did he plan to break this thing between us off? Did he plan on coming back for another taste like nothing happened? I told myself I wasn't going to open my window, that I wasn't going to be that girl who did whatever he said with no questions asked. But in the end, I left it open, with a promise to myself that I'd have a real conversation with him about how I felt. No touching. No sex. At least not before I'd gotten some real answers.

I stand in my walk-in closet, wearing sleep shorts and a matching lace camisole. No. This won't do. I need more clothes. Something frumpy and...unattractive. I don't want him getting cocky, thinking I wore this for him. I shove my shorts down my thighs and pull my top off before switching it out for a pair of baggy sweatpants and a pastel tie-dye sweat-shirt. I stand in front of the full-length mirror in my closet, rolling the waistband a few times so they stay in place. My face is stripped of makeup, hair in a messy bun. I look border-line homeless. *Perfect.*

When ten o'clock rolls around and he's still not here, I start to suspect he's not coming. I climb into bed, swipe my phone and earbuds off the bedside table, and find an episode of my favorite podcast to pass the time. Five minutes. I'll give him five more minutes.

I don't know how long has passed when I jerk upright, finding Thayer standing inside my window. *Shit.* I must have fallen asleep. I can only see his silhouette standing there, his frame tall and imposing. I flip the switch on the small lamp next to my bed, bathing the room in dim light, then I swing my legs over the side of my mattress, moving toward him.

"Hi," I say, the butterflies from earlier returning full force.

"Hi."

We lock eyes, taking each other in, and suddenly, every-thing I had planned to say dies on my tongue. It's only been a week, but I've missed him. His dark hair is perfectly dishev-eled, his lightning tattoo peeking out from the sleeve of his t-shirt. I guess he doesn't care to cover it up now that I've seen it. I don't know who moves first, but all of a sudden, I'm jumping into his arms, his hands gripping my ass as my legs wrap around his waist, our mouths colliding.

Thayer groans appreciatively, his hands squeezing my ass before he hitches me up higher, never once breaking our kiss. He flips us around, slamming my back to the wall next to the window as his tongue continues to fuck my mouth. He's never kissed me like this, his tongue moving slow and sure in a way that consumes me. I'd say he missed me, too.

"Wait," I say, pushing on his shoulders. "No kissing."

"Yes, kissing," he argues, his lips finding my throat. "I want to kiss other things, too." His words send a jolt straight between my legs, and I arch for him, giving him better access. He's hard between my legs already as he nips and sucks the sensitive skin between my neck and collarbone, and I can't keep from rolling my hips into him.

"I'm mad at you," I say aloud, and I don't know if I'm talking to him or trying to remind myself.

"I know." His warm palm slips beneath my sweatshirt, his thumb brushing against my piercing making me shiver, my nipple tightening beneath his touch.

"Explain." My head falls back, every nerve ending tingling.

"Later."

That single word cuts through the haze of lust, giving me the strength to stop this. Unlocking my legs, I slide down his body, then walk back over to my bed, putting some much-needed distance between us. If we're going to do this, I need space.

"Now."

Thayer turns to face me, raising an eyebrow.

"The other night," I start, knowing he's not going to offer information willingly. I'm going to have to pry it from him, piece by piece. "Do you regret it? Do you regret...me?" My heart pounds in my chest, my stomach swirling with nerves waiting for his answer.

The muscles in his jaw flex. He doesn't say anything, but the look in his eyes tells me everything I need to know.

THIRTY-ONE

Thayer

THREE LONG YEARS OF FOREPLAY FINALLY CAME TO A HEAD, AND even in my wildest fucking dreams could I have imagined how good it would feel to finally be inside her. The fact that she was a virgin had me feeling more than a little conflicted. It complicates things, but at the same time, I fucking love that she waited for me. I tried to stay away. I even tried to go back to class. I thought some space from Shayne would do something to dull my need for her, but I should've known it wouldn't work. She was gone for almost a year, and when she got back, it was like no time had passed at all. I made her out to be a villain in my mind, but when I look at her, all I see is my Shayne.

"The other night—do you regret it?" Her eyes beg me to say no. "Do you regret...me?"

I hesitate, not knowing how to answer that, and I see the hurt slice through her.

"Then why are you here?" she asks, her voice growing in pitch. "If you regret me, then why come here?" She walks over to the desk in the corner of her room, retrieving the hoodie I left in her car earlier. "What is this?" she demands, holding it out in front of me. "You fuck me, then you disappear. You take your jacket back, then you leave me this?" She throws it at me and I make no move to catch it, letting it fall to the floor at my feet.

"Coming here was a bad idea."

"Why?" she asks, her tone growing frustrated. "Because you're afraid you might feel something? Maybe even feel something *for me?*"

When I don't respond, she continues.

"Because God forbid you ever show me anything real, right? Every time you start to let me in, you shut down, then say or do something hurtful to push me away."

"You think I don't *feel?*" I finally snap. "All I fucking do is feel since you've been back! And every time I see your face, I'm reminded of the night Danny died. The night I failed him. Because of you. And then I sleep with you, on the anniversary of his death of all days."

She draws back, clearly hurt by my words. But they keep falling out of my mouth, unable to stop. "You want me to talk about my feelings?" I ask, closing the distance between us. Shayne's pretty features tug into a frown, her delicate jaw tensing. "Every time I'm with you, it feels like a betrayal to him."

And there it is. I didn't fully realize it myself until this moment, but it's the truth.

"You blame me," she says in a stunned whisper, and I can tell the thought never so much as entered her mind before. I see the wheels turning as she puts the pieces together. "So it doesn't matter if Grey's innocent, does it? It's because of me. You hate me because you blame *me.*"

"I blame *me* for getting too wrapped up in you. Even knowing what your brother might have done, I still fucking want you. What does that say about me? That I can't stay away from the sister of the guy who most likely killed my brother?

"At first, I was angry. So fucking angry. I wanted to set fire to everything I loved, just to watch it burn. You just happened to be at the top of that list. So I pushed you away. I wanted to hurt you because I was hurting. Then you were gone, and that anger was all I had left. I used it like a lifeline, because as long as I felt that rage, I didn't have to feel anything else.

"Until you came back. You distracted me from the shit show my life had become, and I welcomed the distraction at first. I craved being around you, even just to piss you off. I needed our encounters. I told myself it was okay to touch you, to take a little bit of the fucking comfort it gave me, as long as I didn't let it go too far."

I jam my fingers through my hair, pacing the floor.

"But then I started to forget all the reasons I was so fucking angry in the first place, and suddenly, one day I woke up and Danny wasn't my first thought in the morning." I stop my pacing, looking into her eyes. "It was you."

Tears are streaming down her face now, and she makes no effort to wipe them away.

"So yes. I regret it, but only because I want to do it again." I take a step toward her. "And again. And again. I didn't mean for it to go this far."

She swallows hard, crossing her arms. "Then we should end it now, Thayer." She nods at her own words, as if trying to convince herself. "Because I don't think I can handle losing you again if…" she trails off, angrily swiping at the tears that fall down her cheeks. "You have to be the one to do it. You have to walk away."

Eating up the distance between us with two big steps, I grasp her chin, forcing her to look at me. Her eyelashes stick together, wet with tears, her blue eyes brighter than normal.

"What if I don't know how?"

"Then just…don't."

We move for each other at the same time, our lips colliding. I bend down to curl my hands around the backs of her thighs and lift her up, carrying her over to her bed. There are no more words, only hungry lips and frenzied hands and harsh

210 | CHARLEIGH ROSE

breaths between us. I release my grip on her thighs, and her body slides down mine. I tug on the hem of her sweatshirt and she lifts her arms for me as I pull it over her head, revealing her bare tits. I cup them in my hands, squeezing, and she melts into my touch.

When she was gone, I didn't think I missed her. How could I when she rarely strayed from my thoughts? Our memories plagued me, and if I could've wiped them from my mind completely, I would've. But this past week, I missed her like a fucking missing limb. The lightning might have branded my skin, but Shayne branded whatever's left of my heart.

Shayne's fingers curl under the hem of my shirt, and she rises onto her tiptoes to pull it off. When she still can't reach, I do it for her, dropping it to the floor.

"I probably should've asked you this before, but are you on birth control?"

She nods up at me, her hands on my sides.

Thank fuck. "Next time, I'll come prepared. But right now, I want you bare."

She pushes up onto her toes, her arms clinging to my bare shoulders as she presses her lips against mine. Taking that as permission, I walk her backwards a couple of steps until the backs of her thighs hit her bed. She slides onto her bed, lying flat on her back, and I take a minute to admire the view.

"You're beautiful."

"Then fuck me already." She smiles.

"As you wish."

I drop my pants, kicking off my shoes in the process, then I'm sliding her sweats down her legs. I toss them to join the pile of clothes on the floor before I attempt to bury my face between her soft thighs, but my tongue barely flicks against her clit before she's pulling me up her body.

"I just want to feel you."

Without another word, I hitch her leg up by my hip and push inside. She wasn't joking. She's already wet and ready, but tighter than ever. Her lips graze mine with each shift of my hips, our harsh breaths mingling between us. Her full eyebrows tug together as if she's in pain, but when I slow down, she frantically shakes her head, digging her heels into my ass.

Taking her subtle cue, I sit back on my heels and grip her waist, yanking her closer. I start to fuck into her, not holding back. Shayne braces her hands flat on the headboard behind her, taking it. My eyes are glued to where we're connected, watching my cock disappear into her tight heat. I can tell Shayne's getting close because those sexy little sounds coming from her mouth are getting louder. I lean forward, covering her mouth with my palm, and then I snake two fingers between us to play with her clit.

"I'm coming," Shayne moans into my palm as her nails rake down my back. That combined with the way she contracts around me has me close to the edge.

"Do it again," I encourage her, bringing my hand to lightly grip the front of her throat. She's still spasming around me, but she does it again, applying a little more pressure this time.

I pull out quickly, barely making it before I'm spilling onto the inside of her thigh.

Shayne

"The jacket you took from me," Thayer says out of nowhere.

"Yeah?"

"It was Danny's."

Of course it was. God, I'm an idiot. "I'm sorry. I didn't kn—"

"Don't apologize. That's the only reason I wanted it back."

I climb on top of him, straddling his torso as a thought occurs to me. "So you brought me yours instead?" I ask, walking my fingers up the dips and grooves of his muscular stomach.

"Yeah…" He narrows his eyes at me, his abs tensing beneath my fingers.

"Does this mean we're like *going steady*?" I wiggle my eyebrows. "Do I get your class ring next?"

Thayer bites down on his lip rings, and I can tell he's trying not to smile. Then he's flipping us over and pinning me beneath him, holding my hands to the mattress above my head. "I don't know. What does 'going steady' entail? Because if it means I get to do this—" He slips inside me in one smooth thrust. "Whenever I want, then yeah, we're going steady, Shayne."

I gasp, bringing my knees up to hug his ribs as he grinds into me, staying deep inside, giving me that friction against my clit that I need.

Somewhere in the back of my mind, I know Thayer is going to be my downfall. I'll worry about the consequences later, but right now?

Right now, I'm happy.

THIRTY-TWO

Shayne

WAKING UP WITH THAYER IN MY BED IS…SURREAL. BUT IT also feels right, like it was always meant to be this way. I'm on my side, my cheek pressed against his chest and his chin rests on the top of my head, our legs tangled together. The window's still open and the brisk morning air chills my lower back, but I'm too content to move.

Thayer stirs, rolling onto his back, the movement taking the blanket with him. He stretches his arms over his head, and I can't help but admire the pronounced V-shape before my gaze drifts lower, seeing his already hard cock. Without thinking, I slink down the bed until my face is level with his hips and pull the blanket over my head. I lick the underside of his length and he instantly jerks under my tongue, giving me the confidence to take him inside my mouth. Hands braced on his hips, I do just that, wrapping my lips around the smooth tip. I've never done this. I don't know what the hell I'm doing. But when I feel him shudder, I know I'm doing something right.

"Oh, fuck." Thayer jerks the blanket off my head and lifts his hips to get deeper, his eyes half-mast as he watches me.

I suck lightly and his hands come down on my head to

guide my movements as he slowly fucks my mouth. Getting braver, I wrap my hand around the base of him and start to work his length while I suck on his head, and he bites down on his lip, his head falling back to the pillow.

"Shayne," my mom's voice calls out, making me release him with a pop.

"Shit!" I jump out of bed. I quickly throw my hoodie on, motioning for Thayer to leave through the window. He moves at a snail's pace, swinging his legs over the bed, his massive hard-on standing straight up, still glistening from my mouth. I widen my eyes at him, my heart pounding, but he's in no hurry as he swipes his boxers from the floor before pulling them up. When I hear my mom's footsteps getting louder, I shove him into my closet. I don't even get a chance to close the door before my mom appears.

"Oh," she says, probably taken aback at the fact that I'm standing here in only a sweatshirt—albeit one that's long enough to cover my ass. "I didn't think you'd be up so early."

"I need a shower, so I set my alarm a little bit earlier."

She nods, buying the lie. "I'll be gone by the time you get home from school, so I wanted to make sure I got to hug you." She pulls me in, squeezing me tight. "There are leftovers in the fridge and I'll leave some cash on the counter to get you through the week."

"Thanks," I say into her hairspray-scented hair. When she pulls back, I notice that her makeup is heavier than normal, her hair in perfect, soft curls. It must be a high roller if she put this much effort into her appearance.

"Why is your window open? It's freezing in here," she says, taking a step toward my window, but I intercept her.

"I like it cold."

"Are you okay?" she asks. "You seem…weird."

"I'm fine," I say quickly—almost too quickly—trying to look anywhere but the closet to my right.

"I know this past year has been difficult…" she trails off.

Jesus, Mom. Now is not the time for a heart-to-heart when Thayer's hiding in my closet. And I'd venture to guess that he wouldn't be very sympathetic to our plight, considering he still thinks Grey is responsible for Danny's death. That reminds me, I still need to fill him in on my visit with Grey.

"Mom, I swear I'm okay."

She twists her lips before she decides to let it go. "Okay, well, be safe. Don't forget to lock up when you leave."

I nod, and with a kiss on my cheek, she's gone. As soon as the door closes, Thayer's yanking me into my closet. "You're an asshole," I say as he pulls me against him, my chest pressed against his torso.

"This is news to you?" He smirks, sliding a hand between us and dipping under my hoodie before he slips a finger between my legs, parting me.

"What if she'd seen you?" I close my eyes, grasping onto his upper arms in an effort to stay upright.

"Then she'd know I've been fucking her perfect little angel of a daughter when everyone else is asleep," he says, rubbing me in slow, delicious circles. I sag against him, my cheek pressed against his shirt as he continues to make me dizzy with his words and his fingers. And just when I'm about to explode, he removes his hand.

"Wha—"

"You're going to be late," he cuts my protest off.

"Fuck school," I pout, pulling his hand back to where I need it. "I can miss a day."

Thayer groans, "Yeah?"

"Mhm." Somewhere in the back of my mind, I know my mom is still here somewhere because I didn't hear her car pull out of the driveway yet, but I can't bring myself to stop. A recurring theme when it comes to Thayer. Thayer, on the other hand, doesn't seem to have the same problem, because he pulls his hand away once more.

"Then pack a bag. I'll be back to pick you up in an hour."

That snaps me out of it. "What?"

"You heard me. Your mom's going out of town, anyway. Come with me for a night."

"Where?"

"Does it matter?"

I roll my eyes, knowing damn well I'd go anywhere with him.

"That's what I thought. One hour."

After Thayer left, I jumped into the shower, did my quick ten-minute makeup routine, then blow-dried my hair, leaving it down and straight. I decided to wear a long-sleeved white shirt with a high neck, then threw a dark navy dress with a sweetheart neckline and tiny white polka dots over the top, pairing it with white sneakers.

By the time I pack a bag with a jacket, an extra change of clothes, and my toothbrush, I hear the deep rumble of Thayer's Hellcat pulling up the drive. The sound sends a thrill up my spine, my heart doing a flip-flop in my chest. There are certain things that I will always associate with Thayer. Thunderstorms, lightning, the smell of rain and tobacco, and the sound of his Challenger.

I practically skip out of my house, backpack bouncing behind me. Thayer's waiting for me, leaned up against the hood of his car on the passenger side, arms crossed over his chest. I hurry down the steps, and when he realizes I'm not going to slow down, his arms shoot out to catch me just before I jump into them.

"Hi," I say, unable to keep the smile from my face.

"What's that look for?" he asks, his eyebrows tugging together as his hands squeeze my ass.

"Just happy."

He lifts an eyebrow, a weird look crossing his features, but then he's turning around with me in his arms, walking the short distance to the passenger side door. He opens it, holding me with one hand, before dropping me inside and pulling my backpack off in one smooth motion. He tosses my bag onto the cramped back seat, closes the door, then rounds the front of the car, hopping in next to me.

"So, are you going to tell me where we're going?"

He ignores me, pushing the button that starts the engine, and it roars to life, vibrating my seat. "Freeway or scenic route?"

"Scenic route," I say without hesitation, clicking my seatbelt into place. The interstate would be faster, wherever we're going, but I love the way Thayer drives this thing on back roads. And let's be honest, I'm in no hurry.

"That's my girl," he says, pulling his lip rings between his teeth. The comment is offhanded, but my stupid, girly insides turn to mush anyway.

He lays on the gas, driving out of the driveway and then speeding down the long, winding road that connects Heartbreak Hill to town. A few minutes in, Thayer's hand slides between my legs, gripping the inside of my thigh. That little gesture makes me feel unexpectedly emotional. Memories of Thayer driving us around aimlessly for hours with one hand on the wheel and the other on my thigh pop into my mind, making me miss how it used to be. We thought things were complicated back then when our only worry was being found out. What I'd give to go back to the way we were, to have just one more day of all of us together.

I don't know how much time passes—at least an hour— maybe more, when I finally realize where we're going.

"Amherst?" I look over at him, raising a brow. I know he goes to school here—sometimes, anyway—I just don't know why he brought *me* here.

"You hungry?" He pulls into a parking space in front of a

café with a black awning that reads *The Black Sheep Deli & Bakery*.

"Starved." Confused, but starved. He cuts the engine and we both get out, walking up to the café. Thayer opens the door and I head in first, taking in the cases of pastries and baked goods. Above those are blackboard menus with the day's specials written in neon colors.

"Have you ever been here?" I ask, scanning the menu.

"Where the hell have you been hiding?" some guy with an apron asks behind us, slapping Thayer on the shoulder. *I guess that answers my question.*

"Back home," he says, not offering more of an explanation than that. The man glances at me, folding his tattooed arms over his chest before sending Thayer a knowing look.

"Hey, Home. Nice to meet you. I'm Brax." He holds out his hand and I shake it while Thayer rolls his eyes.

"I'm Shayne."

"You guys hungry? What are you having?" he asks Thayer. "Turkey club and a coffee?" That's oddly specific. He must come here a lot if they know his order by heart.

Thayer looks to me. "What do you want?"

"That sounds good to me."

"Make that two. With a side of ranch and a pink lemonade for her."

"Got it," Brax says, walking behind the counter.

I bite my cheek to hide an amused smile as we slide into a booth, Thayer on one side, me on the other.

"Don't look at me like that. So I remembered what you like to drink. Big deal."

And the fact that I like to dip my sandwiches in ranch. But I let it slide. "So, you brought me almost two hours away for sandwiches?"

Thayer shoves a hand through his hair, seeming uncomfortable, and that's when it hits me. Oh my God. *Is Thayer trying to take me on a date?* "Thought you might like to go somewhere we could let our guard down."

"It's perfect," I assure him. And it is. It's so fucking perfect, because this right here is all I've ever wanted. To go somewhere and just *be* without everyone's eyes on us, picking apart our every move.

Our food comes quickly, and I don't waste any time digging in. We eat in silence, and even though it feels good to be with Thayer, my guilty conscience gnaws at me. I still haven't brought up Christian. Or meeting with my brother. Not that I'm doing anything wrong by talking to my own brother, but Grey is a point of contention between Thayer and me.

"I saw Grey," I say, fidgeting with the tip of my straw. Thayer tenses, pushing his empty plate to the center of the table.

"Yeah?"

I nod. "He wouldn't take my calls, so I showed up at his dorm." I lean forward, my elbows resting on top of the table. "He admitted to having an argument with Danny, but he swears he had nothing to do with it."

"Well, what a relief," he says, sarcasm dripping from every word. "Now I can sleep at night. Do you know many people who would confess to murder, Shayne?"

I flinch at the word *murder*.

"I think…" I hesitate, feeling conflicted as Thayer waits in silence for me to spit it out. "I think he's hiding something from me."

I wait for him to spit out another sarcastic remark at the very least. What I don't expect is for him to reach into his back pocket to pull out his wallet and throw a fifty down onto the table.

"Let's go."

Thayer rises from the booth and heads for the door, not bothering to wait for me or to say goodbye to his friend. I follow him out, kicking myself for bringing it up now and ruining whatever this is. Things were good for two whole seconds, and I had to self-sabotage like an idiot. *Thanks, Dad, whoever you are.*

Thayer's already in the car when I get outside. I slide into the passenger seat, and he takes off without a word. I stay quiet, letting him process or cool off or whatever it is that he needs to do, leaning my forehead against the cool window. Five minutes later, we're pulling into an apartment complex. I look over at him in question when he pulls into a spot and throws the car into park. He opens the door and gets out of the car, then ducks back down when I haven't made a move to get out.

"You coming?"

I step out of the car, closing the door behind me as I take in the tall foreboding building. Thayer heads for the entrance and I follow his lead inside the building, through the lobby, and into an elevator. "Where are we?"

The elevator halts, and we step out into the hall. Thayer comes to a stop in front of one of the doors and sticks a key into the lock. "My place." Pushing the door open, he gestures for me to go in first.

I step inside, gaping at the modern apartment that's completely opposite from Whittemore. It's an open floor plan with large glass windows spanning the entire wall. The living area consists of a single sofa and a TV mounted on the opposite wall. There's a hall to the left and the kitchen to the right. "You live here?"

He kicks the door shut behind him. "Sometimes."

"What else don't I know about you?"

"When did you see him? The day you missed school?" he asks, ignoring my question. I suck in a lung full of air. I guess we're doing this now.

I nod. "How did you kn—?"

"Why didn't you tell me?"

"You went MIA, remember?" I snap before softening my tone. "And…I was afraid."

"Of what?" he asks, his eyes void of emotion.

"Losing you," I say honestly. "I don't…"

"What?" His dark eyes bore into mine, waiting for my response.

"I don't want to feel that again. And there's just so much *shit* between us, between our families...I don't see how this won't end badly."

Thayer steps forward, erasing the space between us. "Fuck our families. I just got you back. I'm not letting you go any time soon."

"What?" My eyes snap up to his. "But what if Grey—?" I can't even finish the sentence.

"Then we'll deal with it."

"So, what now?"

"Now, you walk your ass over to that table."

Heat spreads through me at his words. I look up at him, questioning, and he pulls his shirt over his head, throwing it onto the sofa. I swallow hard, my eyes eating him up.

"Shayne."

Right. Table. I pad over to the small rectangular black table, then turn around to face him, bracing my hands on the edge.

"Up," he says, lifting me onto the tabletop. My palms land behind me to keep myself upright, my knees bent. Thayer's hands glide up my legs and my breath catches when they dip under my dress. His fingers curl around my baby pink thong, sliding it down my thighs. He pulls it past my shoes before letting it fall to the floor.

"Spread your legs for me, baby."

Thayer's eyes are glued between my legs as I slowly let my thighs fall open, feet planted on the table. He brings a hand underneath my dress that's bunched up at the top of my thighs, pressing his thumb against my clit. I gasp, my eyes falling shut at the sensation.

"Show me those pretty little tits."

I lean forward, pushing down the straps of my dress before I pull my shirt off. Goosebumps break out over my skin and my nipples tighten.

"Lean back on your elbows."

I do as he says as he unbuckles his pants, pulling a condom out of his back pocket before he pushes his jeans down his legs. He fists his length, stroking up and down as his hungry eyes look their fill. He hasn't even touched me yet, and I'm practically shaking with anticipation. Wanting to break his control, to push him to touch me, I lick my middle finger before bringing my hand between my thighs. I use that finger to rub myself, and his eyes flare at the sight. I lift my knees higher, only the toes of my tennis shoes touching the table now as I slip my finger inside.

"You're so perfect," he mutters, and then he's leaning in between my spread legs, capturing my nipple with his lips.

"Thayer," I say, arching into his mouth. His teeth tug on my piercing and I hear the condom wrapper tearing open before he rolls it down his length. He helps me to my feet, then spins me around to face the table and I stumble forward, my hand holding on to the edge of the table as Thayer jerks my dress up over my hips. He lifts one of my knees onto the table, and then he's pushing inside me, hands squeezing my waist as he groans in pleasure.

"I'm not letting you go," he says again, his palm gliding up to lightly grip my throat, keeping my back to his chest as he snaps his hips forward. "But if I find out Grey did it, I won't show him any mercy."

"I know."

He presses his lips to my spine, kissing me, and then he's pushing my chest flat against the table.

"Good."

"Why don't you ever go to class?" I ask, coming up behind him as he stands at the kitchen counter, circling my arms around his bare torso. After Thayer fucked me on the table, we went at it twice more. Once on the floor, and once on his couch, right in front of the glass window. Sometime around nine o'clock, we realized we needed sustenance, so he ordered pizza. I'm sore and sated and sleepy, trying to soak everything in before we have to go back to reality tomorrow.

"It felt wrong."

I press my cheek against his back, my hands flattening on his stomach as I wait for him to elaborate.

"Moving on with my life, going to college…Danny was supposed to be here for all of it. It feels like I'm leaving him behind."

My thoughts drift back to when Valen said she hadn't seen him for months. She was as surprised to see him in Sawyer Point as I was. "Is that why you came home?"

He captures my wrist, examining the faint lines the lightning left, his thumb rubbing across the sensitive skin. "I came back for you."

"No, you didn't." I laugh. "You *hated* me." Sometimes, I still think he might on some level. My biggest fear is that he'll never be able to see me the way he did before the accident.

"I never hated you. I hated that I couldn't have you."

THIRTY-THREE

Shayne

Yawning, I TRUDGE INTO THE KITCHEN TO MAKE MYSELF A LATE-night snack after finishing up the homework I fell behind on. Between Thayer keeping me up all night last night and my game after school today, I can barely keep my eyes open. Not that I'm complaining. It was worth losing sleep and the grief Coach gave me for missing practice.

I grab the cheese and butter from the fridge before I pad over to the stove. I move on autopilot, getting the frying pan and buttering the bread, lost in thought, when I hear the sound of breaking glass coming from the other room. I jump back with a scream, and then I freeze with my hand over my mouth. When I don't hear anything else, I blindly slap a hand onto the counter behind me, feeling around for my phone. I back into the pantry, shutting the door as quietly as possible as my shaky fingers manage to click on Thayer's name.

"Shayne?" he asks, concern evident in his tone. I never call him.

I cup my hand over my mouth and the speaker of my phone, trying to keep my voice low. "I think someone just broke into my house." My heart threatens to pound out of my chest.

"We're coming," he says immediately. "Where are you?"

"Hiding in the pantry."

"Good. Stay there. Don't come out until you hear me."

A weird scent hits my nostrils and I inhale, trying to place it. It smells like…burning fabric.

"Shit," I curse.

"What?" Thayer barks into the phone.

"I think I smell something burning."

Thayer's panicked voice yells something to Holden, presumably, and then I hear the telltale sign of his Hellcat. He says something else, but adrenaline has my pulse pounding in my ears, making it hard to hear.

I slowly open the pantry door and peek my head out. When I don't see anyone, I grab the frying pan off the stove and rush out, running toward the front living room, confirming my fear. A small fire blazes on the floor in front of the broken window. "There's a fire," I manage to say before I drop both the phone and the frying pan.

"Shit, shit, shit," I chant, trying to form a coherent thought. *Fire extinguisher*. I know I saw one somewhere when we moved in. I jog over to the entryway closet and open the door, spotting the red container on the shelf above my head. I push up onto my toes to reach it, stretching my arm as far as possible, the tips of my fingers barely grazing it. I jump up, trying to knock it off the shelf, but I only end up pushing it back farther.

I yank a hanger from beneath a coat and use that instead. "Come on, come on." Finally, I'm able to scoop it off the shelf and catch it before it hits the floor. I rush over, willing my shaky hands to comply long enough to do what needs to be done. Pulling on the ring, I squeeze down on the handle, and then a white cloud explodes from the nozzle, extinguishing the fire.

Pounding at the front door makes me jump, but then I see a stunned Holden standing in front of the shattered picture window. I hurry over to unlock the door and Thayer storms in, surveying the place.

"You okay?" he asks, looking me over.

Still in shock, all I can do is nod.

"I'm going to check the woods," Holden says before he takes off, and then Thayer's pulling me into him, prying the extinguisher from my fingers until it falls to the floor.

"You sure you're okay?" His palms cup my face, forcing me to look at him.

I nod again and his fingers curl around the nape of my neck as he bends down to give me a quick kiss on the lips.

"Did you see anyone?"

"No." I shake my head. "I was just making something to eat and heard the window shatter," I say, gesturing toward the huge hole in my window. "And then I called you."

"You didn't call the cops? Or anyone else?"

"Just you. I figured you were closer—" I start to explain, but he cuts me off.

"No, you did good. This is good."

He steps away from me, feet crunching through the broken glass, and then he's crouching down, plucking something from the floor, inspecting it.

"What is it?"

"It's a piece of a beer bottle."

"Nothing," Holden announces, appearing in the doorway before he walks over to Thayer. "Whoever it was is long gone." He flicks his chin toward the glass pinched between Thayer's fingers. "Molotov cocktail?"

"That's what I'm thinking," Thayer agrees. They exchange a look that puts me even more on edge.

"What does that mean?"

"It means this was no accident."

I sit cross-legged on the couch as Thayer and Holden stand in front of me.

"You're going to tell me this is Taylor's work, too?" Thayer says to Holden who shakes his head.

"No. The other shit, maybe. But this is too far, even for her."

"Maybe it was just a random prank," I offer, knowing damn well it wasn't. But the alternative freaks me out too much to consider. They both pin me with a glare, and I hold up my hands in mock surrender. "Or maybe not."

"Besides Taylor, is there anyone else who has something against you?" This comes from Thayer.

"Just you guys," I quip, but my joke falls flat.

"This isn't fucking funny, Shayne," Holden snaps.

I draw back, surprised by how upset he seems to be.

"You're staying here until your mom gets back," Thayer says.

"What?" I stand, the blanket falling from my lap onto the floor. "No. If you didn't notice, there's a giant hole in my living room. I can't leave it like that. And I need to call my mom." Something I'm dreading.

"We'll have your window fixed, but you're not staying there alone. In fact, you're not even going to take a piss alone until we figure out who's behind this."

"Thayer." That's ridiculous.

"This isn't some prank, Shayne. Someone tried to *hurt* *you*. Do you get that? Do you realize what could've happened? A couple more seconds and the flames would've hit those curtains and your whole house would've gone up in flames. With you inside."

"He's right," Holden says, arms folded over his chest. "We already buried one sibling."

Okay, just punch me in the gut, why don't you.

"What about your dad?"

"He stays at his apartment in the city. Now that the

memorial has passed, he has no reason to come around. And if he does, then fuck him. What's he going to do?"

"Tell my mom," I state the obvious.

"Fuck her, too," Thayer spits. "Let's not act like either one of them has ever bothered to be around for their kids."

I want to argue that my mom is there for me in the only way that she can be, that everything she does is to give Grey and me a good life. But it's not the time. And he does have a point. Regardless of reasoning, they're largely absent from our lives. We've always taken care of ourselves. It's what we do.

"Fine." I fall back onto the couch, pulling the blanket over me.

"We'll take you to grab some shit after school tomorrow," Thayer says, and then he's walking toward his room without so much as a goodbye.

"I'll grab you a pillow," Holden offers, scratching the back of his neck.

"Thanks."

He's only gone for a minute, and I'm already starting to doze off, my head resting against the arm of the couch. It's as if all the adrenaline wore off, leaving me completely drained. My mind goes crazy trying to process tonight's events, but my body gives up.

Holden returns, handing me the pillow. He hesitates like he's going to say something, but reconsiders. "Night."

"Night," I say, scooting down and stuffing the pillow under my head.

I don't know how much time passes when I'm startled awake by someone lifting me off the couch. My heart hammers in my chest as my disoriented brain attempts to wake up.

"It's me," Thayer's deep voice rumbles close to my ear.

I relax instantly, wrapping my arms around his neck, feeling the warmth of his bare chest as he carries me up the stairs and into his bedroom. He sits on the bed before he lies back, bringing me with him. His arm is underneath me, holding me close, my head on his chest, my thigh hitched up over his legs, and I slip back into sleep, feeling far too safe for a girl whose heart is in danger of being broken again.

THIRTY-FOUR

Shayne

"**S**HAYNE."

Thayer's voice breaks through my consciousness. My mind slowly comes out of my sleep-induced haze, and I blink up at a ceiling that isn't mine, feeling warmth next to me. Then it all rushes back to me. The window. The fire. Thayer bringing me up to his room sometime in the middle of the night. "I was hoping it was a dream," I grumble, rolling over and burying my face into Thayer's pillow.

He's still shirtless, lying on his back next to me. "Nope. And you're going to be late for school. Holden's in the shower, so unless you want him to find you in my bed…" he trails off, waiting for my response.

I sit up quickly, running my hand through my hair. "I'm up."

Thayer reaches over to hook his hand behind my knee, pulling me over to straddle his stomach. I brace my hands on his chest as his palms flatten on top of my thighs, his fingers slipping under the hem of my shorts, but they don't go farther than that. "You good?"

I nod, tucking my hair behind my ear.

"We're going to find out who did it."

"I know."

The sound of footsteps in the hall has me rolling off him. I stand, moving away from the bed just as Holden throws the door open, looking between us with suspicious eyes. His hair is wet and he's wearing a plain white t-shirt and black sweats that read *Stop Looking at My Dick* across the crotch.

"You are not wearing those to school." I laugh.

"Watch me." He bounces his eyebrows. "Ready to go?"

I look down at my sleep shorts and spaghetti strap crop top. "Do I look like I'm ready?"

Holden claps his hands together. "Well chop-chop, baby sister."

I move past him, heading downstairs to grab my backpack. I hastily shoved some clothes inside, grabbing the first things I saw before Thayer and Holden dragged me out of my house last night, which happened to be a pair of boyfriend jeans with holes in the knees, and a tight, plain black t-shirt. I top it off with Thayer's hoodie, spend two minutes in the downstairs bathroom to brush my teeth, and throw my hair into a pony-tail. I pause, looking at my tired reflection. My eyes are puffy, and my cheeks are red, but I didn't bring any makeup, and truthfully, I don't care enough to try this morning.

My stomach rolls with the anxiety that only let up while I was next to Thayer. I know it was 'just' a window, but the thought that someone might actually want to hurt me—really harm me—has me feeling ill at ease.

"Let's go," Holden hollers, pounding on the bathroom door.

I flinch, taking a deep breath, and wipe the miserable look off my face. I swing the door open, giving him the middle fin-ger. He lunges forward, trying to bite it as I walk by, but I'm quicker. We make our way to the door, and Thayer's standing in the foyer, waiting.

"Watch her."

I roll my eyes. "No one's going to do anything at school." I'm freaked out, but even I know this is overkill.

"Maybe not, but if you watch for the signs, you might find out who's behind it. Pay attention. If someone's watching you for a reaction, if you notice people whispering when you walk into a room—"

I huff out a laugh. "Welcome to my everyday life."

"Not just that. Pay attention to the people who *aren't* talking to you. If they're feeling guilty, they're likely to avoid you."

"Somehow I don't think this person holds any guilt where I'm concerned," I mutter.

He looks to Holden. "Did you fill Christian in?"

"I will at school. Operation Smother Shayne is in full effect," he says, throwing an arm over my shoulder.

Today should be fun. And by *fun*, I mean not at all.

"Are you okay?" Valen asks, squeezing in between Holden and me at the lunch table. Christian sits across from us, doing something on his phone. I sent Valen a text last night, but we were late to school, so I didn't have time to fill her in on all the details this morning.

"Yeah." I shrug, aiming for nonchalance. "Just a little creeped out."

"So, what exactly happened? Someone threw some kind of *firebomb* through your window?"

"Molotov cocktail," Holden says around a mouthful of his burger. The sight of it makes me nauseous. Anxiety from everything going on has killed my appetite.

Valen wrinkles her nose at him. "What is that?" She picks at a piece of her soft pretzel and pops it into her mouth.

"Less dangerous than a firebomb. Usually meant to intimidate or send a message rather than do actual damage," Christian chimes in. "Just be glad you were in the kitchen when it happened."

"That's actually kind of a relief," I say.

"Okay, but it's fire. Fire is never *not* dangerous. Who the hell would do that?"

I shrug, just as clueless as she is.

"Do you want to sleep at my house for a while? You know you can stay however long you want."

"No can do," Holden butts in. "She's staying with us."

Valen raises one of her perfect eyebrows. "She's my best friend. Get your own."

"She's my sister," Holden slings back. "Get your own."

I roll my eyes at their bickering. "I want to stay close to my house until the window's fixed, but I have a feeling I'll be taking you up on your offer soon."

"Fine."

"So, when are you going to see Liam?" I ask, desperate for a change in subject.

"Today. I'm going to leave early to make the drive."

"Douchebag," Holden coughs into his fist and I elbow him in the ribs, making him wince.

"Is he going to make this lingering thing a habit?" Valen asks, sending him a dirty look.

"Unfortunately."

"Get used to it, baby." Holden smiles wide, showing his pearly whites.

"Get a life, *baby*," she mocks.

"Bitch."

"Lurker!"

The bell rings, putting me out of my misery, and Valen stands from the table, dumps her tray, then stomps off toward her class.

"Be nice to her," I say as the three of us stand, heading for the main hall.

Holden jerks his gaze away from her retreating ass. "I'd be very, very nice to her if she'd just let me."

I snort out a laugh. "I'll see you after class."

Once Holden's out of sight, I jog to catch up with Christian who's a few paces ahead of me. "Hey."

He stops, turning to face me as the hall clears out.

"I just wanted to make sure you're okay."

He frowns at me, but there's a sadness in his eyes. A heaviness to them, and I can't remember if it was always there, or if it's a recent development. "I'm fine."

That's what he said that night, too.

"I didn't say anything."

"I know."

"But I don't like keeping this secret," I admit.

"Don't worry about me, Shayne. I'm a big boy."

I shake my head, frustrated. "You're putting me in a shitty situation." I try a different approach.

"Yeah, well, no one asked you to stick your nose where it doesn't belong."

I frown and he rolls his eyes. "I have it handled."

I nod, walking away, knowing we're at an impasse.

"Shayne," he calls out.

"Yeah?"

"I'm glad you're okay," he says, his tone uncharacteristically sincere.

"Back at you."

Class after boring class, I try to do what Thayer said. I try paying attention to my surroundings, but I don't notice anything different from any other day. Taylor still gets her jabs in when she can, and if anything, with Holden and Christian flanking me, I draw even more attention than normal. This is exactly what I wasn't looking forward to. The icing on the cake is when Thayer's waiting for us in the parking lot, standing in front of his car after school. "That's definitely going to feed the rumor mill."

"See you at home." Holden laughs, nodding his chin to acknowledge Thayer before he heads toward his Rover.

Home.

Those stupid butterflies are back at the sight of Thayer standing there in black jeans and black shirt, his lightning tattoo on full display, hands stuffed into his front pockets. I walk over to him, holding my binder to my chest. "I could've caught a ride with Holden."

"You could've," he agrees, opening the door for me.

"People are going to talk."

He shrugs. "Let them."

THIRTY-FIVE

Shayne

THAT'S PRETTY MUCH HOW THINGS GO FOR THE NEXT WEEK. Holden takes me to school and Thayer picks me up most days. They come to my games and even tried to go to my practices until Coach made them wait outside on account of distracting my teammates. Thayer had someone out to fix the window and it was like new after two days. Surprisingly, the only loss was my grandmother's expensive rug, which we tossed, and a burn mark on the hardwood. I'll worry about how to explain that to my mom later.

Every night we hang out together, sometimes with Christian, sometimes it's just the three of us. Thayer brings me into his room after everyone goes to sleep, and every morning, I slip out of his bed, thoroughly fucked, before Holden and Christian wake up to get ready. We don't talk about my brother. We don't talk about Danny. We don't even talk about who has it out for me after the first couple of days. It's become our new normal, and I'm starting to dread going home in a few days.

The bell rings, announcing the end of the day, pulling me from my thoughts. I stand, gathering my things, and when

I walk out into the hall, I'm surprised to find that Holden's not magically there, waiting for me. *Good.* Maybe he's finally realizing I don't need security detail at school, of all places. I make my way through the crowded hallway, heading to get my jacket out of my locker. It's Friday, so I don't want to leave it over the weekend.

People start to whisper and laugh, all eyes on me. Dread unfurls inside me. *What now?* I roll my eyes, pushing past them, but I stop short once I see why they're reacting.

Brother Fucker is spray-painted in bold black letters across my locker. Instinctively, I search out Taylor. She might not have thrown a firebomb through my window, but this...*this* is her brand. And when I see her smug face, I know I'm right.

"Defacing a locker with spray paint and slut shaming? Lacks creativity and originality, but it *is* a classic mean girl move. I give it a solid C."

"If the shoe fits," she preens.

Anger boils in my gut, and I feel myself reaching my breaking point. There's only so much a person can take before they finally snap. I crowd her space, backing her up toward the row of lockers on the opposite side of the hall.

"You're pathetic."

"Me?" she shrieks, her eyebrows hitting her hairline. "You're the one who's obsessed with your stepbrother. Seriously, Shayne. It's creepy."

Heat crawls up my neck and to the tips of my ears. I drop my backpack and shove her shoulders. Her back slams against the lockers, eyes widening, mouth dropping open in shock. "Fuck with me again, Taylor," I say through gritted teeth, "and I promise you, it will be the last time."

Don't hit her, don't hit her, don't hit her.

"What, are you going to have your brother kill me, too?"

I'm going to hit her.

I curl my fingers into a fist before sending it straight into her perfect little nose. Taylor's head slams against the locker, and then she's cupping her nose in shock as a chorus of gasps and cheers alike fill the halls. She looks at me in disbelief for a second, then she snaps into action, screaming like a banshee as she lunges for me.

A pair of arms come around my waist, pulling me away.

"Whoa, whoa, whoa," Holden says. "Calm down, killer." He bends down to scoop up my backpack, throwing it over his shoulder. All eyes are on us as Taylor stands there, chest heaving. She's embarrassed. Most likely infuriated. But she crossed the line.

"You're done," he says, pointing a finger in Taylor's face.

"Holden—"

"Let's go," he says to me, ignoring her as he ushers me down the hall with his hand on my lower back. A teacher pokes his head out of a classroom, looking for the source of the commotion, but we keep walking toward the double doors that lead to the student lot.

I push the door open, but the heavy wind blows it open even wider. The sky is dark with an impending storm, the clouds rolling in. Thayer's car is noticeably absent, and I'm relieved that I have a few minutes to collect myself before I have to see him. My heart is pounding. I've never hit anyone like that before, and I hate that I did. Not because she didn't deserve it, but because that's exactly what she wanted from me. She wanted to get under my skin, to get a reaction from me, and I handed it to her on a silver platter.

We jump into Holden's Range Rover and pull out of the parking lot, making the short drive to Whittemore. Thayer's Hellcat is parked in the circular driveway and Holden pulls up behind it, throwing the car into park before looking over at me.

"How's your hand?"

"It hurts," I grumble.

He chuckles, stepping out of the car. I open my door and jump down, my shoes crunching against the gravel as I follow

Holden up the steps. He heads straight for the kitchen where Thayer stands at the counter, eating a sandwich.

"The fuck happened?"

"Shayne punched Taylor in the face," Holden says with all the glee of a five-year-old tattling to his mom.

Thayer's eyebrows jump, his expression amused.

"She deserved it." I shrug.

"She had it coming," Holden agrees, reaching over to steal the remaining half of Thayer's sandwich, but he smacks his hand away.

"What'd she do?"

Holden relays what happened from the locker to the comment about Grey, and Thayer's dark green eyes meet mine in silent question. I shrug. I don't think she actually knows about us. I think she's bitter that I'm in their good graces again and threw out a rumor that just happens to be true.

"You good?" Thayer asks.

"Of course." I gnaw on my lip, nodding. Why wouldn't I be good? It's not like I'm having a secret affair with my ex-step-brother who thinks my actual brother killed his brother while someone is out to get me, and catty bitches are calling me brother fucker in front of the entire school.

I'm fine.

THIRTY-SIX

Thayer

THE MOMENT HOLDEN WALKS OUT THE FRONT DOOR, I'M HEADING up the stairs, seeking Shayne out. I hear the shower running and slip inside the steamy bathroom, shutting the door behind me. I planned on talking to her about what went down at school, but the moment I see her standing there naked, her back to me as the water pours over her, I lose all coherent thought.

She's fucking beautiful. So different, yet so similar to the girl who moved in three years ago. She's stronger, but still vulnerable. Confident, but humble. Hot as fuck, but inherently innocent. As if she can sense my thoughts, she glances at me over her shoulder.

"Thayer!" Shayne scolds me, whipping around, bringing her arms up to cover her chest. Water from the shower ceiling falls around her, dripping from the ends of her hair, droplets hugging her curves as they slide down her body. She's fucking perfect.

"He's gone." I strip down in record time, and Shayne's gaze falls to my cock, realizing I'm already hard. I walk up behind her, cupping her tits as I dip my head to kiss her neck. She shivers, leaning into me.

"Turn around," I murmur against her skin.

She does as I say, eager for what I'm about to give her. Dropping to my knees, I bring my face level to her smooth pussy and pull my lip rings between my teeth, admiring the view.

"Lift your leg."

She does, propping her foot against the built-in bench. I run a hand up the back of her other leg, bringing my lips to her inner thighs. My teeth nip at the soft flesh, teasing, never going quite where she needs me. Shayne loses patience, spearing her hands through my wet hair, and jerks me toward her. *Fuck, that was hot.* When my tongue slides against her little clit, she bucks against me, unable to keep still. I groan into her, taking her foot and placing it on my shoulder. Sliding my palm over her ass, I hold her to my face, licking and sucking until her legs are shaking with the need to come.

"Turn around," I order in a strangled voice.

Breathless, she does as I say, and then I plant a palm on her back, pushing her forward.

"Ass out. Hands on the wall."

Shayne arches her perfect heart-shaped ass out and I slide my hands over her flesh, squeezing. I spread her, leaning in to lick her. Shayne jerks away with a gasp, not expecting it, but I hold her hips in place. I lick her from clit to ass and everywhere in between. She moans the sexiest fucking sound, pressing her tits against the shower wall, and I know she's so drunk on the feeling that she'd let me do just about anything.

"You gonna let me do whatever I want?" I ask, my voice thick with lust. She tenses at my words.

"Not that."

I laugh against her thigh. "I promise I'll make you feel good."

"Okay." Her voice is barely above a whisper.

I flip her around once more, her back against the wall, and slip a finger inside her pussy.

"Yes," she says as my mouth comes down on her clit

as I fuck her with my fingers. It's not long at all before her movements speed up, becoming frantic. I know she's about to come, so I slide a finger to her back entrance. Shayne tenses up again, but I rub at her as my mouth works her clit. Soon, she's pressing her ass against my finger, wanting more. I gladly give it to her, gently working my middle finger into her ass.

"Oh, fuck," Shayne gasps, and I look up to see her eyes squeezed shut, lips parted.

She's so tight around my finger. I go slow at first, letting her get used to it, but then I move faster as I pull her clit into my mouth, sucking hard. Her taut, little stomach tightens, and her body locks up with her impending orgasm just as I slide my index finger inside her pussy.

She screams—literally screams—and her legs give out. I use my forearm to pin her to the wall, keeping her upright as I pump into her. She contracts around my fingers, legs shaking, as my tongue laves her clit.

"Holy fucking shit," she pants, sliding down the shower wall.

"That was the hottest thing I've ever seen in my life."

"Ditto," Holden's voice says from behind us.

Shayne's horrified eyes snap over my shoulder, and I shield her naked body with my own.

"What the fuck!"

"She was screaming! I thought she was being murdered! I mean, I guess she was, just not in the way I th—"

"Holden! Get the fuck out."

He walks out, slamming the bathroom door behind him.

"I thought he was gone," is all she says.

"So did I."

I step out of the shower, handing her a towel before grabbing one for myself. She wraps it around her, knotting it at her chest. When we step into the hall, Holden's standing in front of my bedroom door with his arms crossed.

"I just have one question," he says, looking between us.

"What?"

"When did you get your nipples pierced?"

"Oh my God," Shayne said, her cheeks turning bright pink. She pushes past him, walking into my room. We follow her in, watching as she disappears into my closet. When she comes out, she's wearing one of my black t-shirts that hits her mid-thigh.

"Why don't you seem mad? Or even surprised?" she asks, pointing a finger at him.

"Wait, did you two actually think you were slick?" he asks, chuckling. "You both disappeared for two days, she sleeps in your bed every night, you eye-fuck each other any time you're in the same room, oh, and let's not forget the night you went down on her while I was on the couch next to you. Thanks for that, by the way."

"But you said—" Shayne exclaims, her face turning even redder.

"I lied." He winks.

"Oh my God," she says again, dropping down onto the edge of my bed.

"All right, well, now that I'm horny as fuck, I'm gonna go find someone to play with. You kids have fun."

Holden walks out and I walk over to my closet, throwing on a pair of grey sweats before I sit next to Shayne on my bed.

"So. That happened."

"It did."

"Are you okay with that? With people knowing?"

"Are you?"

She lifts a shoulder. "We're still figuring things out. I just don't want anyone to ruin it before we have a real chance."

I take her chin between my thumb and forefinger, forcing her to look at me. "Fuck everyone else. It's you and me."

She smiles and I feel it like a jolt in my chest. I miss seeing that smile every day. They don't come as easily as they used to.

"You didn't get to finish."

"You don't need to remind me," I say, adjusting my half-hard dick in my sweats.

She bites down on her lip, dropping to her knees between my legs.

"We should do something about that."

The sound of wind whipping branches against my window pulls me from my sleep. My room is dark, the TV we fell asleep watching earlier no longer on. I slide my arm out from under Shayne's head, careful not to wake her, then I reach for the lamp on my nightstand, but it doesn't turn on. Power must be out. I roll out of bed, blindly feeling around for my phone. When I find it, I turn on the flashlight, heading for my door. I swing it open, finding Holden standing on the other side.

"Check the breaker box?" I ask him. It's probably due to the high winds, but with someone fucking with Shayne, my paranoia is on high alert.

"Not yet. I forgot where Dad left his keys for the basement."

"They're in his desk. Come on."

Holden follows me down the hall and around the corner, into Dad's office.

"So you and Shayne, huh?"

I ignore him, rounding my dad's massive desk, pulling open the top right drawer. I use one hand to shine the light inside and the other to sift through the numerous sets of keys, pens, and other random shit. I finally find the one I'm looking for, pulling on the ring, but it gets caught on something. I shine my phone into the drawer once more, and that's when I realize that one of the keys has slipped beneath something. Something that looks a whole lot like a false bottom.

I clench my jaw tight as a bad feeling hits my gut hard and fast. Somehow, I know whatever's under there is about Danny.

"Come give me some light."

"What is it?" He comes up behind me, shining his light over my shoulder, and I set my phone down onto the desk.

"Let's find out." I take one of the keys and stick it between the board and the drawer front, popping it up, then fit my fingers in between the gap to lift it.

"What the fuck," Holden says as I pull out an orange folder. He leans in closer, shining more light to see the words on the front of it.

"This says Dad checked this out a month after Danny died."

My pulse starts to race, needing answers, but afraid of what I'll find. I open the folder, finding what looks like a CD case inside with a bunch of numbers, followed by a date.

"That's the day he died."

I nod, swallowing hard, and open the case. Suddenly, the power kicks back on, light flooding in from the hall. Holden walks over to flip the light switch, and I take the chair in front of my dad's desk, powering his computer on. His dinosaur of a computer takes what seems like an eternity to boot, each second making my anxiety skyrocket, and I look down at the police report that was in the same folder, but damn near everything has been redacted. Black boxes litter the page, making it impossible to make sense of it.

"You ready?" I ask, pressing the eject button, making the tray slide out. I don't know what we're about to find out, but I know it's going to change everything.

Instead of answering, he sticks the disc into the tray, then pushes it shut.

"Nine-one-one, what's your emergency?"

"I need an ambulance to the falls!"

My heart slams against my ribs when I hear the voice come through the speaker.

"What's the emergency?" the operator repeats.

"He's not fucking breathing!"

My stomach drops and I clench my jaw so hard I'm surprised my teeth don't crack under the pressure.

"Who is he?"

"Danny—uh, Daniel Ames."

My eyes squeeze shut hearing his name.

There's commotion in the background as he yells in response to something that I can't make over the sound of the water. An image of Danny facedown on the shore pops into my mind, unbidden, and I ball my hands into fists, my throat getting tight.

"You said he's not breathing?"

"Just fucking send someone."

"An ambulance is already on the way, sir. Who am I speaking to?"

The caller doesn't answer. The line cuts off, and the recording ends.

But we both know who it was.

Neither one of us speaks for a beat, but then Holden rips the monitor off the desk, launching it onto the floor.

"Why the fuck would Dad have this? Why wouldn't he tell us?" Holden's eyes are glassy as he looks at me, his chest heaving.

"The better question is why is he protecting him?"

Holden steps over the broken parts of the computer, making his way to the shelves that line the wall, half of it filled with books, the other half bottles of liquor. He cracks open a bottle of scotch, taking a long pull as he walks back over to me. He takes the chair opposite me, reaching over the desk to hand me the bottle. Not my first choice, but right now I don't give a fuck. I take it from him, welcoming the burn as it slides down my throat.

We don't talk. We sit in silence, drinking, thinking, *sinking*. By the time the sun comes up, the bottle is gone, and Holden's passed out in the chair. I stagger back to my room, using the wall for support. I pause in the doorway, leaning my weight into the frame as I look at Shayne. Her blonde hair is spread out across my black pillowcase, her pink lips slightly parted, long eyelashes hitting the tops of her cheeks. My sheet is gathered at her hip, exposing the dip in her waist and her arms cover her chest, one hand underneath her cheek. She looks so fucking peaceful when she sleeps. Angelic almost.

And now I have to figure out how to tell her that her brother killed mine.

THIRTY-SEVEN

Shayne

I WAKE UP ALONE. THE SHEETS ARE COLD, TELLING ME I'VE BEEN alone for a while now. I sit up, stretching my arms above my head. Last night after Holden left, I climbed on top of Thayer and rode him long and slow as he lay there with his hands behind his head, watching me move. My feelings for him only get stronger each day we spend together, and if I'm being honest, it scares the shit out of me. But I'm in too deep to walk away now.

I snag Thayer's black shirt that I wore last night, pulling it on over my head. Padding over to my gym bag that I stuffed with clothes from my house, I sift through it to find a pair of clean underwear and a pair of Soffe shorts. After I'm dressed, I grab my phone, walking out into the hall. The house seems quiet. Too quiet. Holden must be still asleep. I use the bathroom and brush my teeth before I head downstairs in search of Thayer.

"Thayer?" I call out at the bottom of the stairs.

No response.

Dread creeps into me slowly. I can't explain why. But it's an overwhelming feeling that something isn't right.

I walk into the kitchen, but he's not there either. I check every room I can think of—the poolroom, the living room, the downstairs bathroom. I open the front door, but his car's parked in front of the fountain. I look down at my phone, scrolling through my call log and click on his name, bringing it to my ear.

No answer.

I give up, heading back upstairs to gather some of my stuff. If he's gone, I'm not just going to wait around for him. When I get to the top of the stairs, a sound coming from the other end of the hall has me pausing. It's a repetitive noise. A *thump… thump…thump…*every few seconds.

Danny's room.

I make my way to his door, hesitating with my hand hovering over the door handle. I haven't stepped foot in here since *before*. It feels like it's off limits. Wrong. But if Thayer's in there…

Taking a deep breath, I twist the handle, pushing the door open. I find the source of the noise. Thayer's standing in the middle of Danny's room, surrounded by trophies and ribbons and plaques, bouncing a basketball.

"Thayer?"

His vacant, bloodshot eyes lift to mine and the look in them sends a chill up my spine.

"Are you okay?" I take a step toward him, but his voice stops me in my tracks.

"Get out." His voice is cold. Emotionless.

"What happened?" I try again.

"Get. Out."

Tears prick the backs of my eyes, threatening to spill over. "You're doing it again, aren't you?" I shake my head. "You're pushing me away," I accuse. He stares at me, not speaking, and my sadness gives way to anger. "How can you do this to me again when you know how much it hurt? When you know how hard it was for me to trust you again? Are you that self-ish?" My voice rises in pitch.

I see the muscle in his jaw flutter beneath his skin, but he still doesn't speak.

"If you let me walk out that door, Thayer, I promise you I won't be coming back," I manage to get the words out without my voice cracking. Tears stream down my face and I hate that they do. I hate that he's seeing me break. Thayer's eyes flash with something, his eyebrows tugging together, but he doesn't say anything. Instead, he turns away from me.

"I guess I have my answer." I swallow past the lump in my throat, feeling my temper flare. How can he be so cavalier when my heart feels like it's being smashed into a thousand pieces? "You're an asshole. I don't know who's worse. The self-serving *boy* who's afraid of feelings, or the idiot who fell for it. Again."

I shouldn't be surprised. Deep down, I always knew it was going to come to this. We ignored harsh truths for temporary bliss. But it doesn't make it hurt any less. I storm down the hall and over to his room, holding on to the anger that courses through me, knowing it's only a matter of time before it turns into heartbreak. I haphazardly throw all my shit into my bag. Unzipping the front pocket, I pull out the makeshift necklace Thayer made with the barn key, squeezing it in my palm before I toss it onto his bed.

It's time to let him go.

Head down, I jog down the stairs, bag over my shoulder. Somehow, my feet get tangled up in the strap to my bag in my haste to get out of here, but two strong hands shoot out to catch me before I fall, steadying me. I right myself, pulling away to find Holden standing in front of me with something that looks a lot like pity in his eyes.

Without a word, I move around him, slip my shoes on my feet, and walk out of Whittemore. For good.

To my credit, I managed to make it all the way home before I broke. I turned my phone off and left it downstairs, then crawled into bed where I've been ever since, with the exception of using the bathroom a couple times. A day ago, I would've been scared to be here alone at night. Funny how heartache overrides fear.

I lie in bed, my cheek against my tear-soaked pillow, wondering how Thayer was able to do a complete one-eighty in such a short period of time. And why? Because Holden found out about us? But he seemed fine afterward. He sure didn't seem to have a problem with it when he was buried inside me five minutes later. It had to be something else. He was in Danny's room when I found him, and my gut tells me what I've been ignoring all along. No matter how much he might want me, his resentment is stronger.

"Shayne?" Grey's voice calls out, startling me out of my thoughts. *What the hell?* I sit up in my bed, quickly drying my face with the bottom of my shirt, then press the heels of my hands against my puffy eyes, taking a deep breath. I drop my hands just as my door swings open, revealing Grey with his brown hair curling over the edges of his backwards Red Sox hat.

"What's wrong?" he says, immediately stepping into my room.

"What are you doing here?" My hoarse voice sounds foreign to my own ears. I haven't uttered a word since I left Thayer's yesterday. *God, I'm pathetic.*

He frowns, his eyes searching mine. "Mom left a message saying she was going to be out of town and told me to come check up on you."

I huff out a bitter laugh. "Well, I'm fine. You can leave now."

"Yeah, you really seem fine," he retorts, sarcasm dripping from every word.

"It's a little late to start giving a shit." I'm being an asshole, and I don't even care. I'm sick of the secrets and lies, I'm sick of always trying to fix everything and everyone, and I'm sick of being an afterthought.

Hard eyes meet mine for a beat, and then he's backing away, closing the door behind him. I flop back down on my bed, staring at the ceiling.

Sometime after the sun goes down, there's a knock on my bedroom door. I blow out a breath, swinging my legs over the side of my bed and trudge toward the door. I open it, fully expecting to go another round with Grey, but instead, I find a bowl on the floor. Oatmeal with brown sugar. And a slice of toast.

My chin wobbles. I miss my brother so much it hurts, but how can we even begin to fix things if he won't be honest with me? I take the bowl and toss it on top of my dresser. I have no appetite to speak of.

I crawl back into bed, put some Netflix on my laptop, and eventually pass out.

THIRTY-EIGHT

Thayer

"**A**RE YOU GONNA TELL HER?" HOLDEN ASKS, ELBOWS leaned up against the kitchen counter.

"Eventually." I have to. I just haven't figured out how. When she found me in Danny's room, I was still raw and half-drunk. I couldn't talk to her, not in there, of all places, even if I was coherent. I stayed up all night thinking about what the fuck that nine-one-one call means for us. I went from resenting her for Grey's part in Danny's death to trying to protect her from the truth in a matter of weeks. The last thing I want to do is hurt her, but judging by the look on her face, I ended up doing it anyway. I could practically hear her heart breaking, and I just sat there, not knowing what the fuck to say or do to fix it.

I knew I fucked up when I saw the barn key on my bed. Shayne loves the barn as much as I do. Maybe even more. The fact that she gave it up tells me all I need to know. She's done. And I can't even blame her.

"You should've seen her face, man. I've never seen her like that."

"Not what I want to fuckin' hear."

If there's one thing I've learned about Shayne, it's that she hates being vulnerable. Especially in front of people. She acts like it doesn't bother her that her mom's never around, that her brother went from being her best friend to a stranger in a matter of months, but I know it does. I see her. When we lost Danny, I still had Holden and Christian. Shayne had no one. Every single fucking one of us turned our backs on her, all for reasons that didn't have shit to do with her.

Sad blue eyes pop into my mind and I swipe my keys off the counter. *Fuck it.* "I'll be back."

Shayne isn't Grey. Shayne is innocent. And she's mine.

Without another word, I stride through the house and out to the Hellcat. Holden doesn't need an explanation. He knows exactly where I'm going. I jump in, start the engine, and speed off toward her grandmother's house.

I don't give a fuck what happened. I lost her once. I'm not doing it again.

THIRTY-NINE

Shayne

THE SOUND OF THAYER'S HELLCAT PULLING UP THE DRIVE sends a jolt of fear straight through me. Not for me. For Grey. I run out of my room and out the front door, thankful for the fact that Grey's truck is parked in the garage.

Thayer's slamming the door shut, prowling toward my door when I step onto the porch. When he looks up and sees me, he stops short, a surprised look crossing his features. He probably expected me to hide away in my room, which I would've if Grey wasn't somewhere inside.

I'm a mess. My hair was never brushed after my shower yesterday, my face is puffy and swollen from crying and it's free of makeup. My hoodie hangs past the bottom of my sleep shorts, and I'm wearing socks that reach the middle of my calves, but Thayer's eyes roam my body, looking at me like he hasn't seen me in months instead of two days.

"You need to go," I say, folding my arms over my chest.

"No."

"Yes."

"Not until you talk to me."

"There's nothing to talk about."

"I disagree." He takes a step toward me. "Last night—" His eyes drift over my shoulder, focusing on something behind me. His face contorts with anger, his entire demeanor shifting. "What the fuck is he doing here?"

"What am I doing here?" Grey asks, his tone challenging as he comes to stand in front of me. "I live here, motherfucker. What are you doing here?"

"Grey, go inside," I say, coming around to stand in front of him, planting my hands against his chest to push him toward the door. He looks down at me, his eyes flashing with understanding.

"Is he the reason you've been crying all weekend?" He looks over my head at Thayer. "Did you fucking touch my sister?"

"You killed my brother. It's only fair I fuck your sister."

"Thayer!" I snap. *What the hell is he thinking?* Humiliation courses through me, my face getting hot. Grey takes advantage of my stunned state, charging past me, and judging by the look on Thayer's face, that's exactly what he was hoping for.

Grey throws a punch, but Thayer dips a shoulder, dodging the hit as he tackles Grey to the lawn. He raises his arm before slamming his fist into Grey's face, the other hand gripping the collar of his shirt.

"Thayer, stop!" I run down the steps, then pull on Thayer's arm, but he shakes me off easily.

"I didn't fucking kill him," Grey grunts.

Thayer lands another punch before Grey somehow gains the upper hand. They're a pile of elbows and fists as they take turns getting their hits in until both of them are beaten bloody. If they don't stop soon, someone's going to be seriously hurt. I run back into the house, grabbing my phone off my bed, and call Holden.

"That was fast—"

"Holden, get over here fast. Grey's here." That's all I need to say.

"Motherfucker. I'm coming."

I drop the phone, running back outside.

"I heard you!" Thayer yells, sending another fist into the side of Grey's face. Grey looks dazed, his eyes rolling for a second before he seems to come to. "I fucking heard it. You were with him when he died."

What?

His elbow comes up like he's going to hit him again, but I don't think Grey can take another blow.

"Thayer!" My scream is desperate and guttural, surprising even myself, and I finally break through to him. He looks at me over his shoulder, fist raised, chest heaving.

"Please stop. Please, please, please," I cry. "He's my brother." My voice cracks on the last word, sounding weak.

Thayer releases his hold on Grey and staggers to his feet just as Holden's Range Rover comes barreling down the drive. He jumps out, taking in the scene before him with murder written all over his face.

Thayer bends down to grip Grey's shirt, pulling him to his feet. "Get in the fucking car."

"Thayer, no."

"I'm not going to hurt him." My face must convey how little I believe him. "Anymore," he tacks on belatedly. "This shit ends tonight."

Grey drags his arm across his bloody mouth, then spits onto the lawn. "Agreed." He ambles over to Holden's Rover, hopping into the back seat. Instead of taking the Hellcat, Thayer climbs in the front next to Holden.

If they think I'm letting Grey walk into the lion's den alone, they're mistaken. Before Holden can drive off, I jog over, jumping into the back seat, then close the door. Thayer's eyes meet mine, and if I didn't know any better, I'd say they were full of remorse. But then he turns away, looking out the windshield.

"Bleed on my seats and I'll finish the job," Holden says, then he lays on the gas, heading for Whittemore.

To say this is awkward would be a massive understatement. Thayer and Holden are on one side of the poolroom, arms folded over their chests, and Grey is on the other. I stand in the middle, leaning against the pool table behind me. The tension in the room is palpable. This is the first time we've all been in the same room together in over a year, and my stomach is all twisted up in knots, having no idea what to expect.

"Start talking," Holden says, breaking the tense silence.

"I didn't kill Danny."

"But you were there when he died." Thayer states it as a fact, his voice void of emotion.

Grey takes a deep breath, then exhales through his nose. "Yes."

My mouth drops open, my head whipping in his direction. "What?" I ask in a stunned whisper. I trusted him. Defended him. How could he keep something like this from me?

Grey looks at me, his eyes contrite, before focusing his attention back on Thayer and Holden. "I was supposed to meet up with him at the falls, but I found him on the shore. So yeah, I called the fucking cops. To *save* him." He works his jaw. "But I was too late."

"That doesn't make any sense. Why wouldn't you just say that to begin with?" I ask, confused. I want to believe him more than anyone in this room, but something isn't adding up.

"I waited for the ambulance. I even tried to give him CPR for fuck's sake. But Samuel got there before they did."

"My uncle?" Holden asks, disbelief evident in his tone.

Grey nods. "He told me I needed to leave before anyone else showed up. Said there was no way anyone would believe that I just happened to stumble upon Danny's body, and they'd take me to jail. I told him I'd already called the cops and he told me he'd take care of it. But then the police showed up before he could talk me into leaving, and they were asking all of these questions like I was some fucking murderer, and I realized he was right. They thought I did it, and there was no way to prove otherwise."

"But my dad had the recording," Thayer says. "He knew that you were the one who called it in. He had the police report. Why would he go out of his way to protect you?"

"Because he's my son."

I jump at the sound of August's voice. It takes a second for his words to sink in, but when they do, my world tilts on its axis. My ears ring and I'm suddenly dizzy. No. *No.* I look over at Thayer who looks about as horrified as I feel. It's not true. It can't be true. But when I see Grey's face harden with contempt, I know it is. Slowly, everything starts to click into place. My stomach rolls, and I legitimately think I'm going to throw up.

"Breathe, Shayne. I'm not your father," August says knowingly, putting me out of my misery. "But I am his."

"You knew," I say to Grey. That's why he's been acting so strange. Well, that and the fact that he was the one to discover Danny's body. That would fuck anyone up.

"Danny found out somehow and told me about it a few days prior. I didn't believe him. I wanted to confront Mom and August, but Danny wanted me to wait until we had all the facts."

"You're my half-brother," I say to Grey as it dawns on me. Why would our mom keep something like this from us?

I look over at Thayer and Holden to see how they're handling the news, but they both stand there, stoic, not giving anything away.

"So, we're back to square one," Thayer says as if he didn't just find out that his dad fathered another child, clasping his hands behind his head. "We still don't know who killed Danny."

"We don't know that someone killed him," August says, sounding surprised.

"I need to get out of here," I mumble, my brain on information overload. I need air. I don't give anyone a chance to respond before I'm heading down the stairs and out into the fresh air. I inhale deeply, pulling as much air into my lungs as I can, and then the dam breaks. I'm crying, *again*, and I can't stop it.

"Shayne," Thayer's voice calls out behind me. I turn around, meeting his eyes. "I wasn't trying to hurt you."

"Then imagine what would happen if you actually tried."

FORTY

Shayne

Thanks to Taylor's creative expression on my locker, I had to go see Miss Thomas *and* the principal the next day. I honestly couldn't even tell you what was said. I sat there, nodding at the right times, giving *yes* or *no* answers. My locker had been cleaned over the weekend, but I didn't care. The damage was already done. The days pass by in a blur. I walk through life on autopilot, feeling that same detached feeling I felt last time I had my heart trampled on. I can't concentrate in class and I'm off my game when it comes to volleyball. I wasn't exactly Miss Personality when our team visited colleges either, so I'm sure I made a fantastic impression on the coaches. That coupled with the fact that I didn't play my junior year—which is arguably the most important year when it comes to scouting—doesn't bode well for me.

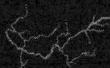

After my mom got home from her trip, Grey finally confronted her. All this time, he knew August was his biologica father, and he never once let my mom in on that fact. The longer she kept it from him, the more his resentment grew. She finally broke down, confessing all the details she'd kept to herself for so many years. Apparently, she and August were having an affair even though he was already married to Thayer's mom. My mom is a few years younger than August, so a teen pregnancy and adultery weren't a good look. Especially back then. Her parents told her she had two options: get an abortion or get out.

She chose to get out.

But here's the real kicker. August never knew. My grandmother called William, August's father, to fill him in on the scandal. Instead of confronting August with the information, he opted for bribing my mom with a nice stack of cash if she left town. William told her that it was what August wanted, and since she was pregnant and on the verge of homelessness, she accepted his offer. Then came my dad, whose identity is still a mystery to me. Honestly, I haven't had the desire or the energy to ask her about it. I have enough drama in my life as it is, and you can't really miss someone you don't know.

My mom was never close with her parents after that, but eventually, they were able to be civil for our sake. That is, until my mom ran into August the first time we ever came to visit Sawyer Point. He took one look at Grey and knew he was his. Cue another fight between both my mom and grandmother and August and William once they put the pieces together. From what my mom says, August wanted an opportunity to get to know Grey. My mom wasn't ready to tell him, and August wasn't quite ready to claim him. So, they got engaged, and he supported us financially, sent Grey to a good college, and the rest was history.

Her phone call with August makes sense now. He wasn't tattling on me for underage drinking. He was warning her because he was afraid that I was hooking up with one of his sons without knowing that Grey was *also* his son.

There are still so many unanswered questions. What happened to Danny? Who was targeting me and why? The 'pranks', if you can call them that, have stopped, but it still weighs heavy on my mind. Is *my* dad going to pop up out of the woodwork next?

But the biggest thing that plagues my thoughts?

Thayer. Always Thayer. If it wasn't clear that the universe didn't want us together before, it sure as hell is now. We've gone through more loss and deception and trauma than most people do in their entire lives, and I haven't even graduated high school.

I'm stabbing a fork at my uneaten salad, lost in thought, when Valen kicks my ankle under the table.

"Ow." I frown at her, and she jerks her chin, motioning toward the cafeteria doors. I look over to see Thayer stalking toward our table with a scowl on his face. A hush falls over the cafeteria as he makes his way toward us, his eyes burning through me like a laser beam.

"Oh, shit," Holden says.

He comes to a stop in front of me, and my heart pounds, not knowing what to expect.

"Can we talk?"

I shake my head, steeling my voice. "Not here."

"You won't answer my calls. You don't answer your door. You're not leaving me much of a choice."

I glance around, not wanting to make a scene. Everyone's watching us with rapt attention, and Thayer doesn't seem to care. If they didn't believe the rumors before, they do now.

"I don't give a fuck about any of these people," he says, reading my thoughts. "I have no problem airing my shit out right here in front of everyone."

That spurs me into action. Standing from the table, I tug on his wrist, pulling him through the lunchroom and into the lobby that connects the gym to the cafeteria. I cross my arms, waiting for him to say something. Thayer reaches a hand out to touch me, but I take a step back, putting some much-needed distance between us. His eyebrows draw together, hurt by the move.

"I can't do this." It hurts. It physically hurts to be this close to him.

"Stay with me. Fuck our families. Fuck everyone else. Stay with me. Be with me."

I shake my head as tears prick the backs of my eyes. "How can you ask me to stay when all you ever do is leave? All *anyone* ever does is *leave me*. You. Grey. My mom. Hell, my own dad left before he even knew me." I sound like a crazy person. I feel a tear roll down my cheek and I swipe it away with the heel of my hand. "What is wrong with me? Because clearly, I'm the common denominator here."

"Nothing is wrong with you," he says vehemently, bringing his hands to cup my face, his thumbs rubbing my cheeks. "I wasn't leaving you, Shayne."

I pull away from his grasp. "You were, though. You found out about Grey and you shut down. You told me to leave without an explanation." I swallow past the lump in my throat, trying to get through my next words without crying. "And now we know it wasn't him and you're here, thinking that changes things, but it doesn't."

"I heard that recording, and all I could do was worry about how I was going to break it to you. I stood there, watching you sleep, and I chose *you*. I chose you over my own brother. Because I'm supposed to be with you, Shayne, and we both fucking know it. And yeah," he says, shoving a hand through his hair, "I had a guilt-ridden drunken breakdown, but that wasn't me leaving you. That was me coming to terms with the fact that I had to let go of Danny to move forward with you. That's why I came to your house. *Before* I knew Grey was innocent."

My tears come hard and fast. He's saying all the right things, and I want so badly to believe him. "There's just too much shit between us. You're Grey's half-brother for fuck's sake—"

"And? How is that any different than when I was your stepbrother? Our parents aren't even together. This changes nothing."

"I feel like all I do is fight for us. And I'm just…tired, Thayer."

"Then I'll be the one to fight. Because I'm not letting you go."

"Well, I am."

I watch the way his throat bobs when he swallows, his jaw clenched tight.

"We both knew this wouldn't last forever, right?" I walk away before I do something stupid like take it all back. When I walk back into the cafeteria, all eyes are on me. It's so quiet you could hear a pin drop.

"Eat your fucking lunch, ya nosy bastards!" Holden yells, breaking the silence. Most people have the decency to avert their eyes. He and Valen flank my sides, walking with me.

"I can't be here today," I say once we're out in the hall.

"Want me to come with you?" Valen offers.

"No, I'm fine. Seriously," I say, forcing a smile when she sends me a doubting look.

"I'll come over later." I nod and she pulls me in for a hug.

"Come on. I'll walk you out," Holden says, tugging me into his side.

We make our way down the hall and through the double doors that lead to the student parking lot. When we get to my car, I climb into my seat, leaving the door open. Holden props his hand against the roof.

"This past year has fucked all of us up," Holden says, seemingly out of nowhere.

I huff out a laugh. *Ya think?*

"But Thayer seemed to take it harder than any of us. He wore that chip on his shoulder, shutting all of us out. But when you came back…so did he. You literally brought him back to life."

My chin wobbles, and then I'm crying again. I sniff, wiping my tears, feeling stupid. But Holden pulls me out of the car and wraps his arms around me, his hand stroking my ponytail. I hug him back, my cheek against his hard chest, taking the comfort he's offering. If there's one silver lining through this whole thing, it's that Holden and I have our friendship back.

"He's stubborn and moody and self-loathing, but I don't think he loved a single thing until he met you."

He said he'd fight for me. I always thought heartbreak was an emotional pain, but the ache in my chest says otherwise. I don't see or hear from Thayer for days. I should be glad that he's letting me go. Why wouldn't he? I made it clear that I planned to do the same. But some part of me wanted him to fight for me like he said he would. The fear of him leaving, along with my stupid pride, wouldn't let me give in so quickly. Why do girls do that? Wait for an acceptable amount of groveling before they give in? All it does is prolong the pain. On both sides.

"The last thing I ever wanted to be is like my mother," my mom says. My eyes fly up to see her in the doorway of my room. I frown, not following.

Hello to you, too.

"You're nothing like her." I didn't know her well, but I knew her well enough to know the two are polar opposites.

"Not true," she says, coming to sit at the foot of my bed. She glances around, taking in the posters and pictures on my walls. "Did you know this used to be my bedroom?"

I shake my head.

"I snuck out of that window more times than I can count."

I want to laugh, but a small smile is all I can manage. I've never snuck out that way, but I have had a boy sneak in. And I'd give anything to have him crawl through that window again.

"I left every chance I could. I spent a lot of my life hating my mother. She always tried to make me fit in this box. She wanted me to be something I wasn't. She was overbearing and made all my choices for me. And I told myself when I got pregnant with your brother that I'd never do that. I'd never intervene in his life the way she did mine. Yet, here I am, making the same mistakes."

"How?" I sit up, hugging the pillow in my lap, genuinely confused.

"I'm not around nearly as much as I should be, for one. I depended on Grey way more than I should've. I took you guys away from Shadow Ridge where you were happy and threw you to the wolves, knowing how the people in this town could be. I was so focused on providing the life I thought you deserved that I neglected to give you the things you needed most."

"Mom. This isn't the same."

"I don't want you to resent me." A tear rolls down her cheek. "I don't want you to run away one day and never come back."

"That will never happen," I assure her.

She wipes her eyes, collecting herself before she shakes her head. "Sorry, I didn't plan on saying all of *that*," she says with a laugh. "I just want to make sure you're happy. If you want to go back to Shadow Ridge, we will. If you want to stay here, we can do that, too."

Am I happy in this moment? Far from it. Could I imagine myself being anywhere else?

"I want to stay."

She blows out a breath, her shoulders sagging a little. "I thought so. Okay. Here's my attempt at doing the right thing and not the mom thing."

"Okay…" I hedge.

"I've known about you and Thayer."

I think my heart stops for a beat. *"Oh?"*

"I found you asleep in his bed right before Danny's accident."

"Oh God," I groan, dropping my face into my hands, embarrassed.

"Obviously, our situation is…complicated. So, I thought it was best that I separate you two."

So that's why she moved us back to Shadow Ridge?

"And I'm not saying it was the wrong thing to do. You were seventeen. When we moved back, I thought he'd be away for college and that you would've moved on. But as soon as both of you were in the same place, you were like two magnets. That kind of love—the kind that doesn't fade with time or distance—it's rare. Like catching lightning in a bottle. And if the only thing holding you back from being happy is the fact that he's Grey's half-brother, then you should be with him."

I blink, not expecting the conversation to take this turn.

"It's not just that," I say, wanting to open up, but not quite sure how. My mom and I have never had the kind of relationship where I felt comfortable talking to her about guys.

"I'm not telling you what to do. You've always been responsible enough to make your own decisions. I'm just letting you know that whatever you choose, I'll support it. And Grey will come around, too."

FORTY-ONE

Thayer

I'M OUTSIDE SHAYNE'S HOUSE LIKE A LOVESICK FUCK UNDER THE guise of checking on her. The truth is, no one has tried anything since the night of the fire, but I can't stay away. I've tried. All the lights are off except the lamp in her room, and her window's open, like I knew it would be. It's barely sprinkling, but the wind is blowing and thunder rumbles in the distance.

I make my way over to the side of the house and hoist myself up and through her window, trying to keep my entrance as quiet as possible so I don't wake her mom. Shayne's curled up on her side and she must have fallen asleep not very long ago because "The Freshman" by The Verve Pipe plays from her phone's speaker on the bed next to her. As I get closer, I notice the tip of her nose is red, like she may have fallen asleep crying, and I feel a pang of guilt. I've been the source of her tears too many times, but I'd kill anyone who dare made her cry.

I brush a wayward strand of hair off her cheek and tuck it behind her ear before I crawl into bed behind her. I kiss the back of her neck, curling my hand around her hip.

"Our scars are called Lichtenberg figures," I say, dropping my forehead to the top of her spine. I'm not even sure she's awake, but I keep going anyway. "You asked me why I'd get a permanent reminder of that night." I use the tips of my fingers to trace the curve of her hip, feeling goosebumps break out over her warm skin.

"It was the night you told me you loved me." I kiss her again where her shoulder meets her neck. I hear her breath catch, and I know she's awake now. "Because in some fucked up way, I felt like that night branded us together, whether we liked it or not." Another kiss. "But more than that, it was the night that I realized I loved you. And I couldn't handle it. My mom left us. Danny had just died. I was fucking scared to love anyone else. So, I did what I do best, and I shut down. I pushed you away. But I wanted to remember what that felt like."

Shayne wordlessly rolls toward me and my hand slides underneath her shirt with the movement, gliding up to rest in between her shoulder blades. Our lips are centimeters apart, but she keeps her eyes downcast.

"I'm sorry." The words are simple, but I don't think I've actually said them before. "Be with me."

Her breaths come quicker now, and I can feel her heart pounding. I don't know what she's thinking or feeling, but she's not kicking me out, so I take it as a good sign. Then I feel her tongue graze my lips, tentatively slipping between them as her hands come up to cup my jaw. She kisses my top lip first, sucking lightly, and then she repeats the motion with the bottom. I groan, letting her take her fill, but when her tongue slides against mine, I can't help kissing her back.

I slide my hands into her hair, holding her to me as I move my tongue against hers. I roll her underneath me, then sit back on my heels to peel her grey shorts down her legs, taking her underwear with them. Shayne lies still, letting me undress her. Her tank top is next. I push it up to expose those perfect tits, admiring how pretty her little pink nipples look with those dainty piercings. I crawl on top of her, my hands pinning hers to the bed as I take one hardened tip into my mouth.

Shayne moans, lifting her hips, seeking friction. I suck on her, capturing both of her wrists in one hand, then my thumb takes care of the neglected side. Getting off on her little gasps and moans, I take my time sucking, licking, nipping, and then I give the same treatment to the other side. Shayne's practically panting now, her eyes squeezed shut like she's in pain with her arms still raised above her head.

I curl her fingers around the slats in the headboard. "Keep them there," I say, standing to get rid of my clothes. Shayne's eyes are glued to me as I tear my shirt off over my head, dropping it to the floor. I kick off my shoes, shoving my pants and boxers down my legs next, and then I'm crawling back over her, kissing my way up her stomach.

"Open your legs for me, baby."

Shayne spreads her thighs for me without hesitation, and I slide in between them.

"Tell me again," I say, positioning myself against her slick heat before lifting her thigh to my waist. "I want to hear you to say it."

She wets her lips, seeming nervous, and I realize my mistake. The last time she said those words, it didn't end well. She needs to hear them from me.

"I love you," I say, pushing inside her. I slide my hands up her outstretched arms, linking my fingers through hers as I start to move inside her. "I tried not to. I didn't want to feel anything for anyone, but then you came along and crawled inside my skin, inside my fucking heart, and you never left. Not even for a minute. I'm done fighting it."

Shayne unlinks our fingers, pushing on my shoulders to flip our positions. She rolls on top of me, pinning my wrists to the bed like I did hers, her warm, wet pussy against my lower stomach. Her hair falls around us, tickling my chest as she leans down. "If you fuck this up—"

"I won't."

"Good." She shifts her hips, angling her ass until my head is nudged just inside her opening.

"Does this mean you love me, too?"

She slides down, taking me inside her. "You're the only boy I've ever loved."

"Show me."

Shayne sits back, bracing her hands on my thighs behind her as she starts to ride me. This position gives me a perfect view of my cock between her lips and I watch, mesmerized, as she slowly slides up and down my length. Her tits bounce once she starts to move her hips faster, and I bring my hands to her waist, slamming her down onto me as I push my hips into her. When I feel her wetness coating me and see her eyes squeeze shut before her head falls back, I know she's close.

"Fuck, I love you," I say, bringing my thumb to press against her clit. She tightens around me instantly, her mouth falling open in a silent scream. I feel her contracting around me over and over, milking me, and I can't help it. I come inside her as she shakes and jerks on top of me.

"Oh my God," she says, flopping onto my chest, keeping me inside her.

Our bodies are slick with sweat, her cheeks flushed as we lie here, catching our breath. After a few minutes, she starts to trace my tattoo, like she seems to do every time we're together like this.

Just when I think she's fallen asleep, she mumbles something that I can't make out.

"What?"

"Like catching lightning in a bottle."

FORTY-TWO

Shayne

We're finally together. It doesn't feel real, but it feels right. There's a chance I might regret it one day, but I know if I didn't give us one more shot, I'd always wonder *what if?* Thayer picks me up from school every day, making sure to kiss me in front of everyone. People talk, but it's nothing new.

The more I think about what Grey told us about that night, the more something doesn't sit right with me. Why was Samuel at the scene so quickly? Knowing what I know about him, I can't shake the feeling that he's at the bottom of all of this. I just don't know how. Christian's been even more withdrawn than usual, and I know that I need to have a conversation with Thayer. I haven't told him about what I saw that night in the parking lot, partly because I promised I wouldn't and was trying to give him the time to do it himself, and partly because it slipped my mind with all of the other chaos unfolding.

I sit at Thayer's kitchen table with him on one side of me and Holden on the other, my plate of untouched pizza in front of me. Holden's having people over later, so I feel like it's better to get it over with now.

"I have to tell you guys something," I say, picking at my black nail polish. They both pause, exchanging looks. Thayer drops his pizza to his plate, pinning me with an expectant glare.

"The night of Danny's memorial thing..."

"Spit it out," Holden says before taking a swig of his beer.

"I went out to the parking lot to find you," I say to Holden. "But you were already gone."

"Yeah?"

I nod. "I saw Christian with his dad, and I don't know what happened or why, but he started beating the shit out of Christian."

I watch them both for a reaction. Maybe this won't be a surprise to them. But their faces give nothing away.

"I ran over to help him, and your uncle wasn't happy that I'd just witnessed it."

"Did he touch you?" Thayer asks, his voice low and threatening.

"No." I quickly shake my head. "He was trying to scare me, telling me how this was 'family business', but Christian stopped him before he could do anything."

"Why the fuck are you just now telling me this?"

"Christian asked me not to. He was supposed to tell you himself." I still don't know if that was a one-off, or if it's an ongoing thing. Not that it's acceptable either way.

"He has been different lately," Holden muses.

"You guys don't seem surprised."

"Samuel's a dick." Holden shrugs. "So are our dad and our grandfather. I wouldn't put it past him. I just don't know why Christian would take it."

"I have a bad feeling about him," I admit. "Grey said he got there before the ambulance on the day Danny died. At first, I just figured he had connections and someone tipped him off about the nine-one-one call, knowing he's family. But why would he cover for Grey like that?"

"He knew Grey was blood," Holden supplies.

Thayer shakes his head. "No. Samuel doesn't give a shit about that. He's gonna beat his own son but protect his half-nephew? That doesn't add up."

"Where is he now?" I ask.

"Fuck if I know. He'll be here tonight, though," Holden says, crumpling up a napkin before tossing it onto his plate.

"We'll talk to him then." Thayer reaches over to grab the leg of my chair, sliding me toward him, then he's pulling to set me sideways on his lap with his hand on my thigh. "Anything else I should know?"

A few hours later, the house is full of people. Taylor had the audacity to show her face after everything. She waltzed in like nothing happened, but Holden cornered her, telling her to leave. She pouted about it not being fair because all her friends were here, so Holden told her if she wanted to stay, she'd have to apologize to me.

I'd like to say that I didn't find a sick satisfaction in watching her fumble over her words with jealousy written all over her face as Thayer hugged me from behind, kissing my neck, oblivious to her presence, but that'd be a lie. Her apology was anything but sincere, but I didn't care. She's irrelevant to me and the people I care about, which is the best revenge for a girl like her.

Christian still hasn't shown up, and I can't say I'm not a little nervous to face him after betraying his trust. Hopefully, he'll understand.

A commotion from out back has me pushing up onto my toes in an attempt to see over everyone and into the backyard.

"Motherfucker," Thayer mutters, pushing his way through the crowd of people gathered in his kitchen, heading for the back door. I'm right behind, still not sure what's happening, but once we step outside, I see Liam, Valen's boyfriend, laid out in the grass, holding his bloody nose. Valen has her hands cupped over her mouth in shock, and Holden's hovering above him.

"By the way, I fucked your girlfriend," he shouts, throwing his arms out.

"Holden!" Valen yells, rushing to help Liam up off the ground, but he shoves her away, refusing her help.

What. The. Fuck.

"Touch her again, motherfucker," Holden warns, taking a step forward, but Thayer steps in front of him, holding him back.

Liam pulls himself to his feet and spits in the grass, wiping his nose with the back of his sleeve before he turns to go back inside, and presumably, right out the front door. I run up to Valen to see what the hell is going on.

"Are you okay? What happened?"

"I need to talk to him," she says, pointing toward the direction Liam went. "I promise I'll call you later, okay?" She gives me a quick kiss on the cheek, and then she's heading back inside.

"Valen…" Holden says, his eyes begging her to stay. She turns to look at him over her shoulder, hesitating, but then she turns back around, disappearing inside.

Valen and Holden? *Holy shit.* I know I've been distracted lately, but how did something like this escape my notice?

Once they're gone, everyone goes back to drinking, and the drama is already forgotten. Holden's eyes are angry and hard, but I can see the hurt he's trying to conceal.

"Are you all right?" I ask, walking up to him and Thayer, rubbing my arms against the cold. I'm wearing fleece-lined leggings, my Sherpa jacket, *and* a beanie, but I'm still freezing. It's as if we've skipped fall and went straight to winter.

"I need a drink," he says, heading back inside for the kitchen.

Thayer and I exchange looks, and I can tell he's just as clue-less as I am. We follow him inside where he promptly walks up to the island counter and takes a swig out of some tequila someone left out, then jams a hand through his hair, seeming conflicted.

"What happened?" I ask.

"Valen is the devil. That's what happened."

I frown, confused, but before I can say another word, Baker and Christian come barreling into the kitchen. Christian's arm is around Baker's neck as Baker drags his drunken body toward us.

Thayer straightens, taking in the sight.

"Found him at the falls. He almost went over," Baker ex-plains, shrugging Christian's arm off. He stumbles, losing his balance, and Thayer walks over to him, jerking him up by his jacket before planting him in one of the chairs at the dining table.

"Stay," he orders, pointing a finger at him like a dog.

"Everyone else, get the fuck out!"

Holden walks out back, making the same announcement. Baker turns to leave, but Thayer stops him.

"Not you."

Baker works his jaw, hesitating, but ultimately, he listens, taking a seat on the other side of the table. Christian starts to slide off his chair and I rush over, catching him before he hits the floor. I shove on his shoulders to push him upright, and bloodshot eyes meet mine so full of pain and something else I can't place.

"Why do you insist on being nice to me?" he slurs. "If you would have just stayed away..."

Ice fills my veins, like my instincts realize something before my mind can catch up, and I stumble back, my butt hitting the floor. People are still making their way out of the house, and someone steps on my fingers, but it barely registers. Suddenly, another piece of the puzzle snaps into place as a single phrase from the night of the fire pops into my head.

Just be glad you were in the kitchen when it happened.

"How did you know I was in the kitchen?" I ask, my voice barely above a whisper.

"Baby, what the *fuck*?" Thayer says, his arms hooking underneath mine to pull me to my feet, but I can't tear my eyes away from Christian. And judging by the way he's looking at me, he knows I've put it together.

"It was you, wasn't it?"

"Shayne," Thayer says, looking between the two of us. "Explain."

"It was him. This whole time—my locker, my tires, the window…"

"*You?*" Thayer says, incredulous. "You were behind it?"

"It was supposed to scare her. I wasn't trying to hurt her—"

"You weren't trying to hurt her? You set a *fire* in her *house!*" Thayer lunges for him with murder in his eyes, but I step in front of him, my hands on his waist.

"Hitting him isn't going to give us any answers."

"No, but it'll feel good," he argues, his jaw flexing in anger.

"Look at him. He's barely conscious as it is."

"I'm drunk, not deaf," Christian says, his voice garbled.

"Why?" Holden chimes in. "Why the fuck would you go through all that trouble?"

I turn around to face him as my brain works overtime trying to work out the last piece of the puzzle. "What did I ever do to you?"

Why would he want to scare me away? And why would he be drunk at the falls? Then it hits me. That look in his eyes I couldn't place…it was guilt. Guilt because—

"You killed Danny."

Christian doesn't answer at first, but then he drops his head into his hands, and his shoulders start to shake.

"You better deny that right fucking now," Holden barks.

Christian looks up at him, eyes shining with tears. "It was an accident."

His admission hits me like a punch to the gut, and I feel Thayer's chest heaving behind me. I tense, knowing I won't be able to hold him back this time. I stick my hand behind me, locking my fingers with his in an attempt to calm him, but it's in vain, because he's on Christian before I can blink.

"You killed my brother!" He fists Christian's jacket, throwing him up against the wall. Christian doesn't put up a fight, and Thayer pulls back his fist, sending it into his face. His head bounces off the wall, his nose spurting blood. "You could've killed my girl." Another punch. This time to the stomach, and Christian doubles over. "You lied to us for a fucking year!" He lands one final punch to his gut, and then Christian's sliding down the wall into a puddle on the floor.

"Thayer, stop!"

I know what he did is wrong and fucked up in so many ways, but all I can think of when I see Christian like this is the scene in the parking lot where his dad doled out the same abuse. I look over to Holden and Baker, but neither one of them moves to help, so I insert myself between them right before Thayer's about to send a foot into Christian's stomach. He stops himself, looking at me like I've grown three heads.

I stand on my tiptoes, bringing my hands to his face, forcing him to focus on me. His nostrils are flared, his jaw set hard. "This isn't going to help anything. Hurting him isn't going to bring Danny back." His eyes squeeze shut as if he's in pain. "We'll make it right," I promise him. "But not like this."

"We were fucking around, daring each other to jump like we always do," Christian says, pulling himself up to sit against the wall, clutching his stomach. "He was being a pussy, talking about how it was too cold. We started wrestling, trying to push each other off, but I got the upper hand."

He stops, leaning his head back to look up at the ceiling as tears roll out of the corners of his eyes. "I fucking laughed. I laughed as he fell. And then I looked over the edge, waiting for him to jump out of the water and flip me off, but...he never came up."

"Finish your story so I can fucking kill you," Holden says, his eyes glassy, arms folded over his chest.

Christian nods, resigned to his fate. "I panicked. I couldn't think, so I called my dad as I ran for the shore. He told me not to call the cops and said he was on his way. I jumped in, looking for him. Then he showed up," he says, flicking his chin at Baker, who's sitting there with his hood on, staring blankly ahead. "He was there doing some shit for his photography class. He saw the whole thing, then jumped in to help me. Eventually, we found Danny. I don't know how long, but it felt like hours."

He inhales deeply, pressing his eyes with the heels of his palms. Shock has all of us paralyzed. I don't even think we breathe, waiting for him to finish.

"We pulled him out, but I could tell..." he trails off, his hands balling into fists. "I could tell he was dead. I didn't know Grey had texted Danny, or that he told him to meet us there. I heard him calling Danny's name, and I looked up, seeing him on the cliff. I panicked. Again. So we ran. The next thing I know, Grey's yelling. He must have seen Danny on the shore. My dad came and got rid of Grey. Made it seem like he'd take the fall if he didn't get out of there."

Hot tears roll down my face, hearing him describe Danny's last moments and what followed.

"He threatened me," Baker chimes in, pushing his foot against the table leg until his chair teeters on the two back legs. "He saw the camera around my neck and smashed it into pieces. Told me he'd kill me if I ever spoke a word of it. My dad had some legal troubles, and he offered to make them go away in exchange for my silence."

"I wanted to go to the police. I wanted to turn myself in, but he wouldn't let me. He said I wasn't throwing college and basketball away over an accident, but we all know it's because he didn't want that kind of scandal to reflect on him. He covered it up and had the records sealed, and that was that." His eyes slide to mine. "Until you came back."

I shake my head, batting the tears off my cheek. "What do I have to do with any of this?"

"Come on, Shayne. You're smarter than that." His head lolls to the side. "They suspected Grey. Grey was gone and your parents split. He was the perfect fall guy. But the second I saw the way they acted with you, I knew it was only a matter of time before they let you back in."

"You knew they'd eventually find out Grey didn't do it."

He nods. "I tried minor shit at first, trying to scare you away, or at the very least, make you switch schools. But that night in the parking lot, you saw something you shouldn't have. And that put you on my dad's radar. I told him I had it under control. That I'd handle it. Because believe me, Shayne. He'd do much worse."

A chill licks its way up my spine. I believe that. Without a doubt.

"He controls everything and everyone around him. If someone steps out of line, he doesn't handle it well. But I'm not playing his game anymore." He stands, wobbling on his feet. "So here's my proposition."

"You really think you're in a position to negotiate?" Thayer asks, his voice low and menacing. "What did we say we'd do if we found out who killed Danny? You were there when we said it, remember?" he taunts.

"We said we'd get revenge—" Holden supplies.

"No matter who it is," Thayer finishes, moving around me, but Christian nods at Baker, signaling something.

"Check your phones."

Thayer pulls out his phone and I lean in to see what it is. It's a video from an unknown number, presumably Baker's. He clicks on the triangle to play the video. It starts out with

Christian and Danny roughhousing on the cliff, laughing and trying to push each other. The camera zooms in, and I can see the wide smiles on their faces.

"I win, motherfucker!" Christian's distant voice calls out, leaning over the cliff with his hands in the air, laughing victoriously. The video is taken from behind, but you can see the moment he realizes something isn't right. His hands lock behind his head as he calls Danny's name, over and over, then he's pulling his phone out of his pocket, running down the path to the bottom. You can hear Baker whisper *"shit"*, and then the only thing we can see is the ground as he runs to help.

Thayer stops the video, most likely not wanting to see what comes next. I don't blame him. Holden does the same, throwing his phone onto the table in front of him.

"He smashed my camera, but he didn't think about my phone," Baker says.

"The whole thing is recorded. This is how you take him down." Christian looks between us, gauging our reactions.

"But it implicates you, too," I say, stating the obvious.

He lifts a shoulder. "I'm ready."

"Talk to me," I murmur, running my fingers through Thayer's hair that's still damp from his shower. His head is on my chest, his arm hooked around me, holding me close. Christian left a couple hours ago with the promise to turn himself in tomorrow. I think I'm still in a state of shock, so I can't even imagine how Thayer must feel. Selfishly, I'm scared he's going to shut down and push me away again. I don't want to fall asleep, afraid I'll wake up tomorrow and everything will have changed.

"I should've known. I should've seen something," he says, sounding like he's on the brink of sleep.

"You couldn't have," I say. "And it's time to stop blaming yourself."

It's somewhat comforting that Danny wasn't killed in cold blood, but somehow, I don't think that would be the right thing to say. Thayer doesn't respond, and eventually, I hear his breathing even out, telling me he fell asleep.

FORTY-THREE

Thayer

SHAYNE'S BODY IS LIKE A FURNACE AGAINST ME WHEN I WAKE UP. Her back is to my chest and both my arms are locked around her upper arms, like I was holding onto her, even in my sleep. I expected to feel like shit when I woke up after last night's revelations, but instead I feel...free. Like maybe I can finally move on now that I know what happened to my brother, even if it meant losing my cousin.

Shayne stirs in my arms, arching her back on a stretch, and then she turns in my arms to face me, sleepy, blue eyes meeting mine.

"You're still here," she says, her voice raspy with sleep.

I pick up her wrist, bringing it to my lips to kiss the scar there. "Where else would I be?"

EPILOGUE

Shayne
4 months later...

OPENING THE DOOR TO MY ROOM, I TOSS MY BACKPACK ONTO
my bed, noticing an envelope on my pillow. I round
the bed, plucking it off from the comforter. Shaking
it, I feel something heavier than paper inside. I open it, finding
the rusted barn key and a note.

Meet me in the barn.

Excitement swirls inside my stomach. After some convincing, Thayer went back to school. It's a miracle he wasn't
dropped from his classes with how little he actually attended.
Even with the distance, we manage to see each other several
times a week, but I didn't think I'd get to see him today. Not
wasting any time, I turn back around, grabbing an envelope of
my own off my desk and stuffing it into the back of my denim
shorts before I sprint through the house, avoiding the moving
boxes that line the halls.

We've still got a couple months left in this house, but we
had to get an early start on packing, especially with all the
stuff my grandmother collected. Somewhere in one of those
boxes is the name, address, and phone number belonging to

my father. Turns out, that was who my mom was with that night. He wants to meet me, but I haven't decided what I want to do yet, so she stuck his information in an envelope for me to open when I'm ready. For the first time in my life, I don't feel like something's missing. I've never felt so whole. And it's not only because of Thayer, but I have Holden and Grey back, too. If only the three of them could come to terms with the fact that they're half-brothers, life would be pretty much perfect. But for now, baby steps.

I take off through the woods that are lush and green now that the snow has melted, heading for the barn. We haven't been out here in a while now that we don't have to hide, and I've missed it. I slow my steps once I get closer, noticing something different. The wood looks newer, and it doesn't look like it's on the verge of collapsing.

"Thayer?" I call out, pushing the door open, finding him standing there in his signature black shirt and jeans with his hands stuffed into his front pockets. "Oh my God," I say, not believing my eyes. Everything looks brand new. There's an actual floor for one, and two couches—the original one and a new one—with blankets and pillows thrown across them. A coffee table sits in between them, and twinkle lights hang from the rafters above.

Thayer walks toward me, scratching the back of his neck. "What do you think?"

"I love it," I say, meeting him halfway. Everything is all fixed up. I bet the roof doesn't even leak anymore. It's still our barn, just cozier. And definitely cleaner. Thayer takes my hand, pulling me over to the old couch before he sits down, tugging me onto his lap. I sit on his thighs with my knees on either side of his legs, and his palms grip my thighs.

"Hi."

"Hi," I say, leaning in to press my lips to his. "This is amazing." I look up at the lights, my hands braced on his shoulders. "But why?"

"I fell in love with you here." He leans forward to kiss the column of my neck, causing goosebumps to prick my arms. "It's where you told me you loved me." Another kiss. This time to my collarbone. "Where I felt you from the inside for the first time," he says, his hands sliding around to squeeze my ass. "And I'll probably fucking end up marrying you here one day, too."

I bite down on my lip, trying not to cry as he sucks and licks the sensitive skin on my neck. A vision of a sixteen-year-old Thayer on the day we met pops into my mind, his brooding yet curious eyes inspecting me as I slipped inside the barn to get out of the rain.

It was my third day living at Whittemore, and I was bored, exploring the property when I stumbled upon it. I hadn't even met Thayer before then, and I was fascinated with him from the moment I saw him. Who would've thought we'd end up here?

"I love you," I say, my fingers tracing the tattoo on his shoulder. "I love you so much it hurts sometimes."

"I love you," he says, his hands sliding up my back, hitting the envelope sticking out of my pants. "What's this?"

I smile, almost having forgotten. "I have something for you, too. Open it."

His eyebrows cinch together as he opens the envelope, pulling the letter out. His eyes scan the paper, and I see the moment realization sets in.

"UMass?" His eyebrows jump up to his hairline.

I nod and Thayer smiles—*really* smiles—and it feels so good to see him do that again. It feels even better knowing I'm the one who put it there. UMass is a mere mile from Amherst, and I ended up getting a Division II athletic scholarship for volleyball. It's a partial scholarship, but it's better than nothing.

"You're moving in with me," he states it as a fact rather than a question, tossing the letter to the table in front of us.

"We'll see." I laugh, knowing I'll be moved in the day I graduate.

Leaning over, he lays me on the couch, his hips fitting between my thighs. His mouth covers my nipple over the fabric of my T-shirt, sucking it into his mouth and my back comes off the couch, arching into him. "I can be very convincing."

My mom was right. Finding a love like ours is like catching lightning in a bottle. And I'm never letting go.

Thayer & Shayne's story is complete, but the saga continues!
Add book 2 to your TBR to find out what happened with
Christian, Holden, Valen, and Grey.

Goodreads: bit.ly/Heartbreakhill2

ACKNOWLEDGMENTS

First and foremost, to the readers, whether you're just discovering me or have been there since the beginning, thank you. I'm so grateful that you've taken a chance on me.

Leigh, thank you for talking me out of my 329374 meltdowns while writing this.

Sarah Grim Sentz! You are an absolute angel. I couldn't have done it without you.

Tijuana, thank you for always sending me encouragement when I need it the most.

Thank you to my amazing editor Paige Smith for sacrificing to get this one done. As always, please don't break up with me.

To the bloggers, thank you for busting your asses all day every day. I appreciate you. I probably won't ever have my shit together, and I'm so beyond thankful for everything you do to fit me into your busy schedules. <3

Lastly, my reader group—my sweet baby Angels—I love you. You're my happy place. Thank you for your endless support.

Continue reading for a look at *Bad Habit*…

PROLOGUE
THEN

Three years ago…

THE FIRST TIME I LAID EYES ON ASHER KELLEY, DRUNK AND bleeding, I decided two things. The first being that he was the most beautiful boy I'd ever seen in my entire life. I was sure of it. And the second thing? He was the kind of boy that I should never, under any circumstances, get involved with. But, even my pre-pubescent self knew on some level that I'd gladly reach inside my own chest and offer him my beating heart if he'd only ask.

What I didn't know then was that would be the first of many nights just like that one. Turned out, Asher's dad was a little bit of a drunk, and a lot of an asshole. If it wasn't his dad, it was some poor soul who decided to cross Asher. He was always looking for trouble, it seemed. Or maybe trouble just knew where to find him.

My brother, Dashiell, was always quick to kick me out of his room on the nights Asher snuck in. It became routine to them. Just another Thursday night. But seeing him tumble through my brother's window never ceased to break my heart and make it beat faster all at once.

Over the past three years, Asher has pretty much become a permanent fixture in our lives. My parents are either oblivious or don't care enough to question why he's always here, or why he occasionally dons a black eye or a split lip. Part of me hates them for it. They've made their feelings on Asher clear. They don't like him hanging around, think he's a *bad influence*.

But Dash is stubborn, and loyal to a fault. So, they tolerate Asher at best.

I'm sitting cross-legged on the floor of Dash's room playing Guitar Hero on his Xbox when I hear the telltale tapping on the window that signals Asher's arrival, and I'm immediately uneasy. Dash was supposed to meet Asher and their other friend, Adrian, at a party earlier. Alarm bells go off, and I drop the guitar, scurrying over to the window on my knees. I help him slide it open, and he hefts himself over the sill.

"Asher? What happened? Where's Dash?" I reach for the lamp on Dash's bedside table, and when it illuminates his swollen, bloody face and T-shirt, I gasp, my hand flying to my heart.

"Asher!" I run to his side and help him to the bed. He stumbles over the laces of his untied combat boots, almost taking us both down.

"Oh my God, say something!" I panic, warring between getting my dad or calling the police.

"Calm down." He chuckles darkly. "You're going to wake up your pops."

"That's exactly what I'm going to do," I snap, before turning on my heels. Someone needs to do something for once. And being a pretty powerful attorney, my dad is someone who can actually help. I feel a hot hand grip my wrist, and despite the circumstances, my already racing heart quickens at his touch.

"Come on," he says in a hushed, gravelly tone. "It's just a little cut. You should see what he looks like," he tacks on with a hint of a smirk tugging at his full lips.

"Is that supposed to make me feel better?" I ask, trying to jerk my arm out of his grasp, to no avail. "Because it doesn't. Not even a little." Tears start to fill my eyes, and his own soften at the sight.

"I'm okay, Briar," he promises, his voice uncharacteristically soft. "Just hang out with me for a while until Dash gets back." Indecision swirls in my gut, and I bite my lip, contemplating my next move.

"Fine." I sigh. "I'll be right back." I tiptoe out into the kitchen, my bare feet sticking to the hardwood floor. I grab a washcloth and run it under the sink before snagging a bandage out of the cabinet. I'm no nurse, but it's better than nothing. When I come back to the room, Asher is sitting on the bed with his elbows on his knees and his hands fixed on either side of his neck. I drop to my knees in front of his spread ones and gently brush his dark hair off his forehead. His eyes snap up to mine—one green with yellow flecks, and the other a honey brown with flecks of green. He swallows, his throat bobbing with the motion. I avert my eyes and bring the damp washcloth up to dab at the dried blood crusted near his eyebrow. He clenches his jaw, but says nothing as I do my best to clean him up.

"Where's my brother?" I question, if only to distract myself from his close proximity. Up until recently, I'm fairly certain Asher has only ever seen me as an annoying little sister. Lately, things have been…different. Like all the air is sucked out of the room when we're in it. And I can't help but wonder how no one else feels it when it's suffocating me.

We've had a few *almost* moments. I thought he might even kiss me once. I was walking out of the bathroom in my towel, and there he was, waiting on the opposite wall with his arms crossed. His eyes raked down my damp body, my long, blonde hair dripping water onto my pink toes, leaving a puddle at my feet. His nostrils flared. I squeezed my towel tighter, and he moved toward me. He extended his arm, and I could feel the heat of his skin at my hip, even through my towel. I sucked in a breath, closing my eyes. Then…nothing. I opened my eyes to see that aloof smirk back in place, his face mere inches from mine. His hand gripped the doorknob I was standing in front of.

"I need to take a piss," he said, moving past me. I

swallowed my embarrassment, rolled my eyes at myself for thinking he might actually kiss me, and scurried back to my room, leaving him chuckling behind me.

"He's at the party," he says, bringing me back from the past. I feel my cheeks heat from the lingering mortification of that day.

"I never made it there," he clarifies. "I just thought I'd chill here for a while." He doesn't elaborate, but I know what he means. Until he cools off. Until the alcohol catches up with his piece of shit dad, and he finally passes out.

Rising on my knees, I blow on the gash above his eyebrow to dry it off a little before applying the Band-Aid. His eyes squeeze shut, and one hand comes up to grip the back of my bare thigh. I freeze, feeling that tightening low in my stomach that only seems to happen when Asher is near.

"It doesn't look that bad now," I say quietly, reaching forward to pluck the Band-Aid off the bed next to him. I feel his thumb rub small circles on the back of my thigh, and I try not to gasp. Crazily, I wonder what that hand would feel like between my legs. I shake that thought from my head and smooth the bandage over his cut with my thumbs.

"Head wounds tend to look a lot worse than they really are," Asher says, clearing his throat and pulling away. I back up, still dazed, as he stands and reaches behind his neck to pull his blood-speckled white tee off his back before balling it up and tossing it to the floor. I think he's going to take one of Dash's shirts, but he doesn't. He plops back down on the bed, exhaling roughly, running a hand through his hair. I gulp watching the way his forearms flex with the motion, and when he lies back on the bed, displaying the muscles on his stomach, I have to look away.

He's always been magnificent to me, with his onyx hair that hangs in his dark, mismatched eyes. His full lips and slightly pointed nose. The dimples that I didn't even know existed for an entire year into knowing him, because the boy never really smiles. Smirks, yes. Taunting, mocking, sarcastic grins. But a full-blown Asher Kelley smile is rarer than a blue moon. Now that his shoulders are broader, his chest and arms bigger, and his jaw more chiseled…he's a man. And he's perfection. Suddenly, I'm all too aware of my small breasts that visibly harden beneath my tank top and my tiny baby pink sleep shorts. I'm looking every bit of fourteen, feeling so inferior kneeling in front of this young god.

Asher scrubs a hand down his face, and I notice that his knuckles are bloody, too, but the sight is nothing new.

"Do you want ice?" I ask as I stand up, gesturing toward his hands.

"What, this?" he asks, examining his knuckles. "I'm fine."

"Do you want me to go?" I fidget with the hem of my shorts. His eyes follow the movement, then move up my body until his eyes lock on mine.

"No." His tone is firm, but he doesn't elaborate. My stomach flips with nerves, and I nod, biting on the corner of my lip.

"Do you…want to watch a movie?"

A shrug. "Sure."

"What do you want to watch?"

"You pick."

I look around for Dash's remote before finding it underneath a sock and start flipping through the channels. I stand in front of the TV awkwardly, not knowing if I should take my spot on the floor or join him. Asher pats the bed next to him, seeming to sense my hesitation.

"I won't bite, Bry."

I sit next to him and settle on one of my favorite movies. No matter how many times I've seen it, I always have to watch it when it's on.

"Really? *Tombstone*?" Asher cracks a real smile at that.

"Hell yes. It's my favorite."

"I'll be your huckleberry," he says, quoting the movie.

"Shut up." I give a weak smile, still feeling helpless in

this situation, but I toss a pillow at him in an effort to appear unfazed.

"Shit!" he growls, bringing his hands up to his face.

"Oh my God! I'm an idiot! I'm so sorry!" I say, crawling over to his side of the bed, feeling terrible for already forgetting.

"Are you okay?" I ask, prying his hands away, but when I do, he's laughing.

"Jerk," I huff, turning away, but he grasps my wrists and flips me onto my back. His body hovers over mine.

"I'm sorry," he says, not sounding sorry at all. "But you were looking at me like my dog just died. I had to do something to lighten the mood."

He still has my hands pinned above my head, and he's close enough that I can smell his spearmint gum and the faint trace of cigarettes.

"I worry about you," I admit, not making any effort to escape. His eyes clench shut, like it physically pains him to hear those words.

"Don't," he says. "The last thing an angel like you should be doing is worrying about a fuck-up like me."

"You're not a fuck-up. And I'm no angel."

Asher drops his forehead, rolling it against my own.

"You are," he insists, his lips trailing from my cheek down to my ear, leaving goose bumps in their wake. "And this is the last fucking thing I should be doing with you."

"What are you doing with me?" I whisper.

"Touching you," he says, rubbing my wrists with his thumbs. A small noise slips from my mouth, and he lowers his body onto mine. Instinctively, my legs part to make room for him. He groans once he fits his hips between them.

"I need to leave," he says, his voice thick and strained.

I lick my lips, mustering up all the courage I can when I ask, "Can I kiss you?"

He makes a pained noise, but he doesn't deny me. He

presses his lips to the skin just beneath my ear, then he trails his lips back across my cheek, down to my chin, and finally, his mouth is on mine. I've kissed a few boys, even though Dashiell, Asher, and Adrian, have done their best to run them off, but this is so much more than just a kiss. At least, for me it is.

Asher licks the seam of my lips before tugging the bottom one into his mouth. He sweeps his tongue inside, and tentatively, mine flicks out to tangle with his. I don't know what I'm doing, but he must like it, because his hips flex, grinding into me. I feel him harden beneath his jeans, and I spread my legs further, wanting *more, more, more*. I pull my hands out of his grasp and bring one to the back of his neck, kissing him harder. The friction between my legs is something I've never experienced, and I don't think anything could stop me from chasing this feeling. I feel it building, much more intense than anything I've ever done alone in the privacy of my bedroom. I wrap my legs around his back and rock into him, uncaring of seeming too eager.

"Fuck. Stop," he rasps. I don't.

"Briar, that's enough," he says, pinning my hands to the bed once again, this time using his demanding tone that brooks no argument. But I don't listen. I tilt my hips up again, and he groans. Before I know what's happening, I'm flipped over onto my stomach, my arms trapped at my sides by his knees as he straddles me.

"You're fucking fourteen, Briar. I'm not even in high school anymore, for fuck's sake."

"I don't care," I say stubbornly. "I'm old enough to know what I want." My hair is in my face, muffling my words. He brings a finger to my cheek and sweeps the strands behind my ear.

"You have no idea what you want," he counters. "What you're asking for."

His condescending tone makes me feel childish and

inferior, and if it wasn't for the fact that I could feel his want for me digging into my backside, I'd probably feel hurt, embarrassed, and rejected. In a brazen move, I arch my backside and move against him.

"So, show me," I say, looking over my shoulder at him. His eyes are fixed on my pajama shorts that have ridden up, exposing my cheeks.

"No," he says harshly. I drop my face into the mattress. God, my *brother's* mattress. I'd tell him to take me to my room if I thought for one second he wouldn't come to his senses and put a stop to this—whatever *this* is.

He shoves off me, horrified, and sits as far away from me as Dash's queen bed will allow. "Fuck!" he yells, tugging at his hair. Seeing him like this is enough to make me feel guilty, but not enough to regret anything.

"Why, Asher?" I ask, tears brimming my eyes. "What is *so* wrong with me?"

When he doesn't respond, I turn to leave, but Asher lunges for me, snatching my wrist and pulling me back toward him until I'm straddling his lap.

"Briar," he says, his eyes searching mine, begging me to understand.

"Say what you mean and mean what you say, Ash. I'm not a mind reader."

"You're *fourteen*," he stresses, as if that's reason enough. And I suppose it is. But this thing feels bigger than our ages. He's not some predator. He's just…Asher.

"Not to mention, my best friend's little sister. Do you know what I'd do if someone even *looked* at my little sister sideways?"

"You don't have a sister," I point out. "And it's different," I insist. I'm not like other girls my age, and I want this. My friend Sophie still plays with Barbies—when no one is looking, of course—and loves One Direction. I like *this*. This feeling with Asher, right here, right now.

"It's not. It makes me sick," he starts, his warm hands smoothing up my back. "It's not right."

I push his shoulders, causing him to fall backward, and boldly, I lean down and press my lips to his. At first, he doesn't react. He simply lies back, allowing me to explore, to kiss and nibble and suck with his hands clenched at his sides. But when he feels my tongue against his lips, seeking entrance, his hands fly to my waist, and he kisses me back. This time it isn't timid or polite. This kiss feels like war. A battle between right and wrong. Moral and corrupt. Honorable and deplorable.

Asher slides his right hand into my hair and positions us so that we're both lying on our sides as he continues his assault on my mouth, on my soul. He shifts his body until his leg is wedged between mine, and I can't help but chase that glorious friction once again. A moan slips free, and I feel him stiffen like he's about to deny me again. I bring my hands to his cheeks to keep his lips on mine and rock into his thigh.

"Please, Ash. Touch me," I beg.

"No."

"Then let me touch you." I reach for the bulge in his jeans, and he smacks my hand away.

"Fuck no. It can't go any further than this."

I could cry tears of disappointment right now.

"Look at me," he orders, hooking a finger under my chin. "Keep your hands to yourself. If you go for my cock again, I'm gone. Understand?"

I nod eagerly in agreement.

"Goddammit, give me words, Briar."

"I promise. Just make me feel…*that*." I feel my face burn with embarrassment, and the corner of his mouth twitches, like maybe he'd be amused if he weren't on the verge of jumping over a line that should never be crossed.

Asher plants each of my hands on his shoulders and gives me a searing gaze, silently ordering me to keep them there. I swallow and give a sharp nod, and he places his own hands flat on the mattress by his head, purposely not touching. I press my lips to his, and he reluctantly kisses me back. I start rocking into his leg, powerless to this feeling. Once I find my rhythm, he clasps his hands behind his neck, watching my body move. Seeing him lying back like a king while I grind into his thigh is the hottest thing I've ever seen in my life.

"Oh my God." My voice is just above a whisper.

I press myself into him even harder. The new angle has my eyes snapping shut and my head flying back. My movements are becoming sloppy and jerky, and I know I'm close to something epic. Life-changing even. I hear Asher shifting again, but I don't dare open my eyes. I can feel my wetness leak through my shorts, and somewhere in the back of my mind, I wonder if that's normal. But Asher doesn't seem to notice, or if he does, he doesn't mind.

I'm climbing higher, higher, higher, when I feel something hot and slightly damp wrap around my nipple. My eyes shoot open to see Asher drawing the tiny bud into his mouth through my tank top. And just like that, I come apart. He holds me in place through my orgasm as he continues to suck until I'm shuddering and shaking in his arms.

I'm practically panting as he uses his palm to brush the sweaty hair off my face and leans in to kiss the damp skin of my neck.

"Thank you," I say dumbly. Because what else can I say after that?

"I'm going to hell."

"We didn't do anything wrong," I say honestly, laying my head on his shoulder, feeling so content that I could fall asleep and stay here forever.

"You didn't do a damn thing wrong. I did. You don't understand it now. But you will look back at this some day and see it for what it is."

"And what is that, exactly?" I ask, feeling my temper rising.

"A man who just took advantage of a fucking child," he spits, looking up at the vaulted ceiling.

"That's bullshit. Don't do that."

"Do what, Bry? It's the truth."

"Don't act as if I didn't practically throw myself at you. That I'm too young to make my own decisions. You didn't take advantage of me. You didn't *take* anything. You gave."

"The only thing I gave you is false hope. You know this can't ever leave this room. If Dash knew…"

"Why would I tell my brother about hooking up with *anyone*? I know this doesn't make you my boyfriend. I'm not that naïve. But maybe when I'm eighteen…"

"This shouldn't have happened," Asher says, grabbing me by my hips and lifting me off him. He stands and reaches for one of Dash's T-shirts lying on top of his dresser. "It's wrong," he says once again.

"Yes, Asher, tell me again how wrong I am for you. I don't think you've gotten your point across." I roll my eyes, sarcasm dripping from every word.

He pulls the plain black shirt over his head, and I watch his muscles flex with the movement. I gulp. Asher's growl has my eyes snapping back up to his.

"Stop looking at me like that, Briar," he warns, his voice lethal and low.

"Like what?" I ask, feigning innocence.

"Like you want what I can't give you."

"The only thing I want is for you to stay."

"I have to tell you something," he says, changing the subject.

"What is it?" And why does it feel like he's about to end our nonexistent relationship?

"I got a scholarship," he says, his mouth twitching at the corner in an almost-smile. "A full ride."

"Are you serious?" I squeal, my frustration from a minute ago all but gone. I'm more excited for him than I've been about anything in my entire life. I knew he was applying, but he told me it was impossible for swimmers to get a full ride. "That's amazing, Ash!"

I throw my arms around his neck, but there's nothing sexual about it this time. Just genuine pride and happiness for him. Ash is one of the best people I know, and he deserves an opportunity to live a life as good as he is. I pull back, scanning his face. He's not easily excitable, but I expected more enthusiasm than this.

"What is it? What else aren't you telling me?"

"It's in Georgia."

For the second time tonight, I feel like that time I fell on the playground in the fourth grade and got the wind knocked out of me. "What?"

"I leave in four months."

I nod, caught between two warring emotions. I'm elated for him, but I'm sad for me. He untangles our limbs and sits on the edge of the bed, resting his elbows on his knees, avoiding eye contact.

"Does Dash know?"

"Yes." He looks over at me, and his eyes soften at his admission.

He never even bothered to tell me.

"I'm happy for you," I say, my voice contradicting the words coming out of my mouth. "This is your chance."

He nods, and we sit in strained silence, unsure of where to go from here.

I try to hold back the tears. To be a good friend and be happy for him, but my chin starts to wobble, and one, single tear runs down my cheek. Asher is in front of me in an instant, gripping my face with both hands, forcing me to look into his eyes.

"Don't waste one fucking tear on me."

I sniff and look away.

"Dash is losing his best friend. And so will I."

"I'm not leaving tomorrow, or next week. We have time."

"Promise me something."

"What's that?"

"Promise me you won't leave without saying goodbye. Promise me I won't be blindsided."

"I promise," he swears.

I nod, feeling slightly pacified. I want nothing more than for Asher to get the hell out of there, but selfishly, right now I can only think about losing him.

"When you leave…"

Asher watches me, waiting. "Yeah?"

"It won't be forever, right?"

"I can't promise you that."

"You really need to work on this whole 'comforting someone' thing. You're really bad at it," I say, pulling back to look up at him. Ash is at least six feet tall, and I have to strain my neck to make eye contact when we're this close.

"I've never had to do it before."

"Why does it feel like we're saying hello and goodbye all at the same time?" After years of tugging at his sleeve and following him like a lost puppy, I've finally gotten Asher's attention in the way I've always wanted. But I'm not naïve enough to think that this could end well.

"Because once I leave, you're going to forget this night ever happened."

I lick my lips, and his eyes follow the movement.

"But you're still here now, so…" I rise onto my tiptoes, circling my arms around his neck. Asher grips my waist and lifts. My legs automatically wrap around him.

"For once in my goddamn life, I'm trying to be the good guy, and you're not making it easy."

"I like you better when you're bad."

Something not unlike a growl is all I hear in response before his lips are on mine once again. Ash walks us over to the wall next to the window, still holding me by my ass. When my back hits the wall, his hands are free to roam. He smooths them up the outsides of my thighs and then either side of my waist. I hold on to his shoulders to keep from melting into a puddle at his feet as I feel it building again, and my hips shift in search of the friction I need, when I hear it.

Giggling. Feminine, *annoying* giggling.

"Shut the fuck up! You're going to wake my parents," says a familiar, albeit irritated voice.

"Fuck," Ash whispers, dropping me like a sack of potatoes, right before Whitley, Asher's ex, appears in the window. She lands in a pile at my feet, and she smells like alcohol and cheap perfume. When she notices me, her face morphs into one of total and utter disdain.

Dash climbs through after her—his preferred method of entry when he has a girl with him—and looks between us. It's not exactly suspicion I detect on his face, but confusion. I feel the need to straighten my shirt or tame my hair, but I'm frozen, afraid of doing anything that will display my guilt.

"What's going on?" he asks, concern coating his tone.

"A little help here!" Whitley slurs in her high-pitched, dolphin sonar voice. Dash rolls his eyes, reaching down to help her to her feet.

"She was looking for you. Wouldn't take no for an answer," Dash explains. "Figured you'd be here when we didn't see your truck at yours."

"I was just, uh, helping Asher with something," I say. Dash reads the meaning of my words, and his head jerks toward Ash, assessing.

"You okay, man?" he asks, keeping it vague since Whitley is here.

"I'm good," is all he says, and the two share a look that even I can't decode.

"What the fuck are you doing here, Whit?" His tone is harsh, but hearing him call her by her nickname reminds me of the fact that they were close once.

"We need to talk," she says, crossing her arms over her chest.

"The fuck we do," Asher snaps. "Go home."

"I can't!" she protests, and I fight the urge to cover my ears. She's always so *loud*. "I didn't drive."

"Jesus Christ," Asher says, scrubbing a hand down his face. "Go wait for me in my truck. I'll take you home." Whitley wastes no time, probably knowing that he'd rescind the offer if she pushed her luck.

"Which is it this time? You pick a fight with some random asshole, or is your dad drunk again?" Dash asks once we hear the car door slam shut.

"The latter."

"Does he look like you?" He gestures to his bloody appearance.

A devious smirk lifts the corner of his lips. "Worse."

"Good," Dash says solemnly. He hates this just as much as I do. It's the most helpless feeling in the world, standing by and watching something so awful happen to someone you care deeply for, and not being able to do a damn thing about it. As much as I hate the thought of him leaving, I feel so much relief in knowing that there's now an end in sight. "Call me tomorrow. I gotta take a piss."

The moment my brother is out the door, Asher's guilt-ridden eyes dart over to mine. "This was a mistake."

"Bullshit," I argue, moving toward him.

"Don't," he says, backing away, and I die inside, just a little.

And before I can pick my stupid, naïve heart up off the floor and form a response, he's gone.

ABOUT THE AUTHOR

Charleigh Rose lives in Narnia with her husband and two young children. She's hopelessly devoted to unconventional love and pizza. When she isn't reading or mom-ing, she's writing moody, broody, swoony romance.

Stay in touch!

Website
authorcharleighrose.com

Facebook page
www.facebook.com/charleighroseprose

Facebook group
www.facebook.com/groups/1120926904664447

Instagram
www.instagram.com/charleighrose

Newsletter
https://bit.ly/2hzVQy4

OTHER BOOKS BY
CHARLEIGH ROSE

Bad Habit

Bad Intentions

Bad Influence

Yard Sale

Misbehaved

Rewrite the Stars

Printed in Great Britain
by Amazon

17448671R00176